D1437216

THE STARS OF CONSTANTINOPLE

THE STARS OF CONSTANTINOPLE

Stories by
ÓLAFUR JÓHANN SIGURDSSON

Translated by Alan Boucher

LOUISIANA STATE UNIVERSITY PRESS
Baton Rouge and London

1992

Designer: *Glynnis Phoebe*
Typeface: *Garamond*
Typesetter: *Graphic Composition, Inc.*
Printer and binder: *Thomson-Shore, Inc.*

Library of Congress Cataloging-in-Publication Data

Ólafur Jóhann Sigurðsson.
   [Short stories. English. Selections]
   The stars of Constantinople : stories / by Ólafur Jóhann
Sigurdsson : translated by Alan Boucher.
     p.   cm.
   Collection of stories translated from Icelandic and previously
published separately.
   Contents: The changing earth—Pastor Bodvar's letter—The
stars of Constantinople—Building pyramids—Interruption—An
old narrative—The padlock—Crying on an autumn morning—The
hand—The blind boy—Journey home—Fire.
   ISBN 0-8071-1778-1 (cloth)
   1. Ólafur Jóhann Sigurðsson—Translations into English.
I. Title.
PT7511.O44A6   1992
839'.6934—dc20   92-6460
                                                     CIP

The translator offers grateful acknowledgment to Anna Jonsdóttir and to Mál og menning, in Reykjavik, for the right to publish these stories in English. All the stories first appeared in books by Ólafur Jóhann Sigurdsson. "The Hand" is from *Kvistir í altarinu* (Víkingsútgáfan, 1942); "Building Pyramids," "Crying on an Autumn Morning," "The Padlock," and "The Stars of Constantinople" are from *Teningar í tafli* (Víkingsútgáfan, 1945); "The Blind Boy" is from *Speglar og fidrildi* (Helgafell, 1947); "Fire," "Interruption," and "An Old Narrative" are from *Á vegamótum* (Heimskringla, 1955); "Pastor Bodvar's Letter" is from *Leynt og ljóst* (Heimskringla, 1965); and "Journey Home" is from *Seint á ferd* (Bókaútgáfa Menningarsjóds, 1972). "The Changing Earth" appeared as *Litbrigdi jardarrinar* (Helgafell, 1947).

Publication of this book has been supported by a grant from the National Endowment for the Arts in Washington, D.C., a federal agency.

The paper in this book meets the guidelines for permanence and durability of the Committee on Production Guidelines for Book Longevity of the Council on Library Resources.⊗

CONTENTS

THE STARS OF CONSTANTINOPLE

THE CHANGING EARTH

I

A few hours after the marvel had happened he could not for the life of him account for having turned old Grani off the moorland ride to follow the rough, winding track along the river instead of hurrying the shortest way home. Perhaps he had intended to look for some sheep, perhaps he had wanted to listen a little longer to the murmur of the river, or maybe some new idea had occurred to him and he wanted to turn it over in his mind, alone. At all events he had turned old Grani off the moorland ride, sharply and impulsively, as though a great deal depended on it, then slackened the reins and whistled a tune—or rather a tuneless snatch which he made up as he went along—quite forgetting that he had to help his father move some peat from the marsh up to the sheep sheds at the edge of the home field, the old sheep sheds.

Not that he had the least deliberate intention of delaying his homecoming, or of loitering out in the fine weather. But it was no easy matter for a sixteen-year-old to fetter his thoughts to peat and the obligations of work on such a mild, still day as this first day of autumn, while the barnacle geese flew honking southward somewhere high overhead and every leaf breathed its gentle, intoxicating fragrance in a final valediction to the summer. Such a day contained an enchantment that drew a veil over everyday cares and awakened a thousand dreams: delicate and evanescent dreams that fluttered about the heart like golden butterflies or soared into space in the wake of the barnacles or led the mind to dwell on pictures of the earth, filling it with a profound and grateful rapture.

Seldom had the earth been so lovely and so rich in colors. It was brown and green, pink and yellow, red and golden, in some places half-withered and faded, but in others still in summer bloom and all but untouched by the cold, northerly gusts of the previous nights. He stopped whistling and gave old Grani his head, gazing at this variegated earth, at the clouds above it, gray-blue and motionless, at the hills and mountains, the stretches of heather and patches of scrub beyond the river, listening to the murmur of the river and breathing the cool, autumnal scent of leaf and grass.

In this way he went on for a good while.

Reluctant even to blink his eyes, he surrendered himself so completely to the colors of the bushes beyond the river that he barely noticed when the track took a sudden turn, to climb steeply over a silvery, moss-grown rise. The horse stepped more firmly, ears pricked. The murmur of the river grew heavier and deepened in quality, like the sound of a bow drawn flat across a low-toned stringed instrument. White eddies flashed in the stream, and a moment later behind the rise a little waterfall appeared, bright and foaming. After this waterfall vanished, the voice of the river once more became subdued and even, the track curved down to the level, and a new prospect was unfolded. There were the moors, golden red and soft as an embroidered cloth worked by the fingers of growth and decay in combination. There was the cart track leading upstream, potholed and unpretentious. And there was the ford across the river.

He braced himself, tightened the reins, jabbed his heels into the flanks of the horse, and suddenly took command. It was as if he had awakened out of a trance. The colors in his consciousness faded into the background, for a short distance ahead, on a hump of pink heather not far from the ford, a girl was sitting. He recognized her at once. Her name was Sigrun Maria Einardottir, from the next farm, seventeen years of age, small and plump, and known as Sigga, Runa, or Runa Maria. She sat there bent forward on the hump of heather and had taken off one of her stockings, while the other was rolled down to her ankle.

II

Hallo, he said, dismounting. At once the girl looked about her and seemed a little astonished when she saw the horse and the boy.

THE CHANGING EARTH

Hallo, she replied cheerfully. She stopped pulling off her stocking and moved herself higher onto the hump of heather, tugging at her skirt, which had ruckled up above the knee. Then she held out her hand to him and smiled. You've come at just the right moment, she said. I never dreamed that I would run into you here. I haven't seen you since last winter.

Where have you been? he asked.

To Gil, she answered. I slipped over there last Saturday to see my cousin.

She tugged again at her skirt, untied her head scarf, and ran the palm of her hand over her dark hair, pressing the pinned coil at the back. Then she spread the scarf out, folded it in a triangle, and knotted it over her head anew. Her movements were as soft and deliberate as if she were handling delicate roses.

You didn't show yourself at the Youth Club tombola this summer, she said teasingly, drawling the words, and the greenish iridescence of her eyes darted him a wavering glance. Why didn't you come?

We were bringing in the hay, he answered, and looked involuntarily at the blue veins in her legs as he bent to pluck a half-withered stalk of cattail grass. I couldn't go.

What a bore, she said sympathetically, and she explained how the tombola of this summer had been the best one ever held at the Youth Club in the district. Things had been lively then! I drew a stick of ground chicory and some pins, she cried, adding in confidence that fortune had also favored her with an ancient, hard, and moldy cod's head which the Moakot boys had presented to the tombola out of sheer devilment. They had put forget-me-nots and white bridewort in the box with the cod's head!

Then she turned her eyes toward the ford, where the water streamed knee-deep over rocks and broken stones, clear and cold, ruffled and murmuring. Bending forward on the hump, she gave a low sigh and began to take off the other stocking.

Look here, said the boy, wouldn't you like to take the horse across the river?

Oh, thank you, yes, she said. I can't tell you how glad I'd be!

But you'd have to ride bareback, he added apologetically. I'm afraid you might get covered with horsehair.

Pooh, as if that mattered.

And also I must ask you to shoo the horse back into the river once you're across. I have to shift some peat on him before evening.

But if he should run away with me? she said. What then? Some horses are so wild and mischievous.

Oh, he's not really at all wild, mumbled the boy a little uncertainly, and gave old Grani a questioning look, as though expecting him to speak or try in some way to refute this disparaging and unwarranted suspicion. But old Grani remained as dumb as ever, mumbled his bit, and laid back his ears with a dejected expression, as if he was affronted, not having run away since he was a colt and having been an example of quietness and docility to all other horses since arriving at years of discretion. The boy shuffled uneasily and snapped the cattail stalk between his teeth. The girl's remark appeared to have undermined his confidence in old Grani and put him on the horns of a dilemma.

Perhaps we might ride double, he said after long consideration, and he stared down at his feet.

Ride double? Why, yes, of course, she exclaimed gratefully, snatching up her stocking. We could ride double, that's quite true! Of course we can ride double!

As in a trance he heard her voice, soft, clear, full of warmth and candor. At once she made him her confidant, admitting that the thought of wading through the river had filled her with apprehension from the moment of leaving Gil that morning. She always got dizzy when she crossed running water; she was so timid and lacking in courage. Maybe her heart was a bit weak, too; she sometimes had a strange pain in her chest and ringing in her ears. His turning up at this moment had really been a godsend to her.

In spite of her confiding in him and the candor of her voice, he remained shy and silent. Sigrun Maria had changed so much since they met last winter. The sight of her affected him in a strange way, awakening a palpitation of a kind he had never felt before, in the neighborhood of his heart. He hardly dared look at her, became embarrassed and blushed, but at the same time noticed all that had changed and been transformed during the summer. She was no longer pale and skinny, as when she had stood outside the church on Palm Sunday, wrapping her coat about her in the frost of April. No, in the course of a few months she had acquired a new shape, a new body. She radiated ripeness: her lips had become soft and full, her breasts swelled under the gaily knit jumper, and the veins in her rounded instep divided and united, blue and branching like little streams.

Heavens, how clumsy I am today, she laughed as she turned her stocking to pull it on. The foot is so awkward and clammy! My feet probably got wet when I walked across that beastly marsh by Gil!

He said nothing and fumbled with the rein in his embarrassment; then he turned his head and stroked old Grani on the muzzle while she was fastening her stockings to the garters under her skirt and lacing her ankle boots. They were beautiful dark-colored ankle boots which her father had probably given her in the spring or summer. He remembered that she had not been nearly so well shod when she had stood outside the church on Palm Sunday, wrapping her coat about her in the frost of April.

Well, I'm ready at last, she said, and picked up her bundle. Shall I be in front or behind?

I don't care, he said. Which would you prefer?

I'd rather be in front, she answered, and taking a firm hold on old Grani's mane she raised herself on tiptoe, compressed her lips a little, and in a single motion heaved herself up onto the horse's back.

When the boy had made two unsuccessful attempts to imitate her elastic spring she laughed, but the moment he was mounted she became serious.

You must hold my waist, she said. Otherwise I might fall into the river!

He obeyed in a daze, holding her carefully as though she were something fragile. There was a clear, sweet sound in his ears, joyful and yet at the same time sad, like the mysterious hum of a bright spring morning. The horse put his nose to the water and twitched his ears for the sake of appearances, but knowing every inch of the ford as he did, felt no obligation to snort before wading out into the clear stream. He stepped slowly and steadily, but when they were in midstream the girl leaned backward and cried out, oh-oh! Hold me tighter! I'm falling!

He tightened his hold on her waist, gripping the sides of the horse with his legs, and did his best to overcome the wave of giddiness that came over him, as if he were going to faint. He felt the rose-patterned head scarf against his cheek, her breast rising and falling, and the warmth that penetrated her gaily knit jumper, but was aware of everything only in a rainbow mist, soft and fluctuating, could not hear the splash of water for the pounding of his own heart, and came to himself with a start when old Grani halted on the opposite bank and began to shake his head repeatedly, as though wanting to be rid as soon as possible of this unreasonable burden.

I'm all right now, said Sigrun Maria, and she slipped to the ground. It was really very kind of you to bring me across.

He dismounted, too, mumbling something into his chest, and did not dare look up, but fumbled vigorously with the knot on the reins.

Did you think I was going to fall? she asked playfully, brushing the horse-hair from her skirt and stockings.

Well, no, he hadn't thought that, not exactly.

You held me so tight, she said. You must be as strong as an elephant!

He flushed more deeply and disparaged his strength, examining the knot on the reins with redoubled care and passing it repeatedly from one hand to the other. The palpitations in his chest threatened to overpower him and rob him of speech. He could scarcely get a word out.

I say, she went on, how old are you?

How old? He was sixteen last Saturday.

Now wasn't that extraordinary! On Saturday? Why, the very day when she had set out for Gil to see her cousin, and was wondering, as she walked over the heath, Could it be somebody's birthday today? But try as she would, she couldn't remember whose birthday it was.

The boy had stopped fumbling with the reins. His eyes were now fixed on a yellow cattail that seemed just waiting to be pulled up and snapped between the teeth. He bent down, pulled it up, and stripped off the ear and root sheath before putting it in his mouth. It tickled his lips.

So you are sixteen, she said.

Yes, he replied.

I shall be eighteen in March. She swung her bundle, gazing thoughtfully over the tawny ridges that lay in her father's land, and moved her lips as if counting to herself. There's only a year and a half between us!

He was unable to refute this, so he busied himself in dismembering the cattail, but Sigrun Maria suddenly recalled a remarkable circumstance which made her gasp aloud.

Do you know, Mama is older than Papa?

No, he hadn't known that.

Yes, observed Sigrun Maria, she's about five years older than Papa! And she continued to swing her bundle, an arch smile on her lips, while the greenish iridescence in her eyes glittered, calling to mind the gleam of moonlight on dark, secret pools, the mutable August moonlight when scent is blended with the dusk. Papa says that five years is no difference of age, she added in a more confidential tone. He says that my late Grandma at Klaustur was twelve years older than Grandpa. And yet they were quite inseparable. They're buried in the same grave!

The boy had no knowledge of either the career or death of the late Grandma at Klaustur and did not venture any comment. He looked about him in embarrassment and was fortunate enough to catch sight of a pair of wild ducks, small and dun-colored, flying up the river. He watched them until they vanished behind the low, curving ridges.

Well, now, said Sigrun Maria. She brushed some invisible horsehair from her skirt, but the smile had begun to fade from her lips and her tone was less confidential. How terribly quiet and serious you are! Are you thinking about anything special?

No, he answered slowly.

Can't you tell me some news?

There's no news to tell, he mumbled, looking down, and he swallowed, picked another cattail, pulled off the ear, and put the stalk between his lips. His thoughts seemed tethered by strange, soft, and delightful bonds, from which he neither could nor would break free. He found the cattail tasteless.

By the way! Doesn't the mail come next Saturday? she asked.

Yes, he replied.

I wish I could get a letter in the mail. I do so enjoy getting letters. I wish someone would write to me. It wouldn't have to be a long letter. Just a few lines.

He was silent.

I do so enjoy getting letters, she repeated looking at him, but when he remained silent she launched upon a new topic.

How was the haymaking with you this summer?

Oh, not bad, he answered. The weather has been so good.

Yes, splendid, she agreed, and glanced for a moment at the clouds in the sky, friendly and peaceful. We did much better with our hay this year, too, but we haven't finished taking up the potatoes yet. Have you taken up your potatoes?

Yes, we did that over the weekend.

And how was the crop?

Well above average, I'd say.

I think ours will be above average, too, she said. They always grow so well in the plots in front of the farm, but the swedes have never thrived in the old cabbage patch by the stable. There's something wrong with the soil there.

She looked up at the clouds again, swinging her bundle, put forward a foot, wrinkled her eyes a little, and tried to conceal a smile. How do you feel about the autumn? she asked him. Will it be a good or bad one?

He was obliged to admit that he had no special feelings about the autumn, in fact he hadn't really given the subject any thought. To him summer had seemed to reign still unchallenged over the earth. There had only been a gust of northerly wind the few previous nights; now mildness and fine weather had returned.

Are you good at forecasting? she continued. What do you forecast now?

I don't know, he replied. I can't forecast.

What! You can't forecast? You really surprise me, she exclaimed, and laughing at his ingenuousness she shook her head mockingly. How stupid you are, boy! Everyone can forecast except you!

I daresay it will be a good autumn, he mumbled, blushing fiercely, and was compelled to examine the knot on the reins yet once more. I dare say the weather will hold fine till Christmas . . .

There you are, what did I say! she cried. I knew all the time that you could forecast just like the rest. It wouldn't surprise me if you were one of the best weather prophets in the district. It's only that you're so proud and secretive! One can't get a word out of you!

She stroked her palm over the back of her neck to find out whether the pinned coil of hair had unwound or moved out of place, and being reassured that it was in good order sighed and looked at the boy questioningly as if hoping that he would say something. The boy said nothing. Gazing at the

music in his heart that he was almost moved to tears in his joy, and he blessed every blade of grass and tuft of moss, the sky and daylight, stroked the rough rocks with hot palms, and prayed to God for the wren that fluttered along the track below the fell and the ptarmigan that roosted on the ledge, that they might never be cold or hungry in winter. Yes, he prayed for all on earth that suffered. The pale, tranquil autumn day had consecrated him to a new life. He was so good. He was so rich. The green world in his heart, with its scent of meadowsweet and moss campion, sounded like a low, sweet-toned consort of strings, inspiring him to help all and show mercy to all, so that he forgave even the bloodthirsty cruelty of the merlins. And when he finally turned homeward to the farm in the twilight, he confided a greeting for Sigrun Maria to the first star in the northern sky. Your adorer, he whispered to the star in the north. Yours till death.

IV

But it looked very much as if the outside world had discovered the secret of this other wonderful green world and, filled with envy, was determined to miss no opportunity of spoiling its beauty, of shattering and dispersing it and obliterating every trace of it from his heart. In this work, man and the elements joined forces. The skies poured down rain, sleet, and hail on the earth in turn; the winds blew, and on the moors the last colors were extinguished, giving way to a universal grayness and gloom. From time to time the boy went out rounding up the sheep with the farmers of the district—with all, that is, except the father of Sigrun Maria. It was raw, wet, and windy, with mud about the pens and the sheep bleating dejectedly, but the farmers made little of it; shaking wet beards they stuck plugs of tobacco in their mouths, shuffled in the mud, chewed, spit, and swore, felt every ewe many times over, tracing pedigrees and like histories and contending on points of breed. When the boy was unduly long in distinguishing an earmark they would jostle or pinch him, inquiring humorously whether he thought that ewe was a woman or had taken to composing a letter of proposal here at the roundup or was perhaps knocking together some verses for a girl. And when he became embarrassed and blushed, there in the cold and rain, they spit tobacco juice and exclaimed triumphantly, Well, well! What a fellow! Who would have believed it?

It took him all his time to guard his green world. They knew nothing of love, he thought. They had never loved, never smelled the scent of meadow-sweet and moss campion in late autumn, never listened to sweet strains of music while others slept or confided to a star in the north the message, Your adorer, yours till death.

He tried not to let their banter affect him, did his best to behave like a man and put in his word when they pulled a ewe out of the flock and disputed vigorously about her antecedents and achievements. But his voice sounded strange. The words got in his way and led him into a blind alley, and the farmers either laughed at him or demonstrated with indisputable logic that he was talking utter nonsense.

He often became silent and depressed, about this time. Sometimes he would sit for hours on the chest in the kitchen staring into the embers in the gloom, saying nothing and hearing nothing of what went on around him, as though he were trying to read his fate in the fire. He took the food which his mother handed him, without a word, and left half of it on his plate.

She asked if he wasn't feeling well.

Yes, he was quite well.

You have lost your appetite, she said. Something has upset you.

No, he said, and continued to stare into the embers.

Then one evening he noticed that his sister was watching him. She stood in one corner by the kitchen range, gawky and freckled, fiddling with her fair braids, and surreptitiously studied him with an expression full of impatient sympathy. She was two years younger than he was and had been confirmed that spring.

Mundi, she said when their mother and brother had gone out, I know why you are so odd.

He pretended not to hear and said nothing.

I woke up the night before last, she said.

Did you now? he said sourly, not knowing what she was driving at.

Yes, she whispered. You talked in your sleep.

He felt the blood rush to his cheeks and his scalp grow hot, and the green world in his heart winced as if it had been stung. He dared not look up, dared not move, for his secret was a secret no more; he had betrayed it himself, in his sleep. And his sister, standing there in the corner, gawky and freckled, had him in her power, although she was two years younger than he was.

No one else was awake, she whispered, and I shan't say a word to anyone about it.

A word about what? he asked, trying to still the tremor in his voice.

About . . . you know, she whispered. And she winked at him and played with her braids for a while in silence. Then she spoke, raising her voice. I say, Mundi, she said, you promised ages ago to mend the lock on my box.

When? he asked.

Some time this summer, she replied. It's so inconvenient not having anywhere to lock things up.

Very well, he said coldly, standing up. Bring a candle. I shall have to do it out in the storeroom.

Must I take my things out of it? she asked.

No, that would not be necessary, though it might be better if she came with him to the storeroom and stayed there while he had a look at the lock. She could hold the screws for him, perhaps, and hand him the hammer and pliers.

She obeyed without a word, and stood by him while he took his time fixing the lock, spinning out the job for as long as he could. He glanced at her and moistening his dry lips whistled a fragment of tune. But when it was evident that the job could be spun out no longer, he turned his back on his sister and cleared his throat.

By the way, he muttered, as if casually, what were you saying just now? That I had been talking in my sleep?

Yes, she answered, and once again her voice became eager with sympathy. You talked in your sleep the night before last.

And what did I say?

Would you like to know? she said.

Yes, he had nothing against it.

You kept saying, My darling.

And had he said nothing else?

No, nothing else, except that once he had said, My sweetheart.

Was that all?

Yes, she said.

It was as though a weight was lifted from his mind. Putting down the chisel, he tried the lock of the box, knit his brow, and gazed thoughtfully up at the storeroom ceiling. He had been dreaming. He had dreamed that he was reading aloud from some book, probably a storybook. He had been reading about some old fellow who was making up to an old woman and kept saying to her, My darling, yes, and My sweetheart, too! He remembered distinctly. The man had been wearing a brown sweater, the woman a blue-check apron, and the book itself had been big and thick—as big as the old book of sermons on the shelf above his father's bed—though he couldn't remember whether the pages in it were all yellow and shriveled like the pages of the old sermon book, but probably they weren't yellow, except perhaps at the edges.

It was the night before last, his sister said after a moment's silence, and a new note in her voice expressed both doubt and disappointment.

Yes, that was right. It had been the night before last.

And didn't you dream about anything else? she asked.

No, he replied with decision, and tried the lock of her box once more; he hadn't dreamed about anything else, he was glad to say. One ought not to attach any importance to dreams. At the most they only meant a change in the weather.

His sister snuffed the candle, fiddled with her braids, and stared awkwardly at the floor. Mundi, she said after a short pause, have you ever heard me talking in my sleep?

He did not answer at once but tightened a screw a little, then turned the key in the lock. Yes, he lied, I've sometimes heard you talk in your sleep this autumn.

Just when? she asked.

Oh, many times, he answered. You chattered in your sleep like anything after you'd been to church the Sunday before last. I imagine Papa would have been a bit upset if he'd heard you.

What did I say? she asked uneasily.

I daresay you know the best yourself, he answered. Here's your box. Well, take it! I might touch up the roses on the lid for you sometime if I get hold of some red paint. They're very faded.

Do you have a paintbrush? she asked.

No, but I might be able to make one out of horsehair.

She took the box and held it in her arms, red cheeked and awkward, sniffed several times, and looking at him entreatingly whispered, Mundi . . .

Oh I know, he broke in, walking out of the storeroom. You needn't be afraid that I'll tell. There's nothing very special about the nonsense of girls who have just been confirmed!

V

But after that he was in a state of constant dread lest he should betray his secret in his sleep. He would look searchingly at his parents, his sister, and his brothers every morning, and more often than not he would seem to read in their expressions that they knew all about the green world in his heart. But as the day advanced he always came to the opposite conclusion. He dared not relax his vigilance for a moment—stopped staring into the embers in the gloom and did his utmost to hide his feelings so that no one should suspect. But he was sick at heart within, for love breeds desire and desire doubt, and the companion of doubt is despondency.

The weather grew colder. Winds from the glaciers played with powdered snow clouds over the mountain, and the earth became white, silent, and frozen. Seldom had the moonlight glided more cheerfully over the frozen snow or the northern lights shuffled more rapidly among the stars. Yet no one was outside but the ptarmigan hunters, the postman, and a few bearded farmers and laborers who declared they had run out of tobacco. He was on the very point of writing a letter to Sigrun Maria and asking the postman to deliver it—just a few lines to let her know that there were some who had not forgotten her, some who sometimes stopped to think a little in the evening moonlight and listen to strains of a wonderful music in their own heart, ever yours. But on further consideration it became clear to him that the news would fly round the district at once, like the report of a stranded whale, that he had started writing letters to Sigrun Maria, for the postman, who was both talkative and something of a wag, would certainly break any promise of secrecy and perhaps circulate verses in which he would be a knight crusader and the girl the daughter of a count. No, he could say nothing to Sigrun Maria until he met her in person and in private. It was even an unanswered question whether she still cared about him at all. Perhaps she had never cared about him. Perhaps she had only been joking, down by the river, when she remarked on the difference of age between her parents and the married life of her Grandma and Grandpa at Klaustur who had been inseparable and were buried in the same grave. He had behaved like a bumpkin, too silent and tongue-tied, making her drag every word out of him, fiddling with the reins, biting his lip, and gaping at wild ducks, instead of talking about farming and the weather and showing some sympathy when she confided in him that she was probably a little weakhearted by constitution and sometimes felt a curious pain in her chest and heard ringing noises in her ears. Of course there was no hope that the daughter of the richest farmer in the district would choose for her future husband a poor, bookish youth who behaved like a fool into the bargain and appeared to have no interest in either vegetable produce or hay crops. No doubt whatever that she had the choice of far more eligible boys.

He sighed deeply and wrote, Your adorer, yours till death, with his finger in a snowdrift by the barn but was startled when he heard a muffled shot in the distance, and hurriedly obliterated his short letter to Sigrun Maria in the snow. He envied the ptarmigan hunters and wished that he too had a shotgun, preferably a double-barreled one, so that he could get away from tending the livestock and shoot himself some pocket money like other people, wander all over the moors, loading and firing at intervals, making the dull reports echo in the still air. He no longer remembered a day in the autumn by the cliffs under the fall when he had prayed to God that the ptarmigan might never be cold or hungry in winter. If he possessed a shotgun perhaps he would make his way to a certain farm in the gathering dusk, all bloodstained and manly, girded with cartridge belt, with a heavy load on his back—maybe fifty ptarmigan. He would knock at the door and ask for a drop of water to drink; he was not quite himself, felt a bit faint; might he lie down for a few moments until it passed?

Yes, he was more than welcome, the master of the house would say. Give Gudmund some of the Hofmann's Drops, Runa. They are very strengthening.

He would lie down, close his eyes, and listen to her footsteps while she fetched the Hofmann's Drops. She would perch herself on the side of the bed and ask anxiously whether he felt very bad.

No, he'd be better in a moment; it would soon pass, she could be sure.

I was so frightened. I thought you were seriously ill. You looked so pale, she would say, and surreptitiously she would stroke his hair in the half-light, and perhaps bend over him and whisper, I love you. Yours till death . . .

After that he would sit up, the lamp would be lit, steaming coffee would be brought, and the master would talk to him about the care of sheep and the weather outlook. You shall stay with us tonight, he would say. We can pass the evening with a game of cards.

Should he accept the invitation? Should he let himself be persuaded by further urging? No, he would show his father-in-law-to-be that he was no idler. There could be no question of staying the night. He had recovered and was well able to get home with the ptarmigan. Many thanks for the coffee and the Hofmann's Drops. Good night.

He would squeeze Sigrun Maria's hand and gaze deeply into her eyes, and when he had gone his way in the moonlight, the farmer would remark to his wife and daughter, He's a smart lad, that Gudmund! As hard as nails!

Ah, there he was again with his mind filled with dreams and fancies! He had no shotgun, no cartridge belt. The most he could do was send Sigrun Maria greetings on New Year's Eve by lighting a bonfire up on the fell if the weather was fine and dry. And then there was no certainty that she would see the bonfire or realize that it was a greeting sent to her through the winter darkness from a secret, greener world down the valley. Probably she would not see the bonfire.

VI

At last the hour came, the hour he had longed for, waking and sleeping since he carried Sigrun Maria across the river. It was a letter that came to his rescue: an unstamped letter to her father. It arrived between postal deliveries late in March and demanded immediate conveyance. *Urgent* was inscribed on the envelope, and *Deliver Without Delay.*

He put on his Sunday best, knickerbockers and windbreaker with a zipper, dipped his comb in water, pushed the letter into his jacket, took the knitted gloves with a fancy pattern from under his pillow, picked a steel-tipped staff from the storeroom, and set off walking in a northerly direction toward the river. The ground was bare and frozen, bathed in a cool, golden sunlight that flooded the landscape, transforming clear icicles into multicolored crystals. He perched on the very hump of heather which Sigrun Maria had used for a seat in the autumn, took off his stockings, pulled the knickerbockers above his knees, and waded out into the stream. The water did not seem to him at all cold: there was a spring note in the river, and the fine gravel in its bed tickled his heels. He dried his feet in a perfunctory way on the far bank and allowed himself no time to worry about the red patches he had had to stick on his rubber shoes in the winter. Sigrun Maria would scarcely notice those conspicuous, glaring patches when they met at long last! He continued on his way, swinging his staff, and quickened his pace over the ridges on her father's land, whistled a tune, talked aloud to himself, rehearsing everything that he was going to say to her, blushed with happiness, and heard her answer echoing back to him out of the distance. It was like a fanfare of trumpets in his heart.

But when he saw the farmhouse on the level land at the foot of the hill, something strange happened in his head so that he forgot everything he was going to say. This was in fact not just a farmhouse but a fine mansion with tarred roof, white gables, and large, questioning windows, and with a magnificent weathercock on its ridgepole. As he drew nearer to the house he felt himself grow smaller in proportion, stopped swinging the staff, and began to walk slowly and deliberately, fixing his eyes on the ground in front of his feet as though threading an indistinct path through a bog, and able to think of nothing but the glaring red patches on his rubber shoes. What disastrous footwear! How on earth could he expect Sigrun Maria to look favorably upon him when he was wearing such ugly, worn-out shoes!

There was no one outside. He knocked on the door three times, then stood like a condemned man on the step, hand clenched about the staff, waiting.

The master himself came to the door, bald and thickset, with a little tuft of hair on the tip of his nose and money wrinkles round his eyes.

Hallo, boy, he said in a deep voice. So you're on your travels, eh?

Yes, replied the boy and he fumbled hastily in the breast of his jacket. I have a letter for you here.

Eh? A letter for me? Who's it from?

I don't know, he said, and felt the sweat springing to his brow. It was brought over from Hjalli yesterday evening.

THE CHANGING EARTH

Ah, I daresay it's some confounded cadging from old Brand at Thufa, said the master of the house, and he cleared his throat several times as though he had an irritation in it. Let me see!

He took the letter and examined the writing on the envelope, his head to one side, and muttering to himself, Urgent, Deliver Without Delay. Well if this isn't old Brand's scrawl there's something wrong with my eyes!

Shaking his head, he sighed. Then he said shortly, Come in, boy, come in, and led the way to the parlor, where he pointed to a chair on one side of the table, and sitting opposite tore open the letter.

Health and greetings to you, kinsman, he read aloud. God grant that these lines find you and yours all well . . . There, didn't I say it was from old Brand?

He thrust his fingers into a vest pocket, pulled out a quill and began to pick his teeth while he read the rest of the letter in silence. From time to time he snorted, clicked his tongue, knit his brow, and groaned.

The boy sat motionless on his chair, scarcely daring to breathe and wishing he had never set out with this tiresome and seemingly endless letter. He saw that one picture on the chest of drawers in the corner was of Sigrun Maria in her confirmation dress. And he heard her voice outside in the passage.

Cadging for one thing after the other! He has his nerve, I must say! exclaimed the farmer finally, and took the quill out of his mouth. Then he slipped the letter back into its envelope and threw it carelessly onto a carved shelf. You wouldn't have seen a white wether of mine with a brown belly among your flock, I suppose, my lad?

A white wether with a brown belly? No, it hadn't been seen down the valley, that was certain.

It never came back to the sheds the night before last, the imp of darkness, said the farmer. I don't know where it can have run off to.

After that he went out of the room, leaving the door open behind him. You there! he called. Give the visitor some refreshment. I have to slip across to the barn.

The atmosphere in the room seemed to become more relaxed and warmer after he had gone. The boy was unable to take his eyes off the picture on the chest of drawers. The fanfare of trumpets in his heart was renewed, and the green world redolent with the scent of meadowsweet and moss campion. A light step could be heard in the passage, and a moment later Sigrun Maria appeared in the doorway. She was wearing a blue jumper with white stripes, had wound her braids in a coil and stuck two arched combs in her hair.

No-o, is it you? she cried.

Yes, it was he.

How are you, she said, giving him a soft hand. Thank you for last time.

The same to you, he said.

Are you looking for sheep?

No, he had brought a letter for her father.

Who from? She inquired curiously. Then in the same instant she glanced up at the carved shelf, and snatching down the letter, ran her eyes over the closely written pages. Hurriedly she slipped them back in the envelope. Oh, it's only from old Brand at Thufa!

She moved a chair over to the window, ran the palms of her hands carefully over the coil of her braids, and tugged once or twice at her jumper so that the white stripe stretched across her breasts.

Coffee will be ready in a minute, she said. Are you in a hurry?

Oh no, he murmured, not especially.

Then perhaps you can tell me some news as well?

He did not answer her at once but stared very hard into his cupped hands and cleared the lump in his throat. All that he had made up his mind to say to her when half running among the shrub-covered hills, swinging his staff, had gone into hiding now and was not to be drawn out however much he groped after it in his mind. He could no longer remember anything. But he was not going to give up. He would not behave churlishly, be silent and tongue-tied, and make a fool of himself a second time. Yes, there had been some heavy snow that winter, he said, and he began to talk about farming and the weather, hot in the face and stiff and hesitant in his speech at first but gradually with greater ease and a firmer control over his tongue. It was just as though an elderly farmer were chatting with his neighbor. He remarked that the hay had been of the very best quality that winter, thanks to an exceptionally good summer; none of it had been spoiled by getting overheated or gone moldy in the barn. Indeed, this could be seen in the livestock: sheep had seldom been in better flesh. He recalled the still weather of Advent, the frost in January, the snowstorms of March, and the recent thaw which had cleared away most of the snow in a couple of days, so that now there was excellent pasture for sheep and horses everywhere. There was hardly likely to be severe frost from now on; at the most maybe a few snowflakes around Easter; then spring would come, and it would undoubtedly be mild and fine. He added that he could see no reason to suppose that lambing would not be highly successful, for the ewes were in such excellent condition.

Sigrun Maria nodded assent from time to time, plucked at the hem of her jumper, and stared out of the window blankly. Then suddenly she broke in: There's one thing I'm certain about, and that's that the boys of this district are quite the dullest of any of their age!

He was so taken aback that he could not say a word.

You're always talking about ewes, she continued. You can never find anything else to talk about except ewes. Pooh! I'm getting so tired of this ewe talk of yours that I can't bear it any longer. Why don't you talk about something interesting?

He was silent.

Sigrun Maria looked out the window and sighed. Why didn't they ever have any entertainment here in the winter, she demanded, like the public prosecutor, with the answer ready: Because the young men of the district only thought about cows and sheep. They were so dead that they couldn't even dance properly. They never opened a book, knew nothing about poetry, and couldn't be bothered to buy foreign stories that described interesting events. She knew a seventeen-year-old boy in the neighboring district who bought the *Weekly* and composed beautiful poems. Nobody bought the *Weekly* in this district!

I have a few books, the boy stammered. You can borrow them if you like.

They'll be nothing but old sagas, of course, she said. Do you imagine that any young person could enjoy reading those old sagas of yours? They're nothing but *thee* and *thou* and *yea* and *nay!*

He did not venture to explain to her that he had not only Njala and Laxdaela but also three or four volumes of poems and one love story, for his heart was in a whirl and there was a heavy sound in his ears. He just stared into his hands and tried to summon up a topic of conversation that would offer a way out of this impasse and enable him to regain control over his tongue. The fanfare in his heart had been dispersed like a flock of frightened birds.

Have you been ill this winter? he inquired after a long pause.

Me? Ill? she exclaimed, and she began to laugh. What made you suppose I might have been ill?

You told me you had rather a weak heart when I took you over the river last autumn.

I, a weak heart? she said. No, now you're making things up!

Words seemed to fail her, and she fell back in her chair radiating merriment.

A weak heart! I've never heard anything like it! Why in the name of goodness should I have a weak heart at my age? And after she had laughed heartily at this absurdity she felt constrained to go to the door and put her head out.

Mamma, she called, Gudmund thinks I have rather a weak heart!

At that moment her mother came in with coffee and stayed for a while to hear the visitor's news. She was curious to know if the cows had given a good yield after calving, whether there had been any incidence of calving fever, whether they had all been well this winter.

Yes, answered the boy, they had all been well.

That was good news. Health comes before everything, she said, nodding her head, and she went back to her work in the kitchen, pulling the door to behind her.

There was a silence in the parlor. The photographs on the chest of drawers assumed a strange expression, and the air once more became cold and tense. The boy sipped at the boiling-hot coffee and looked to neither right nor left. Sigrun Maria too sat motionless on the chair by the window and did not utter a word. He sensed that she was staring fixedly at the prominent red patches on his rubber shoes, so that he blushed with shame, sweat beading his brow, and drew his feet under him, pressing them tightly together. Good Lord! If only he were wearing decent shoes! It was all because of those glaring red patches!

I say, she remarked, you haven't touched the fritters.

Yes, I have, he replied, and tried to still the twitching round his mouth.

THE CHANGING EARTH

Or the doughnuts, she added. You haven't tasted the doughnuts I made yesterday evening.

He mumbled into his chest that he couldn't eat another thing, was quite full.

I'm going to get myself a cup, she said, standing up. Maybe you'll have a better appetite if I drink to keep you company.

She darted out to the kitchen for the cup and was back in a moment, then pulled her chair up to the table and drank to keep him company.

Are my doughnuts bad? she inquired.

No, he answered.

Then, please, she said, eat one for me.

He had to obey, for her voice reminded him suddenly of a spring breeze passing over the meadows. She also prevailed upon him to have some of the fritters, which she had made that morning, she said, for she had been certain that someone would come today. She always dreamed before the coming of visitors. And when they had finished their coffee she wanted to look in his cup and see if she could read anything interesting in it. But there was nothing of interest to be read in the cup, for the cream had spoiled all the pattern. How silly of her not to have remembered in time! She had meant to ask him not to put cream in his coffee so that she could read his fortune, but somehow it had slipped her mind! Well, it didn't matter. Perhaps they should play a hand of rummy? Or Black Peter? She always enjoyed a game of Black Peter.

No, the boy hadn't time. He had hung around too long and must hurry home.

All the same, before you go I'm going to cast one star for you, she said, and began to search for the cards in the top drawer of the chest of drawers. Have you ever had your star cast?

No, that had never been done.

Who knows but I might see something strange? she said, and pushing the coffee tray to one side, she pursed her lips and knit her brow a little, shuffled the cards, and then laid them out on the table according to complex and mysterious principles. But no sooner had she completed the star than she caught her breath and struck her thigh.

Jeremiah! Never in all my born days have I seen such a star! There was no great difficulty about telling the boy's fortune: it all lay there before her eyes! The knave of hearts and queen of spades were half-engaged, though they hadn't yet made any formal marriage contract or started wearing rings. The knave of hearts was poor, as things were, but would probably enjoy an unexpected stroke of luck—receive a legacy from a distant relative or a sur- prise money order from some kind gentleman. The queen of spades, on the other hand, seemed to be quite well off; in fact, she hadn't a moment's peace from suitors of all ages. See, there were knaves and kings all round her, but she cared nothing for them. She just made fun of them and would look at no one but the knave of hearts. They would probably announce their engage- ment in a few months and set up house after two or three years on a good property. Well, now! What a star! There were four children beside the queen!

The boy listened to the fortune-telling with a crimson face, forgetting the patches on his shoes, and stole a glance at Sigrun Maria. Her cheeks were red, too, and the green iridescence in her eyes darted hot, gleaming sparks. She picked the cards up from the table and put them back in the top drawer of the chest of drawers, but when she saw that the boy had risen to his feet and was getting ready to leave, she remembered that he had not yet seen the photographs.

Look, she said, this one is of me in my confirmation dress. Do you rec- ognize me?

Yes, he recognized her.

But don't you think I've changed? she asked. I was so skinny and childish when I was confirmed.

Yes, he answered, she had changed.

And here is the picture of Grandma and Grandpa at Klaustur, she said, peering over his shoulder so that her breath played on his cheek. See how happy they look! They were always so good to each other.

He trembled all over with joy and felt the heart bound in his breast. She stood at his side quite motionless for a long while, breathing more rapidly and staring like him at the photograph of Grandma and Grandpa at Klaustur. He was on the point of putting his arm around her, thrusting up against her and whispering, I love you, yours till death, when she moved away, put a hand to her mouth, and cleared her throat. The sound of heavy footsteps could be heard outside the door.

Well, she said, Papa is back from the barn. I really must go and help Mamma in the kitchen.

He took his cap, thanked her for the coffee, and said good-bye. She walked with him out to the step, so that he should not take all the wit of the house with him, and gave his hand a parting squeeze, blinking her eyes winningly in the pale April sunshine.

You're a dreadful fellow, she whispered, not to want to play Black Peter with me!

Perhaps we could have a game of Black Peter . . . some time later, he stammered.

Yes, of course, she agreed. Some time later.

After that he walked homeward among the shrub-covered hills trying to solve some of the many riddles which this journey had posed to his heart. But his head was so confused that one solution canceled out another. Sometimes he was convinced that Sigrun Maria loved him and considered herself engaged to him. Sometimes he felt that she had merely been playing with him and found him dull; he was a dreadful bore, couldn't dance, had no idea of decent books, and could hardly get a word out without blushing and sweating. And sometimes he hopped, swinging his staff, and sang, because Sigrun Maria had read their future in the card star: they would announce their engagement in a few months, then set up house on a good property and have four fine children. She had blushed herself, and become confused, on reading their future in the star. Then she had pointed out to him the picture of Grandma and Grandpa at Klaustur, peered over his shoulder, breathed on his cheek, and said, They were always so good to each other!

By the river he removed his stockings, and waded out into the stream, which ran clear and glittering in the sunlight. But the water was so cold that it hurt his feet and made him grit his teeth. The gravel on the bottom no longer tickled his heels as it had done when he waded across that morning, and he must have been mistaken about the spring note in the water, for its murmur was dull and monotonous.

He could think of no relatives with one foot in the grave and a mind to bequeath him their possessions. Nor did he know of anyone likely to send him a money order so that he could rush off to the goldsmith in the village, buy a ring, and announce their engagement.

VII

In June the moss campion bloomed on the hill and the meadowsweet lined the stream in the marsh. The rim of the fell glowed in the red of evening, and the nights were bright and still. Nevertheless it seemed to him as though the time would never pass. The days crawled by, filled with work and restlessness. The blaze of sunset awakened doubtful questioning, the twilight a melancholy yearning, and the night dreams. He gazed to the north when he was alone, forgot his work, and sighed. He had, it was true, seen Sigrun Maria in church at Easter and Whitsunday, but not a word had he been able to say to her in private, for she had hardly moved from her parents' side. He had intended to tell her, privately, that he was expecting some books from the south, interesting novels which she was welcome to borrow, and at the same time to slip into her hand a small poem that he had written on the first day of summer. But that, too, had come to nothing. Everything had gone wrong. Everything turned against him or slipped from his grasp. He had no hope of seeing her again before the Youth Club tombola.

The spring passed, and nothing of interest happened, except that shortly before midsummer the roadmen came on a truck and pitched their tents to the north beside the river. The legislature had suddenly converted the parish road into a county highway and provided a sum of money for its repair during the summer, while the local foreman had rounded up some men from the village and sent them up-country to work for the money.

Most of the men were young and exuberant, had pipes and cigarettes, drank sweet coffee and ate hardtack in their tents, grew moustaches and wore check caps—all except the truck driver, who had a cap with a shiny peak.

Tip her! he would shout to the spreader on the road, and pushing the peaked cap onto the back of his head he would move his pipe into the corner of his mouth and blow thick clouds of tobacco smoke. Steady! Let her go!

They went home on the truck every weekend, spent their pay on the spot, they said; it didn't go far, for they knew so many girls in the village, who had to have trifles of all kinds. Lively girls, man! Spirited and lighthearted girls who liked to fiddle with a moustache and had nothing against slipping out a window and playing hide-and-seek while Papa and Mamma were asleep in bed resting for the next morning's quarrel!

THE CHANGING EARTH

In the evening, after work was over, they would sometimes break into strange, foreign songs. They would climb a hill near the tents singing "Donna Clara," "They'll be taking me to prison in the morning," and "Ramona, Ramona," and their songs could be heard far away in the evening stillness— especially the voice of the truck driver, for it was so loud and clear. When the truck driver's voice reverberated in the distance, the summer evening seemed to change its character and become filled with a strange restlessness.

At last the news went round the countryside that the committee of the Youth Club had decided to hold a tombola in the schoolhouse at Grund on the second Sunday in July. There was to be a draw for five lambs promised by some farmers when the flocks came down from the fells in the autumn. Besides these, various useful donations had been made. For example, if one were lucky one might become the owner of an excellent Primus stove, an enameled washbasin, a blue coffee pot, two pounds of lump sugar, or some matches, wicks, and lamp glasses. Then there was to be a dance in the evening, when the most renowned musician of the county, Palli from Bali, would play his accordion. The entertainment would begin at four o'clock, admission one krona, tombola tickets fifty aurar each. All come! The Committee.

As soon as this important news had spread round the district, the days began to stretch themselves out to an extraordinary length. Haymaking started. The boy swung his scythe, sharpening the blade twice as often as occasion really demanded, and gazed to the north, following every wisp of cloud with his eyes. God let the weather be good! God let these rows be got under cover before the weekend, so that he needn't be kept in the fields, as happened last year! When he saw light trails of cloud above the fell, he was filled with anguish and dread, fearing a downpour toward the end of the week, followed by dry weather on Sunday. But when the time came, all went better than he had dared hope. They were just gathering in the rows at about six o'clock on Saturday evening as the roadmen drove past in their truck waving their check caps.

The evening was so red and silent, so tranquil and sweet-scented, that he stayed awake far into the night composing a new poem for Sigrun Maria. Tears came to his eyes as he put it in the envelope with the other poem, together with some sprigs of moss campion and forget-me-not. In the morning he intended to slip down to the stream and find a fine spray of meadow-sweet.

Yes, the day of the tombola was brighter and clearer than he had dared hope. He put on his Sunday best, lacing the new boots which he had bought when the wool was taken in, put the envelope containing the poems in one pocket of his tunic and a bag of candy in the other, anointed his hair with milk-separator oil, and went furtively time and again to the mirror to comb it. And he was so absorbed that he did not notice that his sister had also got herself ready to go until he bumped into her before the mirror just as he was about to leave.

Would you rather ride Blesa or old Grani? she asked.

He stared as though he had been stung. Who had told her that she might go to the tombola?

Papa and Mamma, she answered, sparkling with anticipation.

He inquired what business she might have there; she was too young to be going to entertainments; she couldn't dance.

No more can you, she said, examining her freckled face carefully in the mirror. She was going to try her luck and see whether she couldn't win a lamb or Primus stove or some useful article such as a lamp glass or an enameled washbasin. Mamma had always wanted a Primus stove.

He flushed with vexation and tried to find other objections. She didn't have to think she'd draw a lamb or a Primus! No, she wouldn't win a thing in the tombola, not a single thing! Besides, she couldn't pay for herself. She had no money. She had better stay home!

Yes, his sister replied, certainly she could pay for herself. She had nearly all her pocket money since last year, as well as the money for Golta's wool and the six kronur she'd been give at her confirmation.

You can't let strangers see you in those knickerbockers, he said. They're so ugly.

Yours are no better, she answered, and turned away, a sob rising in her throat and tears to her eyes. It was a riddle to her why he was making this fuss. She wasn't going to ask him to pay for her. She was going to pay for herself. If he didn't want to go with her he could just ride on ahead.

He walked away from the mirror and looked out the window. His parents and brothers were standing outside on the terrace by the horses, but the harness had not yet been brought from the storeroom. He turned and ran his fragment of comb through well-oiled hair, taking care to avoid the tearful eye of his sister, for she had always looked up to him and been good.

Oh well, perhaps she had better come, then. But she would have to hurry. It was getting on toward three o'clock, and there was a long road ahead of them. They'd draw neither lamb nor Primus if they didn't show themselves at the tombola until after everything had begun.

His sister wiped her eyes, adjusted her braids, and brushed some fuzz from her knickerbockers. The light had faded from her face, her lips quivered, and the freckles on her face seemed darker than before. Continuing to look for invisible fuzz on her knickerbockers, she remarked in a trembling voice that she was asking whether she had better ride Blesa or old Grani.

Blesa, he answered in a gentler tone, and was sorry he had made her cry. Old Grani was so slow and had such a rough trot. And she didn't have to worry about her knickerbockers. There was nothing the matter with them; they were at least more presentable than his. Good heavens! He had only been teasing her, for he knew very well why she wanted so much to go to the tombola. But he wouldn't tell anyone; he'd be as silent as the grave.

His sister smiled, her eyes reflecting warmth and gratitude, and recovered her spirits as she looked in the mirror and put on her red woolen cap.

You know nothing at all, Mundi, she said. You're talking nonsense!

After that they set off. The tents of the roadmen north by the river were silent and deserted, and nothing was to be seen about them but picks and shovels, paper and rubbish, jars and fuel cans. The clear stream glittered, and the cold, murmuring water splashed up round the horses in the ford. What a glorious day! The skies were flooded with sunlight, the scent of blooming shrubs and grasslands mingled with the heat haze in the air. Obsidian cliffs flashed in the distance, and everywhere the earth was green—almost as green as the world which he guarded in his heart, almost as lovely and wonderful. In the evening there would certainly be a heavy fall of dew and a pungent scent in the bushy hollow to the west of the schoolhouse. Perhaps the best thing would be to give Sigrun Maria the poems and flowers when the last beams had died in the thickets and the sky's dewfall was beginning to water plant and leaf.

VIII

They unharnessed the horses and put them in the paddock at the bottom of the home field. Then they helped each other brush the dust from their knickerbockers, and walked up the track to Grund and the little schoolhouse on the north side of the farm.

The committee of the Youth Club was busily engaged in putting up the refreshment booths on the newly mown grass round the schoolhouse, and people were standing about in groups, gossiping and laughing, exchanging news and blinking in the sunlight. The raffle was just about to start. The entertainment subcommittee announced that all was ready in the schoolroom, the sale of admission tokens would begin shortly, people would be able to buy coffee in the refreshment booths into the early hours of the morning, and the dance would commence as soon as the raffle was over—seven o'clock at the latest. Where was the musician himself, Palli from Bali? He had not yet come with his brand-new accordion with the five-row keyboard which he had got from Reykjavik in the spring, but he would not let them down, that lad. He would turn up on time, as always.

Brother and sister walked hesitantly in among the crowd about the schoolhouse, said hello, answered questions, and took note of everything. They seemed both to be looking for somebody in the throng, for their eyes wandered from one to another, expectant and searching. There might still be some to come; perhaps some were late and now on the far side of the ridges and slopes on their way to the tombola. For instance, a group could be seen coming from the east, across the levels. Three riders cantered on easygoing mounts up to the paddock and sprang from their saddles, but no one knew the horses, no one recognized the piebald or the bay. No, those were definitely people from outside the district on a journey—possibly from Bakki, or perhaps Moar.

He did not catch sight of Sigrun Maria before the committee had announced the sale of admission tokens. All of a sudden there she was standing at his side in a new blouse and striped skirt, a sunburned cheek turned toward him and her eyes fixed on the door of the schoolhouse, where the chairman of the entertainment subcommittee was selling blue ribbons and pins at a krona each. Her appearance was a little strange: her face seemed chubbier and the dimples deeper, for she had cut off her braids and put waves in her hair. A silvery brooch gleamed at the neck of her blouse.

Hello, he said, and he held out his hand to her.

She did not answer at once, but looked round slowly, as though preoccupied, and he had to repeat his greeting.

Hello, she said at last, and nodded to him. Are you here?

Yes, he said. Thank you for the last time.

The last time? she repeated, not remembering. When did we see each other last?

Late in March, he replied.

No, no, you're making things up! she said and laughed teasingly. I saw you at church on Whitsunday!

I came to your house, he stammered. I came with a letter in March.

Oh yes, that's quite true, you brought a letter for Papa!

Are you here on your own?

No, she was not on her own; the work people had come with her. But Papa and Mamma couldn't be persuaded to come, as usual. They would never go to amusements.

The raffle is beginning, he said.

Yes, what are you thinking of, boy? You'll never draw a lamb this way!

Aren't you coming too?

Yes, in a minute, she said, and she fingered the brooch at the neck of her blouse. I never have any luck. It makes no difference whether I draw early or late.

He asked if he might buy her a token.

Me? she exclaimed astonished, and looked about her. No, thank you. Buy one for your sister.

He hurried to the door, took out his purse, and jingling the money told the chairman of the entertainment subcommittee loudly and distinctly that he wanted to buy two tokens: There you are, two kronur, thank you. He handed his sister one of the ribbons, ignoring her protests. There had never been any question of her paying for herself; he had really invited her to the tombola. Then he glanced back over his shoulder, but Sigrun Maria had walked over to the refreshment area and was deep in conversation with some girls. He could hear her bright, clear laughter as he worked his way through the door into the schoolroom. A fanfare of trumpets seemed to float through the green world in his heart, mingling with the scent of moss campion and meadowsweet. He was so carried away that when the treasurer of the Youth Club inquired sharply how many tombola tickets he intended to buy, he was startled.

Three for me, he replied. And three for my sister.

Pay, please, said the treasurer.

Forgetting to shake the purse, he picked out the money carefully, then turned and was going through the door.

What's the matter with you, man? the treasurer called after him. You forgot to draw!

He checked himself and explained that he had been looking for a friend he had to talk to—Siggi from Haedarendi, it was.

All right, draw! directed the treasurer.

Assuming an air of nonchalance he thrust his hand into the box and pulled out three folded slips of paper, which he held clenched in his hand, while his sister tried her luck and drew three more from the heap, silent and serious, for she had counted on winning either a lamb or a Primus stove. Then they moved to one side and unfolded the slips. But alas, fortune had passed them by! The boy had drawn an eight and his sister a twenty-three, and the rest were blanks.

What do these numbers mean?

The club secretary examined the slips and then handed them respectively a toothpick and a box of matches. Here you are, he said smiling. A box of matches and a toothpick are better than nothing!

His sister looked dejected. She had had her heart set on getting something useful, at least a lamp glass or an enameled washbasin. She had no use for the box of matches; there were plenty of matches at home. But she might be luckier if she tried again. She had the money. She could pay for herself. Aren't you going to have another try? she asked her brother.

Not just now, he replied, and went outside into the sunshine.

They had begun selling coffee in the refreshment booths, and the smell of it came to him as he hunted for Sigrun Maria. Where could she have gone? He looked all round the schoolhouse for her, peered into the booths, and wandered among the groups on the grass with the same exultant fanfare

sounding in his heart. He was sure to find her soon. Perhaps she had gone
into the farmhouse to say hello to the old woman. Perhaps she had met with
some of her girlfriends—the girls from Gil, for instance—and left the crowd,
walked southward across the valley, or westward into the thicket, where the
evening sunbeams were still dancing among the leaves. In fact he could see
some girls there now, making their way between the bushes, and he hurried
to cross the fence, toothpick in hand, into the thicket, where before long he
came upon a pair of his former confirmation classmates. The girls smiled at
him, said that they hardly recognized him, he had grown into such a giant,
and gaily inquired where he was off to.

He was looking for a friend he had to talk to—Siggi from Haedarendi.

We saw him back at the schoolhouse earlier, they told him.

Yes, but he walked out into the woods, he said.

It's odd that we haven't seen him, they remarked to each other and fid-
geted with their scarlet headbands. What's that you're holding in your hand?

Only a toothpick, he replied.

A toothpick! What are you doing with a toothpick?

I drew it in the tombola.

And didn't you draw anything else?

No, he said, and hurrying away to avoid further questions he advanced
into the thicket and threw the toothpick down a hole.

The evening was warm and still. He wended his way between the bushes
and circled the rises and hollows, a leaf of sallow in his mouth, but saw
nothing except the thrushes and whimbrels, droning hawk flies, glittering
spider webs, and some little moths that flew only in brief starts and were
waiting for the dew. Gradually the murmur from the schoolhouse faded into
the distance, peace and silence took possession all about him, and the sunbeams poured through the foliage of twisted branches, warming the bark.

He sat down on a grassy hump in a low area between bushes, and pulled
a cattail apart, quietly and thoughtfully. What would he do if she suddenly
came to him, in her light blouse and striped skirt? What would he say if she
sat down beside him on the hump of grass and asked him whether he had
forgotten the card star she had cast for him in early April? Dear Lord, he
mustn't stammer now, mustn't sweat and behave like an idiot! What a silly fool
he had been not to ask her to talk to him in private when they had met earlier

beside the schoolhouse. She was sure to have whispered, Yes, let's go into the woods. Then they could have plighted their troth, here in this hollow.

IX

The sun slipped ever farther westward, strewing the sky with gold. Sigrun Maria came out of the schoolhouse, put a hand above her eyes, and scanned the road to the south. He hurried up to her and cleared his throat.

Oh, there you are, she said.

Yes, he said.

What did you draw in the tombola?

Nothing.

Well, that was unlucky. Had he drawn nothing at all?

Well, yes, a toothpick.

A *toothpick!* She didn't call that anything! She had drawn a lamb.

That was good.

And her cousin at Gil had won the Primus, but she had returned it immediately, for she had both a Primus and an oil range.

I see, said the boy, and glanced round to make sure that no one was listening to their conversation. Will you have some coffee with me?

They're going to start dancing soon, said Sigrun Maria, still gazing at the road to the south. Palli from Bali has come.

Then brushing the dark locks back from her ears, she assumed an oddly vacant expression. Coffee? No, thank you—she drawled the words absently— I don't feel like any just now. I had a cup with my cousin only a few minutes ago. You should offer your sister some. There she is, over by the booths.

Maybe you'll feel like having a cup later, he suggested.

I don't know, she said. Yes, maybe.

At that moment someone called his name. It was a young girl with thick braids and a scarlet headband. She told him that she had found Siggi from Haedarendi—and here he was.

That spoiled everything. He was forced to leave Sigrun Maria without having mentioned a walk in the woods. Why on earth did he have to pretend he was looking for Siggi from Haedarendi, this ungainly, adenoidal youth who waddled like an old man and wagged his head? He invented a pretext, heard the reply in a daze, saying yes and no alternately, and was on the point of walking away. But Siggi from Haedarendi pursued him, talking without cease on his favorite topic: sheep and lambs, horses and cattle, the haymaking at home, and the fox's lair which had been found north on the moor that spring.

You haven't seen my chestnut, the five-year-old, he said in conclusion, working himself to a pitch of enthusiasm. Papa broke him in.

The boy nodded.

He's here in the paddock, added Siggi from Haedarendi, pointing. You can have a short ride on him now if you like.

They'll be starting the dance in a minute.

Well, come all the same. We won't be a minute, said Siggi from Haedarendi, and he continued describing the chestnut and all his good points until the boy finally gave in and hurried with him down to the paddock.

When they returned the schoolhouse echoed to the sound of the dancing.

Palli from Bali was standing on a box at the far end of the room, and he played one tune after another on his new accordion, swaying to left and to right and jerking his head in time with the music, even closing his eyes, for fun, just to show everyone that he could play blindfold if he wished. He seemed as though transformed into a sorcerer who controlled the dancers with strange enchantments. He made them hop and circle, advance and retreat, take sidesteps, rock themselves, and stamp their feet together. All obeyed, all yielded to the magic of the accordion and did their best to follow the beat of the music—all except Mangi, the hired man, a black-bearded bachelor of fifty, who tenaciously danced some kind of a reel, stomping and swinging round the floor with a terrified girl in his grasp, whirling her in dizzy circles, and took snuff when Palli from Bali rested, dried the sweat on his brow, and declared with a bellow of laughter, Now things are moving, lads!

The schoolroom shook to the music and dancing, while the dust eddied in an orange sunbeam which fell in a shaft through the west window. But time passed, time flew by on invisible wings, taking no account of those who sat in the corner and waited. Soon the orange sunbeam would fade in the windowpane and a faint blue veil envelop the earth. There would be scent among the thickets, moths on the wing, and soft gleam on leaf and flower.

Then the evening glow would vanish over the mountains, all things droop and be silent, and night would come, breathing coolly on the grass and closing the petals of the flowers—the July night with its stillness and clear skies, a night of dreaming and loving, translucent as a spring among the rocks.

And still Sigrun Maria danced . . .

He clenched his cap in his hand, moved to the window, and gazed for a moment out across the woods. There could hardly be much difficulty about moving one's feet here and there, turning in circles, going forward and then backward, taking a few steps to one side, and then whirling oneself in another circle. He could scarcely be more ridiculous than Mangi, the hired man, who flew past him just then holding his sister, wide-eyed and pale with giddiness. Why not try? The sun was barely above the brow of the moor now, and soon it would sink out of sight, drawing this long-wished-for day in its wake. If he continued to sit here on the bench, dreading and despairing, nothing would happen. But if he danced with Sigrun Maria he would surely have the chance to whisper a few words to her and ask her to come and talk to him about something important out in the woods. Putting his arms around her, as when he had carried her over the river, he would squeeze her hand, gaze into her eyes, and say in a low voice, I have a letter for you in my pocket. There are some poems.

The accordion stopped. Palli from Bali rested, and the dancers sat down on benches round the wall, while the dust gradually settled in the sunbeam from the west window. Now things are moving! announced Mangi, the hired man, shaking his snuffbox, and for a time there was silence. Palli from Bali was in no hurry. He flourished a white handkerchief, mopped the beads of sweat from his face, and whistled quietly to himself, as though recalling a new tune. Then with a few magisterial clearings of the throat he let it be known that the intermission was over.

The boy rose to his feet. He was trembling at the knees a little and felt the blood surge to his cheeks. He hesitated, and was on the point of either sitting down again on the bench or rushing through the door, but then walked across the floor, walked as though in a trance straight up to Sigrun Maria.

Hanging his head he asked, Will you dance with me?

With you? she said in a surprised tone and glanced involuntarily at his knickerbockers. Have you ever danced before?

No, he hadn't.

Do you know how to dance, then?

Not exactly, he replied awkwardly, and tried to master the quiver in his voice. But maybe he'd learn quickly.

Sigrun Maria shrugged her shoulders and said nothing. She stirred on the bench, fingered the silver brooch at her throat, smoothed her striped skirt, and seemed unable to take her eyes off his knickerbockers. He noticed that people were beginning to stare at them and listen but stood as though nailed to the floor waiting.

I'll dance with you some time later in the evening. I'm going to rest now, I'm so tired, she said at last, biting her lip. Why don't you dance with your sister? There she is, standing in the corner.

At this moment Palli from Bali stepped onto his box and drew the accordion apart, and the schoolroom filled with sound. Two men from another district bowed before Sigrun Maria, pretending not to see the boy, but she shook her head and wouldn't dance: she was tired and needed a little rest. Later she stood up and went outside into the bright evening.

He took his cap and followed.

Shading her eyes with her hand, she stood gazing for a long time down the road, out across the countryside, but gradually her expression lost its eagerness and her shoulders sank. He moved closer and asked hesitantly if she would care for a cup of coffee.

No, she sighed, I don't feel like coffee.

Aren't you feeling well?

I have a tiny bit of a headache, she said, putting her hand to her forehead. Also I'm dying of boredom.

What? He stammered in his surprise. D-do you f-find this boring?

She snorted. It's no fun dancing with these boys. They're as clumsy as a herd of cattle!

He stood beside her without speaking, twisting his cap in his hands, not sure whether he was included in this condemnation. The evening light played on her cheeks, filling the hollow at the base of her throat with gold, and glittered on the silver brooch at the open neck of her blouse and the black buttons down the front. Then she stopped gazing out across the countryside, glanced to the west, and asked suddenly, What's the time?

I don't know, he replied. I suppose it must be getting on toward eleven.

Don't you have a watch?

No.

Really, you surprise me, boy, she said. I thought that you would have a watch at your age!

He dared not look up, ashamed of his poverty, but Sigrun Maria changed the subject. She was afraid that the Youth Club was bound to lose on this social: so few had come, she said. Far fewer than last year. And the roadmen, she added, why haven't they shown themselves? The club surely deserved to make a few kronur off them.

The roadmen went home yesterday. They always go home on Saturdays.

I think they could have come along this evening, she said. And the Youth Club should have made them pay three kronur a head for entrance; they're rolling in money, those fellows.

Once more she turned her eyes toward the thicket, where the sunbeams were pouring their rays over the soft green shadows in the hollows. Once again her expression became warm and gay, the dimples deepened in her cheeks, her brow lifted, and the gold at the base of her throat quivered.

I say, she remarked, have you seen the little rowan tree over there in the woods?

No, he replied, and he blushed with joy, for her voice was different. Now it was like a summer breeze moving across a meadow.

Nor have I, she said giving him a look. I'd love to see whether it's as pretty as the rowan tree at home on the hillside above the house.

S-so would I, he stammered, and was just about to take the bag of candy from his pocket and ask if they couldn't slip across to the woods, when a strange sound reached his ears. It penetrated the tones of the accordion, the hubbub of the refreshment booths, his own secret green world, changing his joy to a strange uneasiness. They turned, and both at the same time saw a truck approaching over the levels, roaring and rattling, and the roadmen standing in the back singing the verse about Ramona.

Oh, look! cried Sigrun Maria. Here they come! I knew it all the time!

The boy said nothing.

And singing, too! she said.

He was at loss for words. He forgot to take the bag of candy from his pocket and rolled his cap between his hands.

And waving at us! she continued. And they're going to drive right up the track!

He moved closer to her, staring in front of him and feeling an unfamiliar shadow fall across his inner world, swift and silent, like the darkness before a hailstorm.

And they never closed the gate behind them! What a wild crowd they are!

Sigrun, he whispered, shall we go into the woods!

Into the woods? What for?

To see the rowan tree.

No, my dear boy, I dare not. I'm too afraid of the spiders! She laughed, and rushed away from him, rushed into the schoolhouse to tell her friends that the roadmen were coming.

X

He stood alone in the evening sunshine, no longer hearing a clear, exultant fanfare in his heart; only the roar and rattle of the truck as it wound its way circumspectly along the narrow track, emitting small clouds of blue smoke. Suddenly the music came to an end and people flocked out of the school-house and refreshment booths to watch the truck. The roadmen laughed. They jumped down from the back with eyes only for the girls, whispered together, and nudged each other, throwing out their chests. Then they lit cigarettes and crowded round the club treasurer to buy entrance tokens. They trooped into the schoolroom together and gazed about grandly, like knights, full of glamour and mystery, with their narrow moustaches and tobacco-stained fingernails. They had a half-empty bottle of home brew with them and thought themselves capable of anything. Now there'd be a bit of life in the place—dancing and song! The truck driver took off his peaked cap, turned to Palli from Bali and spoke for his companions: Turn it on, man! he said. Let her go!

And once more the schoolroom resounded to the dancing.

The boy stood in the doorway and watched Sigrun Maria spin round the floor in the arms of the truck driver, with a smile at something he was whispering to her. A greenish fire, restless and intermittent as moonlight on running water, flickered in her eyes. Her dancing was different: she moved quickly and softly, swaying more supplely to the beat of the music, and spun in flying circles. When the beam from the west window caught her face, she closed her eyes for a moment as though unable to bear the light. But the beam soon faded, and suddenly it vanished, for the sun had set and a blue shadow veiled the window. The dust could no longer be seen.

He overheard the truck driver say, It's always more fun dancing after sunset! And the tone of his voice, impudent and ironic, pierced and ran like a shadow through the world of the heart.

He took refuge outside and drifted round the schoolhouse, seeing everything in a mist and still not believing that he had suffered defeat. It could not be that Sigrun Maria had forgotten him, forgotten the ride across the river, forgotten the card star she had cast for him last winter. No, she simply enjoyed dancing, she could not get away from the truck driver, and she had no inkling of the poems that awaited her in the envelope, along with the flowers, forget-me-nots, moss campion, and meadowsweet. He had just been on the point of telling her about the two poems when the roadmen appeared. And she had been talking about the rowan tree in the woods.

He crushed his cap in his hand, feeling a sudden hatred for the truck driver—a hatred for his glances, his movements, his voice, and even his black peaked cap that stood out from the headgear of the district. A dark wave seemed to rise about his heart. He clenched his fists, the cloud before his eyes thickened, and his lips trembled. Then he stood still, confused, and tried to hide his emotion. One of the girls who had been confirmed with him was standing there in front of him, smiling.

Mundi, she said, why are you carrying on like that?

Me? he mumbled. Like what?

Rushing round the house, she said, fingering the band in her hair. And swearing, too!

Yes, he had lost his pocketknife.

What a shame! Was it a good one?

He should say so. A twin-bladed clasp knife.

I'll look for it too, she said, and began to search about.

But the boy hadn't the least hope of the knife's being found now. It was lost and given to the trolls! Perhaps it had slipped out of his pocket down by the paddock, or in the thicket. It was pointless making any more fuss about it.

Shouldn't we see if we can find it by the paddock? she asked, looking down at her feet. I'm so good at finding things.

It's no use, he replied, and hurrying away from her he went into the schoolroom and continued to watch the dance.

He leaned against the wall and saw that the truck driver was still whispering to Sigrun Maria, clasping her to him, and putting his thick lips against the dark wavy lock of hair. And Sigrun Maria was listening! Sigrun Maria was whispering something back to him, a strange look on her face and her cheeks flushed. From time to time she shook her head, sometimes nodded, and sometimes laughed at his words, opening her eyes wide and darting at him wavering greenish glances that seemed somehow to have grown deeper and hotter since the sun set. She had never been so beautiful.

He fled from the schoolroom again and wandered round the house and down by the booths, not knowing how the time passed, and finally got into conversation with some boys who had gathered round the truck. They were standing by the hood trying to spell out what was on the nameplate. Chevrolet, they remarked to one another, that must be a good make.

No, he said, Fords were much better.

How do you know? they asked skeptically.

He had read about it in a paper. Chevrolets were useless rattletraps that no self-respecting man would ever want to own. Besides, there wasn't the slightest difficulty about driving them; any fool could learn to do it in a few hours.

Sheer nonsense! said someone, and quoted as evidence the farmhand from Reykjavik who had stayed at his home the previous summer. The farmhand had been of the opinion that Chevrolets were sturdier than Fords.

He said nothing. He was outnumbered and could think of no suitable reply, was powerless even to take his revenge on this gleaming black vehicle that reminded him involuntarily of the peaked cap of its owner. He was so lonely and miserable that in his extremity he walked up to Siggi from Haedarendi and asked him where he was going.

Home, said Siggi, and added that he intended to mow that night while the grass was still wet with dew and take a short nap in the morning. He was eager to give his horse a canter.

I'll go with you down to the paddock, he said, as though reluctant to part with this friend of his. Don't you think you'll be sleepy tonight?

Sleepy? No, Siggi from Haedarendi would not be sleepy. He was determined to stay awake; he had been taking things easy and amusing himself all day.

You didn't dance, said the boy.

Well, if he didn't know how to dance it was all the same to him. He had no desire to learn that sort of tomfoolery! Rounding up sheep was much more fun than going round in circles with some girl in one's arms. It was true that ewes could sometimes be awkward and contrary, but womenfolk were more contrary still; so said Papa.

Then he saddled his horse, fondled it, and rubbed its nose, combing out the mane with strong fingers. He asked the boy whether he had ever seen a more serviceable-looking mount.

No, never.

And no one is going to drown, riding this old fellow, said Siggi from Haedarendi, pointing at the neck of the horse. Look at the Saint Peter's prints!

The boy examined the whorls in the horsehair and nodded. He was so stricken and woebegone that he would gladly have stood there beside the paddock far into the night listening to new stories about the horse, until the dance was over and Sigrun Maria came to prepare herself for the homeward journey. But Siggi from Haedarendi would hang around no longer and was in a hurry to be off; he was going to stay up all night and mow a good patch of the home field before it dried in the morning sun. He would ride straight along the earth track on the north side of the ridge and give his horse the rein across the levels by the lake. Good-bye!

He was gone.

The boy gazed after him for a while and pulled a cattail from the turf wall of the paddock. Then suddenly he turned and quickly walked back along the path to the schoolhouse. What had he been thinking of? Why had he wandered off down here with Siggi from Haedarendi? Good Lord! Who knew if he hadn't allowed happiness to slip through his fingers yet once again! Palli from Bali had taken another rest and was probably refreshing himself with coffee, for the people were standing in groups round the booths or had strolled out over the new-mown grass together. And there was one couple just vanishing into the thicket.

He stopped dead halfway along the path, went pale, and trembled. He felt a sharp pain in his chest as though he had been stabbed, went strangely weak at the knees, and stared bewildered into the bluish vapor that hung like a veil over the woods, transparent and motionless. He no longer heard the happy laughter of the people. For a long time he stood without moving, as if turned to stone. But when he came to himself, he was half running through the uncut grass of the home field, on his way to the thicket. Slowing down a little, he glanced back over his shoulder, even gave himself time to adjust his cap and make a detour to the gate in the fence. If anyone should ask what he was doing, he would say that he was looking for his clasp knife.

It was silent among the bushes, with a cool sweetness in the air. The grass was already damp with dew, and there was a gloss of moisture on the leaves. He tried to follow the faint path that wound between the hummocks but soon lost it and was uncertain which way to take. Moths fluttered about him, gray and golden, a marsh snipe flew up from under his feet, and somewhere a redwing chattered. The grass was not wet enough yet for him to be able to trace footprints. He paused, holding his breath, and listened. What business had he there in the woods? What did he mean to do in the peace and silence of the July night? Did he perhaps intend to chase the moths or show the poems in his breast pocket to the snails? He became hot with shame and anguish, clenched his fists, glared balefully at the glittering cobwebs, and made up his mind to turn back. But when it came to acting on his decision, he continued to drift through the thicket, searching and peering, as if he had lost control over his will. He had to make sure whether he had been mistaken.

And suddenly he knew.

Peering over a stunted birch, he felt something snap within him, felt a cold torpor creep through the world in his heart and take away the fragrance that had reminded him of the moss campion and meadowsweet. There was no longer any room for doubt. The peaked cap lay between two hummocks in the hollow, and the truck driver held Sigrun Maria in his arms, pressing her to him and drawing long kisses from her lips. And her lips were red and thirsty. She seemed to have forgotten the spiders that ran in the moss and spun their webs in the branches behind her. She neither saw nor heard.

He drew back and walked quietly away so that they should not be aware of his presence. Another string snapped within him, and his heart was no longer able to repel the rising torpor. The earth, too, had become colder under his feet, transformed in a moment to emptiness and desolation. The woods seemed naked, and the moths had suddenly lost the silver on their wings.

When he got back to the schoolhouse the people had begun dancing again. His sister was waiting by the booths, lonely and disconsolate, for she had lost the matches and lampwicks she had won in the tombola, and besides no one would dance with her except Mangi the hired man: her knickerbockers were so ugly.

I was looking for you, Mundi, she said in a low, toneless voice, as though talking in her sleep. Shouldn't we be starting for home?

Yes, he replied, and suddenly he remembered that he had once promised to buy some red paint and touch up the roses on her box. Let's go, he said.

They rode home without saying a word to each other. He stared into the night, feeling the flowers wither in the envelope with his poems. It was good not to be riding alone.

XI

Thus in mid-July happiness had abandoned him and grief taken up her abode with him instead, changing the horizon and turning the summer colors of the earth into a faint green mist. The days suddenly lost their fragrance and crept past silently, while the evenings cast heavy shadows on him, letting the angel of sorrow revive all those memories which brought pain and bitterness. He was convinced that God had never inflicted such torment on a living soul before. It even occurred to him to put an end to himself. He leaned on his scythe down in the marsh, gazing into a deep, sinister pool, and decided to end it all that evening when his father and brothers went home from the water meadows, to bid farewell to this aimless existence and throw himself headfirst into the pool. Tears came to his eyes. What a fate! He pictured his own funeral, the oration and the weeping, wondered whether Sigrun Maria would follow him to the churchyard and how she would take the news of his death, and made repeated journeys to the pool to shed a few secret tears. But as the day advanced and the time of parting drew near, he noticed that the water was both muddy and swarming with beetles. He had always had a horror of water beetles, so he put off making an end to himself that evening. It would be much cleaner to drown himself in some pool of the river—if he could be sure that the roadmen would not find his body.

His mother was beginning to comment on his silence and lack of appetite, on how haggard and dark about the eyes he was, when he received a package and postal cash demand from the *Weekly* in Reykjavik. Hurrying to get his pen and inkwell, he took the package, sat down in a corner of the living room, and wrote on it in large letters, Return to Sender. Then he remarked that the publishers must have got the name wrong, it was a mistake, he had never dreamed of becoming a subscriber to the *Weekly,* it was such rubbish!

He lay awake in the night recalling a certain journey, listening to the angel of sorrow, and seeing his own body revolve in the eddies under the fall. The next day, though, he felt an unexpected change of heart. It was so long since he had read a decent book! In fact he had read nothing worthwhile for many months, for his thoughts had been constantly turning on other things. He whetted his scythe, chewed a juicy stem of sedge, and made up his mind to allow no leisure time in the coming winter to go to waste. He would read and read. He would fix a candle at his bedside and stay awake late into the night, devouring one book after another and writing down everything that seemed to him beautiful or significant. But how was he going to get hold of the books? Did he perhaps intend to borrow them, tramping the district like a beggar and making a laughingstock of himself? For book buying he would only be able to put by a few kronur at the most, when the sheep were driven to slaughter. And were he to tramp the district, the farmers would doubtless only smile in their beards and kindly tell him that he was welcome to this volume of sermons if he wanted it. Also the earmark catalog!

All at once it became clear to him that if he stayed at home that winter he would abandon himself to gloom and despair to a greater degree than ever before. No, the right thing would be to avenge himself on Sigrun Maria by leaving this wretched place, by going to Reykjavik and tempting fortune. He would be able to find something to do down south. He could read innumerable books and learn languages, compose elegiac poems, and meet editors in person. Perhaps he would be able to get the elegiac poems published, with a picture of himself, pale and interesting. Perhaps he would return home the following spring wearing new clothes and bringing a pile of books with him. It would spread round the district that he had made a great impression in the capital and aroused interest by his difficult and melancholy poems. The man must surely have a secret sorrow.

Forgetting the anguish in his heart, he set to work energetically to mow the sedge, and that evening told his parents that he had decided to leave home in the autumn. He was going to spend the winter down south.

Is that so? said his father. Did he perhaps imagine he would be able to get work in these difficult times, with unemployment all over the country? Perhaps he thought that people could live on air in Reykjavik?

I'm going, he replied, refusing to be discouraged.

His father asked where he intended to live and what he would do for a living and how he proposed to eke out a miserable existence in the town without money and without anything. His mother had a word with him a few days later and tried to make him realize that he was still far too young to be setting out into the world. There were so many lures and temptations in Reykjavik; he ought to wait for a year or two. Who knows but times might change?

But their reasoning, prayers, and admonitions had no effect. Some inward voice seemed to whisper that he had to surmount all obstacles. And before long his thoughts were racing down long, straight streets, brilliant with electric lighting, rambling among fashionable houses, and engaging in conversation with strange people. Gradually the earth emerged from the faint green mist that had clouded it, the cotton grass swayed its white tufts in the morning breeze, the cinquefoil drooped in the stillness of the August evenings, and once more a fragrant scent was wafted over the segment of water meadow as the sun dried the dew on meadowsweet and butterwort. He swung his scythe visiting an imaginary photographer and assuming an expression of bold resolution as though capable of anything, for his photograph was to appear in a widely known periodical, together with a long poem about a young man of heroic disposition. The poem might begin something like this:

> From crest to crest I climbing go,
> Gazing on the world below:
> No fetters shall withhold me . . .

Suddenly he stopped mowing and looked around in the marsh, shame-faced and blushing as though caught red-handed. Good heavens! He had been whistling! And he hadn't given a single thought to Sigrun Maria all yesterday or the day before! What was more, he had begun composing a kind of epic for a journal in the capital, and imagining conversations with strange girls! What had come over him? Was he so inconstant in his grief, so fickle and capricious, so quick to forget? He relaxed his shoulders, conscious of only a very small pain in his heart, swung the scythe more slowly, and concentrated on devoting his remaining days to grief and mourning. Never would he know another happy day. Never would he try to smile or laugh. Yours till death! He would be like a bird that has lost the power of flight and song, like a tender plant that has been nipped by the frost and can never wave its soft head in the sunshine again. Perhaps it would be better, after all, to go to the river and throw himself into the pool under the fall, he whispered tragically, watching the godwit flutter across the blue sky knowing nothing of sorrow. But soon afterward he began whistling again and was racing along strange streets in his mind.

XII

The summer passed.

Peace reigned on earth and in the sky. There was a grayish powder of snow on the distant peaks, and early autumn in the heather. He gave old Grani his head and turned to the contemplation of the silent hills, pink and yellow, russet and fawn, or watched the barnacles fly honking to the south and finally disappear into the fair-weather cloud above the fell. Involuntarily some chord within him vibrated, gentle and sad as the string of sensitive musical instruments, for he, too, was saying good-bye and setting forth. He would be starting for Reykjavik the next morning.

And how had the summer passed?

He was both surprised and annoyed: It had not passed at all. It had slipped from him like a meaningless dream that leaves nothing behind. He had wasted weeks and months in futile despondency, tortured himself waking and sleeping, bound himself in imaginary chains, and brought himself to the point of taking his own life. What folly! He had scarcely allowed himself time to notice the meadowsweet, the cotton grass, or the cinquefoil, to gaze at the cloud cities of the sunset or the mirages near the glacier, to look at the rainbow in the marsh and the sun-bright clouds that hung motionless in the sky, reflected in the pools and watercourses. He had barely heeded the milfoil on the turf walls of the cabbage patch, or the flowers of the potato plants that shone like stars in the dusk as he came home from the meadows. And now all was fading and withering, now he was saying good-bye to this district, which he had found so unspeakably melancholy and depressing during the months of summer.

He began to think about his proposed stay in the capital, frowned, and clenched the knot on the reins tightly, feeling something like doubt and fear blended with the tone of the chord within him. But then he straightened his back, whistled a snatch of tune, and kicked his heels into the horse's sides, as though the hardest stretch was already behind him and the depression and unemployment overcome. Yes, he would show what he could do! He would never give in! He would fight to the bitter end!

The horse quickened its pace, shook its mane, and twitched its ears, for the track was approaching some dark patches on the ground where the roadmen had camped that summer leaving behind jars and rubbish, empty bottles, fragments of glass, and old shoes. There was somebody walking by the ford—somebody who had come down from the heath, wearing a light-colored blouse and striped skirt and holding a small bundle in one hand, who waved gaily: Aren't you going to say hello to me, boy?

He would have fled, would have urged old Grani off the track and disappeared behind the rise. But escape was impossible, for Sigrun Maria continued to wave and call, and even came to meet him and asked whether he was blind. He felt her voice penetrate him, turning all within to confusion and awakening both a glimmer and an echo in his heart. He suddenly felt himself like a prisoner who had served only half his sentence.

Hello! she said laughing as she tugged him from the horse. I thought you had gone to sleep on the animal!

He stared at her dazed and unable to get a word out.

What's the matter? she exclaimed. Have you lost your voice?

No, he said, continuing to stare.

You don't say hello to me, she said. You just gape at me as if I'm some kind of freak!

He looked away and pretended to be adjusting the bridle on the horse. Could this be Sigrun Maria? Could this plain, stout, clumsy-looking girl have once caused the earth to be transformed from autumn to spring and become veiled in the soft green of an early morning in July? Could it be that he had lain sleepless night after night, overwhelmed by sorrow, had suffered and despaired, all on account of this round, chubby face that made him think of fresh milk and cheese? He leaned against the horse, not knowing what to believe. It was as if he began to see straight after an optical illusion.

How pale and run-down you look, she said. Have you been ill?

No he replied.

Isn't it odd that we should meet here again? she said, and drawing closer to him she brushed the curls from her forehead and lowered her voice. I remember so well that day when you carried me across the river. I was on my way home from Gil then, too. And the weather . . . the weather was exactly the same as it is now.

Ah well, he said.

It's odd that we should meet here again, she repeated, swinging her bundle. You came riding up along the river then, but this time you came down from the moor. There, you see what a good memory I have?

Yes, he agreed, you certainly have!

She caught the tone of his voice and said nothing for a moment but looked at him. Then, gradually, the dimples in her cheeks deepened and her eyes darted their green flashes at him.

You shirked dancing with me at the tombola this summer, she said. I promised to dance with you during the evening, but when I went to look for you I couldn't find you anywhere.

Did you by any chance look for me in the woods? he asked.

In the woods? she replied, putting her head to one side as though trying to remember. No, I didn't go there.

It was just as well, he said. You might have been frightened of the spiders.

She stopped swinging the bundle, brushed a sprig of moss from her sleeve, and sniffed. But, Mundi, why are you so grouchy?

I'm not grouchy.

Oh yes you are, she said glancing at him out of the corner of her eye. I don't know what I could have done to annoy you.

Nor do I, he said, and looked involuntarily at the patches where the roadmen's tents had stood. He had bought candy, composed poems, and picked forget-me-nots, moss campion, and meadowsweet for this plump, insincere girl who still thought she could twist him round her finger and treat him as a plaything. He had behaved like an idiot at the tombola this summer, chasing her around, rushing after her into the woods, hating the truck driver, and deciding to drown himself in a pool. Suddenly it all seemed to him so ludicrous and farfetched that he could not restrain a smile.

Sigrun Maria shifted uneasily and gave him another glance out of the corner of her eye.

What are you laughing at? she asked.

Nothing, he replied, and watched two wild ducks flying up the river as in the year before.

Why can't you be more pleasant? she said. One can't get any news out of you, and then you start laughing and giggling just like a half-wit.

By the way, he said, you need to cross the river.

Of course, she replied. Aren't you going to carry me?

Yes, you're welcome to the horse.

Perhaps you'll come with me up over the heath as well?

No, I can't manage that.

What have you got to do?

Various things, he answered.

How dreadfully disagreeable you are, she said shaking her head. Will you hold my bundle for me while I get on?

He took the bundle and gazed after some barnacles that were flying in wedge formation to the south, until she inquired whether he didn't think it might be better for him to sit behind her, so that he could hold her if she became giddy from the current.

No, I'll wait here, he replied. You drive the horse back when you're over.

What? she said, surprised, not understanding. Aren't we riding together?

All at once her voice had become so warm and intimate that it reminded him again of a spring breeze passing over the meadows. He felt a pain at his heart, as if opposing forces were tugging it. Then he pulled a cattail and glanced quickly at the patches where the roadmen's tents had stood that summer.

I'll wait here, he repeated.

But the horse? she said. It may run away . . .

No, there's no danger of that. He's very quiet.

Yes, but what am I to do if I become dizzy?

You can just close your eyes and hold on to the mane.

Well, good-bye. I won't waste more time being nice to you, she said with a haughty jerk of the head. It'll be your fault if I fall in the river!

When she reached the opposite bank she jumped to the ground, drove the horse back into the stream, and gave it a whack with her bundle.

You'll never know what I was going to tell you! she called as she went. Then she walked up from the riverbank without looking back and vanished behind the shrub-covered ridge.

The boy continued to take leave of everything for the last time. He did not want to go back home at once but turned old Grani up onto the silver-white moss-cushioned rise where the waterfall echoed in the hollow. A mist seemed to have cleared from his eyes. He saw the foaming water wash against the boulders, still clouds reflected in the slack, saw the heather, the thicket, and the birch trees, all in a powerful new light. He was aware in a single instant of both the withering of the leaves and the surging vigor of the roots, drank in the cool autumn-heavy scent, feeling that wherever he went this land would go with him, giving him strength and abiding in his soul like a secret treasure.

He was young. He was free. He was released from a spell.

And he had no inkling that in a few years' time once again the earth would be transformed, would be bathed in a brightness lovelier than the spring skies, a glamour more indescribable than the clear heavens of an early morning in July—and later become dark and desolate, as cold and lifeless as the night that closes around the heart when we die.

PASTOR BODVAR'S LETTER

I

My dearest daughter,

    God grant that these lines find you and your husband in good health. I haven't much news to tell at present, for little of note has happened here since I last wrote . . .

The Reverend Bodvar Gunnlaugsson, or more properly Bodvar Gunnlaugsson, pastor emeritus, gazed for a moment at the snow-white sheet of paper and tried to remember when he had last addressed his daughter on a similar sheet—whether it had been a fortnight or over three weeks ago that he had gone out about midday in bright sunshine and down to the post office with an airmail letter to Svava B. Andrews, 505 Woodhaven Blvd., Queens, Long Island, New York, U.S.A.

Perhaps I should say a short while ago, he thought. How dreadfully forgetful I'm becoming.

Instead of adopting this expedient—reconciling himself to a trifling imprecision and continuing the letter—he leaned back in his chair, adjusted his spectacles, and gazed out the window at the rowan and birch to which he had grown so attached, at the roofs of various colors, and at the clouded sky. The sun was not visible, but the weather was as calm and mild as it had been the day before, midges on the windowpane and redwings singing somewhere in the neighborhood. Pastor Bodvar listened absently to their song, contemplating the light gray clouds, until his right hand stirred restlessly. He put down his pen and took from a vest pocket the gold watch presented to him by parishioners on his retirement nearly six years before.

Well, well, he said to himself, half past two.

He screwed the cap on his pen and sighed. Perhaps he would think of something entertaining to tell his daughter if he had a breath of fresh air first, went out for a while and took a little walk—down to the sea, for instance, or round the Pond. He had not been idle today. He had slipped out to the dairy and the fishmonger's for his wife, glanced through the morning paper, and cleaned his pipes of various lengths, before settling down at his desk. He then reread the proofs of a short article, or rather meditation—an old sermon in a new dress—which he had written for the *Church Gazette*. It was to appear under the title "The Power of Prayer." He had not found many errors overlooked previously, and none of them had been serious ones. Nevertheless, he had decided to go over it again later, reread the proofs a third time, either this evening or tomorrow morning. After his lunch of haddock and milk pudding, he had switched off the radio announcements and smoked his pipe in the living room, going through the paper again, reading at random, but stopping when he came to the obituary of a tailor who had in fact been unknown to him. He must have dropped off then, for when his wife called from the kitchen, telling him to come at once if he wanted his coffee hot, he had awakened with a start.

At once, she had repeated.

As soon as he had emptied his cup, he had retired to the study and taken his *Pages from the Past* from the drawer of the desk: this was a substantial manuscript that had been gradually growing over a period of three years, especially during the winters. Reading the last page over carefully, he had written a brief comment in the margin. Then, with an effort to recall a long-vanished term, he had begun to write: We were a lighthearted company, my schoolmates and I, and we found many ways of amusing ourselves.

At the next sentence he hesitated, stopping halfway to consider how best to record a comical incident but aware of some kind of music penetrating the walls and door. Dance music? Dance music at this time? Ah, of course, it was Saturday. Naturally Gudrid had switched on the radio, remembering the hospital choice program. Extraordinary how a sixty-year-old woman could find any pleasure in that rubbish, rattling and thumping, caterwauling and wailing, which the blessed people chose for their nearest and dearest in the hospital, with loving wishes.

We were a lighthearted company, my schoolmates and I, and we found many ways of amusing ourselves. Once there was a great to-do in our class . . .

Gudrid now suddenly broke with her usual habit and switched off the hospital choice, probably because a song which had nothing in common with the bleating and bawling had begun:

> Leise flehen meine Lieder
> durch die Nacht zu dir.

The notes of Schubert's song left a strong impression in Pastor Bodvar's mind so that the amusing incident in the classroom long ago seemed to fade and grow dull, in spite of favorable circumstances. He had given up the attempt to capture it and, taking the manuscript carefully from the desk as though it were something fragile, slipped it back in its hiding place and locked the drawer. He then pulled out another drawer and began to go through its contents, including some curious-looking stones which he kept in an old cigar box.

Leise flehen meine Lieder . . . durch die Nacht . . . zu dir.

What was he looking for? Or wasn't he looking for anything? He had opened a third drawer, run his eye over a two-month-old letter from his daughter, gazed for a moment at the snapshots of her, and then decided to send her a few lines. In the top left-hand corner of the envelope she had written, From Svava B. Andrews, 505 Woodhaven Blvd., Queens, Long Island, New York, U.S.A.

II

Half past two. After half past two.

Pastor Bodvar supposed that his wife had begun either to crochet scarves or to sew flags, but as he opened the study door she emerged from the bathroom.

It's half past two, he said. I thought I'd slip out for a while.

Where are you going? she asked.

I thought I might stroll round the Pond, he said, or go down to the sea.

Fru Gudrid straightened the cloth on the little chest of drawers in front of the big mirror. Maybe I'll come with you, she said in an indifferent voice, looking in the mirror. Why don't we take a walk down to the Pond or in the Park?

She's painted her lips, thought Pastor Bodvar. To think of such vanity in a woman of sixty!

Why are you shaking your head, my dear? she asked him.

I'm not shaking my head, he answered.

Yes, you were, she said. I saw you in the mirror.

If I was shaking my head, then I was shaking my head, thought Pastor Bodvar, and he sighed without replying. He put on his black coat in silence and took a black hat from the hook in the cupboard.

My stick, he muttered, peering in the cupboard. What has become of my stick?

Fru Gudrid laughed. You may well ask! The first thing you did was take it out. She pointed to a silver-mounted walking stick, a birthday present from several parishioners. You might reach me my coat, she added. The gray one.

Pastor Bodvar helped her into her coat and waited, stick in hand, while she knotted her scarf and put on a new hat—a brimless pot which he considered both ugly and gaudy, at all events on a sixty-year-old woman.

Have we no scraps of bread? he asked as she took a pair of cotton gloves from the top drawer of the chest. A little something to give the birds?

Fru Gudrid was still gazing in the mirror. Is there any call to be pampering the birds in the height of summer? she asked. I was going to make bread soup tomorrow.

Pastor Bodvar looked beyond her, rubbing the knob of his stick. Haven't you enough for bread soup even if we give a little to the birds? he inquired, as though from a distance. A few scraps, he added, just for the fun of it.

Fru Gudrid buttoned her coat.

I have never regarded it as fun to throw bread away, she remarked. Going into the kitchen, she opened a cupboard and felt pieces of bread of varying degrees of hardness in the bin. Then she found a paper bag and put three of them in it, adding a fourth after a moment's hesitation.

That's all you're having, she said, shutting the cupboard. She dusted invisible crumbs from her fingers and put on her cotton gloves. Have you got your keys? she asked, standing again before the mirror.

Pastor Bodvar assured himself that his bunch of keys was in his pocket before nodding in reply. Well, anyway, I have mine, too, she said. I don't care to leave keys lying in an empty apartment.

Pastor Bodvar cleared his throat and looked beyond her as before.

Shouldn't I, ah, shouldn't I carry the bag?

No, I'll carry it, she replied, starting to go. How I hate that black hat of yours in the summer. I've asked you time and again to get yourself a gray one.

Pastor Bodvar stopped rubbing the knob of his stick.

I shall buy myself a new hat when I can afford to, he said.

Afford to! Fru Gudrid clicked her tongue impatiently. How much will you get for that long article of yours in the *Church Gazette?*

Nothing, he answered shortly. You know very well that I never take any payment for what I write in the *Church Gazette.*

Fru Gudrid seemed to find this amusing. Well, well, you can afford to give article after article to the *Church Gazette,* but you can't afford to get yourself a hat!

Pastor Bodvar refrained from asking whether he had ever deviated from his rule of handing over to her his pension untouched, as well as the greater part of the small grant which the National Assembly awarded him annually for his literary work. He edged his way through the door, pretending not to notice his name on the highly polished brass plate, walked carefully down the stairs, and did not look back when his wife latched the door behind her.

A thickset, bald-headed man—the owner of the downstairs apartment—was standing by a car outside the house. He held a small trout rod in one hand and a camera in the other.

Pastor Bodvar raised his hat. Good afternoon, he said. Are you going to the country?

The man glanced at Fru Gudrid. Hardly that, he answered. We are just running out to Ellidavatn to spend the weekend at our cabin.

Ah yes.

Pastor Bodvar paused, suddenly regretting that he was unable to offer a small cigar. Lovely, hmm, lovely mild weather today, he said, leaning forward a little. Maybe we shall have some sunshine.

Perhaps.

The man slipped rod and camera into the car, then straightened himself and looked at the sky. According to the forecast there will be sunshine tomorrow, he said. An area of high pressure over the country.

Pastor Bodvar looked at the sky in his turn.

It should stay dry at all events, said the man. Actually I'm rather partial to this kind of warm, dull weather.

Pastor Bodvar was partial to it, too. You're planning to do a bit of fishing, of course, he said. Isn't the trout fishing at Ellidavatn quite good?

You can pick up the odd tiddler, replied the man. I do it mostly just to practice my casting.

I see.

Have to keep my shoulder supple, said the man amiably. Going to Haukadal in the west next week.

Quite so. Pastor Bodvar responded to the other's tone and smiled. You'll be fighting salmon then, he said. They're fine ones there.

Caught a seventeen-pounder last year, said the man.

Fru Gudrid, standing a short distance away staring into space, waited no longer. She started off in a northerly direction along the quiet road, coughing very distinctly. Took it on a fly, said the man. Half an hour landing it.

Ah, indeed.

Pastor Bodvar raised a hand to the brim of his hat in token of leave-taking and began to hurry after his wife, tall and lanky, pale of cheek and somewhat bent at the shoulders. Fru Gudrid sighed as he caught up with her.

Ai, those people downstairs, she said.

Now, then! thought Pastor Bodvar.

Is that supposed to be some kind of modesty, calling their summer cottage a cabin? she asked. What did he call the car?

Pastor Bodvar did not reply.

They're very conscious of owning a car and a summer cottage, she said.

Pastor Bodvar deferred his answer until they had turned the corner and walked a few paces along Tungata.

It's only natural that prudent folk should be well off these days, he said. She laughed.

He had been determined to change the subject, to try to avoid bickering and argument out of doors, but her laughter compelled him to protest.

It can hardly be a matter of great moment that our neighbors give themselves a little weekend relaxation, he muttered.

Who said it was? Fru Gudrid seldom raised her voice when she wanted to put him in his place in public but spoke very slowly and quietly, as though admonishing a child. Only natural that prudent folk should be well off— I must say, this comes as something of a surprise to me! she said. And since when were you so remarkably interested in salmon fishing, I'd like to know?

Pastor Bodvar gazed at the ground in front of his feet, renewing his resolution not to be drawn into an argument with his wife out of doors.

Prudent folk? What nonsense! she exclaimed. Do you suppose they'd be quite so high and mighty if they hadn't been left a large sum of money a few years ago?

Pastor Bodvar adjusted his spectacles, which had begun to slip down his nose. High and mighty? he thought, involuntarily recalling the time when his wife had spent the small legacy from her father. What had she suggested just after they returned from the old man's funeral?

Such a crying shame it was that we couldn't have bought the downstairs apartment, too, said Fru Gudrid. When those people moved in I knew they'd give us trouble.

Us? Pastor Bodvar posed a silent question. Who had been to blame for the constant friction, sometimes over the heating bill or the use of the common washhouse, sometimes over the stairs or the garden, and sometimes about nothing at all? Who had started it? he asked himself. Who wanted to manage and control?

I knew it, said Fru Gudrid. Somehow I had a feeling that they would be difficult neighbors.

Pastor Bodvar could no longer restrain himself. How would you have felt about having drinkers in the house? Some people have to put up with that, he said. To my mind Harald is the easiest of men to get on with.

Oh, he's a harmless creature in his way, but a fool. It's mainly Hrefna I'm thinking about, said Fru Gudrid.

Pastor Bodvar still protested. Hrefna has a quick temper, perhaps, but I have no reason to complain about her, he said. She's always been polite to me.

How kind of her! Maybe it's not so hard to be polite to a man who says yes and amen to everything! For a moment Fru Gudrid lost control of the admonishing tone in her voice.

A quick temper, perhaps! She behaves as though she owned the whole basement and the garden as well! I don't know what she thinks she is, that . . . that barren creature!

Pastor Bodvar did not answer his wife, restraining the urge to point out that she was really finding fault with the one who governs all things. Can't understand her attitude, he thought, and he gazed gloomily at the rowans in the gardens and two low-roofed houses that always looked so friendly, being more or less unchanged since he had been at the Latin School. He intended to mention them in *Pages from the Past* and write a short chapter about one of them—or rather, record an incident which had taken place there—if he ever managed to finish the section on his school days, to say nothing of the whole book. It had gone badly of late. There had been little progress; seldom had he been able to sustain the necessary mood for more than a moment, whether owing to rheumatism or spring fever or something else. Four pieces, he thought, and he looked critically at his wife, at the brimless pot of a hat which he considered both ugly and gaudy, at the white cotton gloves and the rustling paper bag. Four pieces for the dear birds. That was all. Four pieces!

I don't let anyone push me around, said Fru Gudrid. She needn't think that she can make me defer to her overbearing ways!

Pastor Bodvar said nothing, it is true, but lines of dissent were beginning to form round the corners of his mouth, when a small boy came running out of the baker's on the corner of Vonarstraeti and Tjarnargata. The aroma that filled Pastor Bodvar's nostrils as the door closed behind him recalled not only newly baked doughnuts and currant buns but also his early school days, those winters at the Latin School. No one nowadays made such good currant buns as old Bernhoft had, no one such excellent doughnuts as old Veiga of blessed memory. He crossed Tjarnargata with traces of the aroma still in his nostrils and glanced at the paper bag in his wife's hand. Then all of a sudden he stopped, raising his stick.

Gudrid!

What's the matter? she inquired.

Wait for me there, he said in rather a strange voice. I'll only be a minute.

Having said this, without further explanation he turned and hurried away, as if in a state of some emotional disturbance, and headed for the bakery, not looking back. This time I won't! he thought to himself, swinging his stick. No, this time he wouldn't give in, whatever happened.

He raised his hat to the white-overalled girl and hastily gave his order: A French loaf. Yesterday's bread will do, he said.

We have no loaves from yesterday, answered the girl.

Pastor Bodvar nodded compulsively: Then I shall have to have a new one, he said. It's for the birds on the Pond.

Large or small? asked the girl.

Er . . . large, said Pastor Bodvar. A large French loaf.

He leaned his stick against the counter, unbuttoned his black coat, and felt in the pocket for his old purse. As he did so he caught the baking smell and involuntarily compared it with the remembered aroma of old Bernhoft's of former years.

It was lucky, hmm, very lucky that you weren't closed.

We close at four o'clock on Saturdays, said the girl as she wrapped the French loaf in a sheet of thin paper. She pushed it across to him and named the price.

Ah yes. Pastor Bodvar picked some small coins out of two compartments in his purse and laid them on the counter in front of her. He was no longer nervous, but deliberate in his movements, looking about him absently as he returned the purse to his pocket and buttoned his coat. Old Bernhoft hadn't had glass-fronted cupboards and glass cases like these, if he remembered rightly. The doughnuts of poor old Veiga of blessed memory would certainly have been lighter and somehow more shapely altogether, and he missed the hot cinnamon smell of freshly baked currant buns, for there was no flavor to equal cinnamon, he thought, unless it was almonds. But just as he was about to take his stick and the bread to the birds, he received a sudden shock that made him go pale.

Three French waffles and a honey cake, said a female voice with a slight drawl beside him.

Pastor Bodvar recalled the song by Schubert that Gudrid had switched off. It occurred to him that he had fallen asleep at home and was dreaming of that voice. A moment later he glanced furtively at the woman who had asked for French waffles and honey cake. She was not dark haired, though, but fair, not about twenty but at least thirty-five. When she also asked for oatmeal cookies and sugar rolls, her voice sounded quite different. He dropped his stick on the floor and bent down so incautiously to pick it up that a stab of rheumatism passed through his back.

Adjusting his spectacles on his nose, he walked thoughtfully to the door.

Your bread! the assistant called after him. You have forgotten your bread!

Oh yes, thank you.

Pastor Bodvar paused on the sidewalk outside the shop while two cars drove past. A mental lapse, he muttered. An extraordinary mental lapse. Then realizing that he had started talking to himself in public, he shook his head and wandered across the street, the fingers of his right hand clutching the bone knob of his stick, and in his left the soft French loaf, a present for the birds which he had felt absolutely compelled to buy. He walked very slowly, scarcely aware of the bread now, for the Schubert song was like a distant echo in his mind:

> Leise flehen meine Lieder
> durch die Nacht zu dir;
> in den stillen Hain hernieder,
> Liebchen, komm zu mir.
>
> Flüsternd schlanke Wipfel rauschen
> in des Mondes Licht . . .

Suddenly the echo died, as though Fru Gudrid had switched off Schubert's song a second time this Saturday. She was waiting by the Pond, standing on the bank with open paper bag and throwing very small fragments to the mallards that splashed and quacked at her feet. She was distributing her pieces among some turbulent drakes with silky green heads but ignoring a number of ducklings that were driven back every time they ventured into the fray.

Finished, my pets! All finished!

She shook some imperceptible crumbs from the bag, crushed it into a ball, and threw it upon the water.

The corners of Pastor Bodvar's mouth contracted in sharp disapproval. Why did you do that, woman? he exclaimed. How could you be so untidy?

Pish! Fru Gudrid's laugh was her only reply to his remonstration. She pointed before her at two mallard drakes that had broken away from the group to pursue each other with a great deal of splashing, each trying to peck the other's tail.

Look, she said, laughing, see how they carry on!

Pastor Bodvar looked at the drakes but did not withdraw the reprimand from either his expression or his voice. I can't understand you, he said. You wouldn't throw rubbish in the Pond if it was yours.

Oh, don't you think I have the right to dispose of an empty paper bag?

Not in the Pond, said Pastor Bodvar. The Pond will not be the pride of the town for long if everyone makes a habit of throwing litter into it.

Pish! What a fuss about nothing!

Wrong is wrong, said Pastor Bodvar. The Pond is the pride of the town and shouldn't be made into an exhibition of slovenliness.

Tell the birds not to do their business in it then! Fru Gudrid seemed still in a good humor, in spite of her mocking remark. Even a little teasing. So you've been buying white bread! she exclaimed.

Pastor Bodvar recollected himself. Yes, as a matter of fact, I have, he said, and he tore off the wrapping. A large loaf, he added.

He intended to let the ducklings benefit by his resolution, broke one piece after another from the bread and tried to toss the pieces to them, but to his chagrin saw that the fat, aggressive drakes always forestalled them. Finally, unable to restrain himself, he cried, What greed! Just see what confounded rogues those drakes are!

Fru Gudrid smiled. They know how to take care of themselves, she said.

I might have known, thought Pastor Bodvar. She was sure to find an excuse for them, of course.

He stepped forward, his walking stick under his arm, tore a few more fragments from the loaf, and flung them out on the water, but when all went the same way his irritation redoubled. Get away with you, you wretches! he called to the drakes. Why do you have to crowd together there?

Fru Gudrid moved closer, smiling again. The poor creatures, she said, and stretched out a hand. Shall I . . .

Pastor Bodvar turned away. I was going to give the ducklings something, he said. There's no kindness in pampering those wretches.

They know how to take care of themselves, repeated Fru Gudrid, and she waited for him to give her the bread. Now, let me . . .

No! It's my bread.

Fru Gudrid raised her eyebrows interrogatively.

To the best of my knowledge this is my loaf!

Fru Gudrid became slightly haughtier in her manner.

To the best of my knowledge I bought this loaf with my own money, said Pastor Bodvar, and he took the stick from under his arm. I have no intention of throwing it away—not on those wretches!

The smile on Fru Gudrid's face had faded, though it did not vanish entirely.

Well, well, she said. I must say!

You must say? Pastor Bodvar sniffed abruptly and glanced at the drakes. You've fed them already, he said as they moved off, then added in a low voice, as though to himself, Four, hmm, four pieces.

The smile still lingered on Fru Gudrid's face, cold perhaps but not at all angry.

Second childhood, she remarked. You're behaving like a willful child.

Now, then, thought Pastor Bodvar, of course she had to remind him that she was fourteen years younger than he was.

So far as I'm concerned you may keep your bread, she added. If it's too good for me to touch, there's no more to be said about it.

What do you mean? asked Pastor Bodvar. I thought you said you didn't like throwing food away . . .

PASTOR BODVAR'S LETTER

Ai! Fru Gudrid shook her head. Your wits are in good enough order when you have a mind to twist my words, she said. But I have no intention of bickering with you about this bread of yours. I just can't be bothered, my dear man!

Pastor Bodvar was silent. Somehow he felt that he had given way after all—got the worst of the exchange as usual and behaved like a fool into the bargain. He that governs his temper excels the conqueror of cities. The fact was that he didn't understand why he had become so angry. Maybe the mallard drakes had been the last straw. Those ornamental ruffians, greedy and aggressive—how very foolish of him to let their behavior upset his balance. He decided to refrain from all argument and simply cleared his throat as they walked past a small boy with a cheerful-looking woman feeding the ducks south of the old Trade School. Mother and son, he thought. No disagreement there—and he stopped a short distance away by the stone jetty on the main road, tore off a fragment of the soft, white bread, and tossed it to some ducklings that were swimming close to the bank.

Little mites, he murmured. Quack-quack, quack-quack.

He did not have to wait long for a response. Quite a crowd of ducks came flocking to him as if they knew him. The drakes were less obstreperous, so that the ducks and ducklings got at least every other morsel. Pastor Bodvar did not look at his wife, but he was aware of her standing beside him, gazing out over the Pond, probably at the terns on the islet, or perhaps the pair of swans—mutes or whatever they were called, from Germany, that had been presented a year or two before. He had no longer felt annoyed but rather a little conscience-stricken. Idiotic to be bickering and squabbling, he thought, and longed to make up with his wife so that they could both enjoy this walk to the fullest. But when he was just about to remark that it was a mistake to let these mute swans drive out their native whoopers, even if they were a gift from the Germans, she suddenly jerked at his arm.

Sigurhans, she said, don't you notice anything?

Pastor Bodvar started. Eh? Notice what? he exclaimed.

Do you need to ask? Are your spectacles misted over?

Fru Gudrid pointed both to right and left and counted, deliberately, up to five.

Five! she repeated with a show of surprise. Five paper bags floating here by the bank! I'm not the only one who disposes of the bag after feeding the birds!

Pastor Bodvar stopped tearing a fragment from the French loaf and looked quickly at the mother and child as though taking leave of them. There is no discord there, he thought, moving away from the stone jetty. No bickering there.

I understood from what you said that my paper bag was quite unparalleled, said Fru Gudrid. I was beginning to think that I had committed some sort of sacrilege!

He that is slow to wrath is more than champion. Pastor Bodvar heard the new note in his wife's voice, glanced at her face, and recognized the waxen smile. Sacrilege? he repeated as though to himself. I never said that.

You should be more upset about these paper bags, said Fru Gudrid. I understood from what you said that you had never witnessed such sloppy behavior.

I never said that . . .

Oh, then what was it you were mumbling, about litter and untidiness?

I said that the Pond was the pride of the town . . .

The pride of the town, eh? Well, was I denying it? she asked. I'm not so senile that I forget everything the moment I hear it! I understood you to say that I had wrought havoc on this pride of the town with a single paper bag, and an empty one at that!

Pastor Bodvar glanced across the street. The Free Church, he thought to himself. His head shook involuntarily, as if in reply to a secret admonition— undertaking not to lose self-control opposite a house of God where he had once read the funeral service over an old schoolmate and true friend.

I have not been known hitherto for sloppy behavior, said Fru Gudrid. How in the world was I to know that it was nothing short of sacrilege to throw away an empty paper bag?

There was no doubt about it, thought Pastor Bodvar. She proposed to follow up that waxen smile of hers and punish him for buying the loaf, to pay him back with cheap mockery and nagging until he had no choice but to sue for peace and defer to her again and yet again.

I'm sorry for you, I really am, said Fru Gudrid. Being married to such a slattern.

Quack-quack! Pastor Bodvar paused and held out the bread. He threw several fragments to three ducklings that seemed to have lost their mother, calling them mites and muttering that he had been sure they were going to take more, as he moved on at his wife's side. This one loaf won't go far; it's half finished already.

Sigurhans, you've no need to buy yourself a new hat, said Fru Gudrid. I see now that the old one suits you very well.

She glanced at the hat and laughed. The pride of the town! she said. Green with age!

Perhaps it was the proximity of the Free Church that restrained him from answering her back. Perhaps it was the decrepit bus that rattled by with a prolonged roar, leaving behind it an evil-smelling cloud of black smoke.

Sigurhans! he repeated to himself when most of the cloud had blown away. *Sigurhans!* He wondered how Gudrid had discovered his intense dislike of his second name, which caused him to try and keep it secret, only writing it when compelled to, as on census returns. Somehow she had become aware of it, though, for she called him Sigurhans only when she wanted to take him down a peg, tease and torment him. Somehow she must have detected his sensitivity over the name, just as to her jibes over their difference in age. Sigurhans! she said, Sigurhans! Maybe the object was to anger him, so that she would have the occasion to remind him that he was a minister of the faith if she remembered rightly! *Pastor emeritus,* he thought then, as if the Latin words had suddenly appeared before him inscribed in italics on a brass plate: a pastor emeritus, an acknowledged man of peace, ought certainly to have control over his temper.

He held out the remainder of the French loaf in his left hand murmuring, I could really have done with two.

You mean hats? asked Fru Gudrid with a note of caution. Have you at last realized that you need a more summery hat?

Pastor Bodvar opened his eyes wide and shook his head at this question, displaying all the wonder that the occasion warranted. No, he said, you must have misheard me. I was referring to loaves. Loaves for the ducks.

Very well, so I misheard you, did I? Fru Gudrid also opened her eyes wide. Maybe I misheard too that you proposed to take nothing for all that stuff you were correcting this morning?

In this way they moved along Free Church Street, goading each other. But when they reached the Bandstand Gardens they fell silent and began looking round among the bushes behind the statue of Jonas Hallgrimsson the poet. Scattered among the twisted birches there were tall clumps of cranesbill against the ragged gray bark, together with several exotic orna-mental herbs which Pastor Bodvar was unable to identify, except for what he believed to be a variety of poppy. The statue—oh yes, there stood the poet with a dandelion in one hand, as if anxious to lead the thoughts of the way-farer away from bitterness and dissent, to draw attention to the heartfelt words which the pastor emeritus had pondered in his "stuff," the little study on the power of prayer he had been correcting that very morning:

> Father and friend of all that is,
> tend thou this garden at my prayer;
> all buds and blossoms guard and bless,
> I pray, both here and everywhere.

The reddish-colored milled lava on the pathway crunched softly under-foot. Had all been well he would hardly have walked by the statue in silence but would have paused, nodded, and remarked that there was their good poet, and after a few more steps he would have stopped again and pointed out the second statue—of Thorvaldsen, most famous sculptor of Scandina-via—and then discussed the garden, its trees, flower beds, and newly mown lawns. Dissension, he thought, constant dissension—and in the same instant became conscious of a fragrant aroma, just like freshly cut hay, though there was none to be seen. Had Gudrid not taunted him with their difference in age nor called him Sigurhans he would have asked her whether she could smell that particular aroma, and whether it did not give her pleasure to see the tall sedge lining the banks here. But he asked her nothing, remained as silent as she, with the reddish-colored lava crunching steadily under their feet, until they reached the pool at the southern end of the Pond.

Ah, greylags!

Pastor Bodvar tore off a generous lump of bread as the words escaped. Greylags with goslings!

Fru Gudrid looked at the geese in silence, but finally assented.

Yes, so they are, she said.

Pastor Bodvar heard no undertones in his wife's voice, so he pointed at the miscellaneous crowd of birds on the islet where a warrior of ancient times towered on his pedestal. Hmm, eider ducks and drakes, he said.

Fru Gudrid gazed out at the islet with an indifferent expression but again assented.

Yes, so there are, she said.

There was no need for Pastor Bodvar to refer to the poster with colored pictures on his left in order to distinguish a goldeneye from a scaup. There was a teal, too, and there a shoveler or spoonbill. Quack-quack! But having listed the species that he recognized and torn several fragments from the loaf, he raised his bent index finger to point higher.

That statue, he said, isn't it supposed to be Thorfinn Karlsefni? Fru Gudrid looked up and assented yet again. You called it Thorfinn the other day when we walked this way, she said.

Ah yes.

Pastor Bodvar gazed dubiously at the white patches and streaks that marked the statue, especially the helmet and shield, where arctic terns had found it convenient to perch. I seem to remember that it's supposed to be Thorfinn, he said. Wasn't there something about it in the paper lately?

Fru Gudrid nodded. Yes, she remembered something of the kind.

That the place was perhaps unsuitable? he said. Weren't they proposing to move it from the island?

Fru Gudrid nodded again. Yes, she believed she had read in the paper or heard on the radio that the statue was to be moved.

That's what I thought.

Fru Gudrid shifted her gaze from the islet, turning to look about her—silent, it was true, but without a cough or other indication that she might be bored. Pastor Bodvar also turned away from the pool and crossed diagonally over the bridge of dry land between it and the Pond to the north, intending to take a look at the birds there. Little mites, quack-quack! he exclaimed, tearing off some more bread. You're not so badly off up here!

Fru Gudrid made a sound of interrogation.

I meant the ducklings, explained Pastor Bodvar. It's good for them to be able to take shelter in the sedge if they are scared. Sometimes the black-backed gulls take advantage of them, the infernal bandits! They . . .

Fru Gudrid interrupted. Look, she said, now it's getting brighter.

Sunshine flooded the gardens as though a curtain had been drawn back, while a gentle breeze sent ripples over the gray water. Pastor Bodvar narrowed his eyes against the glitter of the Pond and was in total agreement with his wife: it was getting brighter now, as the weather forecast had predicted—a dry spell for the next day, with a ridge of high pressure over the country. Fine and clear, he declared, throwing scraps to the birds—the same blessed calm everywhere.

Fru Gudrid narrowed her eyes, too, and looked around, pulling at the top of a white cotton glove. She agreed. Yes, she said, it's a change to see the sun.

Regarding the weather there was no difference of opinion. Neither of them questioned the forecast on this occasion; in fact it had begun to clear up a good while before, a ridge of high pressure over the country. Pastor Bodvar filled the interval with some tentative clearing of the throat and said quack-quack but felt deep down that he had been unfair to his wife—awkward and petty, for instance, in not letting her touch the bread, which was now almost finished, barely a quarter of the loaf remaining. He was not sure how she might take it if he were to hand her the rest, inviting her to bestow this remnant on the birds. Perhaps it would only serve to awaken the disharmony between them again and cause further unpleasantness.

Little mites, he murmured, deciding after some consideration to make no reference to the remnant of the bread—this quarter of a loaf—but to revert to the difference made by the sight of the sun and the prospect of fair weather. He was on the point of saying, How beautifully bright it is, when his wife cried out, quite loudly, No! Can it really be?

III

Pastor Bodvar had not accommodated himself to her tone of voice before she added, Isn't that Gussi?

Gussi! Pastor Bodvar looked back with an expression of surprise mingled with dismay. Gussi? Here?

He saw the man almost immediately, knew him, and heard the sound of his shoes crunching on the reddish lava of the path. The man was bare-headed, as of yore, with that characteristic walk of his and the rough voice that seemed to have changed little, and not at all for the better.

Goo-da, goo-da! I thought it was you, now!

Fru Gudrid pulled off one of her gloves as she walked to meet him.

Hallo, how are you? she said. I thought it was you, too!

They shook hands, using the familiar form of the pronoun to each other, but Pastor Bodvar straightened himself and hastened to adjust his spectacles.

How do you do? he said, taking the initiative and suddenly dropping his tentative manner. He had assumed an authoritative, almost a stern demeanor. How do you do?

The man greeted him in his habitual fashion, the handshake limp, eyes evasive, impossible to tell whether he aimed to be playful or ironic, whether he was smiling or smirking. I thought it was you! he repeated, and putting down a sizable bag with a broken zipper, he took a packet of cigarettes from his shirt pocket and a box of matches from his trousers pocket, cocked his head to one side, and seemed on the point of offering Pastor Bodvar a cigarette. It's a long while since I last ran into you two!

Fourteen or fifteen years, said Fru Gudrid. Only twice since you moved to Eystrihofn!

No, thank you, I never smoke cigarettes, said Pastor Bodvar, scarcely glancing at the packet the man had extended to him but choosing rather to look at his wife, at her summer hat, that brimless cylinder of fashion that seemed gaudier than ever in the sunshine, more unsuitable than ever on a sixty-year-old woman. What was she saying? Fourteen or fifteen years? That he had only run into them twice since moving to Eystrihofn? What a remarkable memory!

Well, I can't offer you a cigar. Never smoke fence posts, said the man in his rasping voice, which was as suggestive of a mallard drake as the sheen on his black hair. The high and mighty appreciate them, I dare say, he added, putting the cigarette packet back in his shirt pocket. They're devilish expensive, I know!

Didn't we last meet on the quay at home? asked Fru Gudrid. You were fetching some part for a machine, weren't you?

Very likely, answered the man. Shifting the cigarette into the corner of his mouth, he shielded the flame of a match in his palm and inhaled the smoke, then stood, legs wider apart than before as he straddled the neck of land, dirty jacket open and the two top buttons of his shirt undone, exposing a tanned throat and hairy chest. Well, now, he said smiling—or smirking—is the pastor giving bread to the dilly-ducks?

Yes.

Pastor Bodvar flung fragments of various sizes without noticing whether the drakes or the ducklings got them. The same slapdash look, he thought, the same conceit, and the same big mouth. "Never smoke fence posts . . . The *high and mighty* appreciate them"! When was this young fellow going to grow out of the habit of talking like a cheeky boy in his teens? Young fellow, huh, past forty. He'll be forty-five this autumn, I suppose. Wasn't he nearly nineteen when he undertook to paint the house?

You were standing on the quay, said Fru Gudrid. If I remember rightly you were on an errand of some kind for the Operator, some business to do with machines.

I may well have been, replied the man absently, and he turned the cigarette round with the tip of his tongue, gazing at the ducks with shifting eyes. How damned greedy they are over the bread!

Bigmouthed and irresponsible, thought Pastor Bodvar. We should never have had any dealings with him.

Now the Operator's become quite a little moneybags, said Fru Gudrid. Does he still make so much profit on the boats and the salting plants?

He makes a profit on everything he touches, replied the man. He even made a profit out of me, the damned scoundrel.

Fru Gudrid laughed. Out of you? she said. How did he manage to do that?

The man exhaled a cloud of smoke. Put the touch on me! he replied with a grin. He continued to stare at the ducks.

Hmm. Pastor Bodvar was conscious of something at the back of his mind that he had to remember. Hmm, he repeated in a sharper tone. So you're here in town.

Here in the city, corrected the man.

Precisely.

I'm glad to say, the man added.

Oh, and what do you mean by that? asked Pastor Bodvar.

Fru Gudrid raised her left hand and touched the cylinder on her head with her fingertips. Are you getting tired of Eystrihofn? she inquired.

The man did not answer either question immediately but removed the cigarette from his mouth with a laugh.

See, they're fighting over the bread! he exclaimed. Then, gazing in a westerly direction, he stuck the cigarette between his lips again.

Oh, I suppose there's bloody little to choose between them. Adalfirth, Eystrihofn, and Midhofn, he added with a shrug. Adalfirth is still the biggest and always had the most to offer—at least in some years.

Silence.

What does he mean? wondered Pastor Bodvar.

Eystrihofn has brightened up a bit since the fishery limits were pushed out, and the fellows at Midhofn think they'll make their fortunes now that the harbor wall has been enlarged, the man continued. But needless to say, these places will always be bloody provincial dead-ends compared with Reykjavik, the capital itself, where . . .

But you didn't dislike living at Adalfirth? interrupted Fru Gudrid.

The man ignored this.

. . . where you have the country's most highly respected institutions, he said. The banks, government, National Assembly, liquor monopoly, university, high court—yes, the bishop of Iceland, too, and the thermal heating service. Here a man can walk among fine folk and institutions, borrow in many banks, and pray for the government in many churches every Sunday . . .

Fru Gudrid burst out laughing. To hear you talk, Gussi, she cried. You're still as droll as ever!

Now she can laugh, thought Pastor Bodvar.

My greatest regret is that I didn't kiss the dead-end good-bye years ago, said the man.

Pastor Bodvar flung the last fragment of bread. Do you mean that you have moved here now? he asked.

Moved here more than a year ago, the man replied. Dawned on me at last that I should be living near the nation's leading institutions.

Quite so.

Pastor Bodvar crumpled the wrapping paper in his hand and, after a moment's hesitation, pushed it into his coat pocket. The clown, he thought. The good-for-nothing windbag.

Fru Gudrid touched the brimless cylinder again with her fingertips. What? she exclaimed. More than a year ago? And you haven't called on your old friends!

Hasn't been much of that, said the man. Truth is, I've had other fish to fry.

Indeed? said Pastor Bodvar.

Except maybe on Sundays, the man continued. But then I'm busy praying for myself and the government.

Fru Gudrid laughed. You really are incorrigible! she cried.

Pastor Bodvar removed the stick from under his arm and clenched his fingers around the yellow bone handle. Have you some kind of work here? he asked dryly, swinging the stick.

The man smiled—or grinned. I'm not drawing a pension yet, he replied. I have to slog away.

A hit! thought Pastor Bodvar, and involuntarily he became more formal. How are you employed? he inquired.

Oh, I do this and that.

The man inhaled and blew smoke from his nostrils and the corner of his mouth. This and that, he repeated in his harsh voice, cocking his head to one side. There's plenty to choose from here, too, at least in the summer: the pick of jobs of every confounded kind, both weekday and weekend. A man doesn't have to crawl on all fours to collect a few miserable crumbs, like he did back in the dead-end in the old days.

He runs from one thing to another, thought Pastor Bodvar. Never sticks for long at anything, as ever.

Fru Gudrid brushed a lock of hair from her ear: Perhaps you sometimes do a bit of painting? she suggested.

The man glanced quickly at her with an arch gleam in his eye, a glint that died the next moment like a spark in damp shavings. No, he replied, I haven't done anything of that sort since I came south.

We want the roof of our house painted, said Fru Gudrid. Perhaps you would take it on some time before the autumn comes.

Pastor Bodvar dropped his stick. At once the man bent down for it. Here, he said, your stick, Pastor Bodvar.

You could suit your own convenience, said Fru Gudrid. Paint it whenever the weather is fine—in the evenings, or on weekends.

What? On days off?

It isn't a big job, Fru Gudrid continued. Only the roof and the window frames.

The man shrugged his shoulders. Hadn't I better be praying for myself and the government? he replied. No, I haven't touched a paintbrush or stirred a can of paint since the devil knows when, back home in the dead-end. I'm not taking on the painting of a grand house here in the city.

What nonsense! exclaimed Fru Gudrid. You who painted our house at Adalfirth inside and out!

The man's eyes shifted from the stick in the aging hand of Pastor Bodvar to the bag at his own feet, and then to the narrow neck of land between the Pond and the pool, the sedge and the ducks.

Well, I can't take it on, he answered. You'll have to get someone else to paint it for you.

It wouldn't be much trouble for you to put a couple of coats of paint on the roof and window frames, said Fru Gudrid. Why, you could do it with your eyes shut!

Not now, the man replied. Not since the rheumatism got into my wrist.

Rheumatism! In the wrist! Fru Gudrid's laugh had a different note. Do you expect me to believe that you've got rheumatism?

The man cocked his head to one side. It's either rheumatism or a touch of inflammation in the tendon, he replied, as if with malicious amusement. Besides, he added, I've become so scared of heights that I avoid going up anything, if I can.

Pastor Bodvar stopped rubbing his thumb against the bone handle and silver band of his stick. Your wife—wasn't she unwell? he asked a little tremulously, suddenly remembering what had been at the back of his mind. How is she?

Sveinbjorg is getting on fine if you clergy know what you're talking about, answered the man. She's dead.

What's that? Dead?

Died the year before last, said the man. Her health broke down about five years ago.

I'm very sorry to hear that.

Pastor Bodvar adjusted his spectacles, but he could detect no regret in the man's face. Poor Sveinbjorg, he thought, to be dragged about from place to place after him, losing her health and dying in the prime of life, that well-mannered, capable girl. He began to move his thumb again, rubbing it over the initials and date on the silver band.

I'm sorry to hear it. Hadn't you two children?

The man removed the cigarette stub from his lips and threw it in the water.

Three, he replied.

And are they here in Reykjavik, too? asked Pastor Bodvar. With you?

Where else would they be? said the man.

Where they could get some sort of an upbringing, thought Pastor Bodvar.

The boy is really here, there, and everywhere, the man went on. Sometimes at sea, and sometimes on the air base with the Yankees. He's doing all right.

At Keflavik Airport?

Yes.

How old is he? asked Pastor Bodvar.

Eighteen, the man replied. Does all right everywhere.

And your daughters? How old are they now?

Twelve and six, answered the man, spitting out a piece of tobacco that had lodged in his mouth. They're getting on fine with my Lulla, and . . .

Fru Gudrid interrupted him. Lulla? she said.

My new lady, replied the man. They think of her just as a big sister. She's only twenty-five.

Pastor Bodvar's features relaxed, his Adam's apple sinking against his white collar, while the thumb of his right hand came to a halt in the middle of the date on the silver band.

I see, he said after a short silence. Then you married again?

Well, as good as, answered the man. I suppose you clergy would call it a scandalous liaison! His voice developed the tones of a mallard drake.

Fru Gudrid did not laugh but broke into a fit of coughing while Pastor Bodvar gazed at Thorfinn Karlsefni and the man's bag.

Hmm, he said. From where does the person come, if I may ask?

My Lulla? She's Faroese. Brought up on dried meat, whale blubber, and Danish aquavit, the man replied. And we are expecting our first addition to the family in a month's time.

Hmm, said Pastor Bodvar, thinking, Poor girl, to find herself in the clutches of a lout like this.

I daresay we'll do our best to produce two or three more brats, added the man. The government has taken to paying for it! He stared boldly at nothing in particular. We have to find something to do with our Sunday evenings—after all the church services and prayers!

Is he trying to provoke me? thought Pastor Bodvar.

Does it not stand written that the Icelanders and the Faroese shall multiply and fill the earth? Or am I getting rusty on the Old Testament, ha ha? A bit shaky on the Book of Genesis?

Pastor Bodvar ran his fingertips over the ornately engraved initials, then clenched his hand slowly round the smooth bone handle of the stick. Is he trying to provoke me? he wondered again, but decided not to answer the man, pretending that this specimen of wit had been lost to him owing to a burst of sound from the airport. The next moment a four-engined giant lifted into the air and flew northward over the Bandstand Gardens and the Pond with such a roar that Fru Gudrid put her hands over her ears while Pastor Bodvar hunched his shoulders and grimaced as if in pain. The man, however, seemed elated by the noise.

That one's off to America.

He stood in his tracks, legs apart and jacket wide, gazing exultantly after the aircraft, until its hum was barely distinguished from other distant sounds.

Devil of a racket it made! he remarked at last, spitting out another piece of tobacco that had lodged in his mouth. It's because of the calm weather.

Yes.

Pastor Bodvar became conscious that his wife was shifting impatiently on the neck of land, but for a while he ignored this and looked neither at her nor the man, only at the discolored water, on which there was now not a ripple to be seen. Marvelous weather today, he said, as though absently but not without a slight tremor in his voice. A ridge of high pressure over the country.

I don't set too much store by these high-pressure ridges of theirs on the radio, replied the man. All the same, there's nothing but the pure gospel of good tidings to tell now, ha ha! Absolutely perfect weather!

Fru Gudrid moved away a fraction and coughed again. Pastor Bodvar leaned in silence on his stick, touching neither the initials, B.G., nor the date underneath, 1953. The man's eyes shifted evasively, and he moved his tongue in his mouth as if searching for something to spit.

Absolutely perfect weather.

When neither of them responded, he shook the box of matches in his trousers pocket, spit, and made a motion to leave them.

Ah well, we can't stand here talking our heads off!

Hmm, are you on your way to work? asked Pastor Bodvar.

Well, I'm on my way to a friend of mine over in Framnesveg, in the west of town, the man replied. We're going to have a run in his motorboat out here in the Sound.

I see. Pastor Bodvar grimaced as though the sun, which had clouded over but now appeared again, were too bright for his eyes. Do you perhaps go in for fishing—for lumpfish maybe? he inquired.

Lumpfish are usually beginning to get scarce in July, the man replied. Besides, I have to admit that I've always thought the lumpfish rather a nasty fish.

He stopped rattling the matchbox in his pocket and bent over the bag with the broken zipper. Death and damnation! Did I forget the packets? he muttered to himself, and seizing the bag by one handle, he pulled from it a pair of thick woolen socks, a dirty peaked cap, and a crumpled scarf, then forcing it wide open as though he wanted to let Pastor Bodvar see the contents underneath, displayed two Thermos flasks, an unattractive piece of dried fish, a small bottle with a gilt top, cartridges in ornamented cardboard packets, and the jaw of a singed sheep's head, together with slices of bread, in a plastic bag.

Everything in order. Everything in first-class order, he muttered, and stuffed the socks, cap, and scarf back into the bag. Then gripping it by both handles, he straightened himself.

No, he said grinning, we don't interfere with the lumpfish. We just go for a run to enrich our spirits and strengthen our faith. We usually have the old blowpipes with us to give the seabirds a puff if they don't behave themselves. Maybe we give the odd eider duck a beakful, too, ha ha ha, just so that it doesn't forget to say its prayers!

Pastor Bodvar had begun to swing his stick, and his head had started shaking. Lawbreaker! he was thinking. Murderous lout!

The man again made a movement to go but then glanced at the ducks and closed one eye as if aiming a gun. They are tame, this lot, he said. Maybe they'll find their way out to the Sound when it gets cold in the winter!

He went without shaking hands—merely nodding to them, slovenly and shifty eyed in the sunlight, throat tanned, chin dark with stubble, hair glossy black. Well, so long, both of you, he said, so long!

Good-bye, said Pastor Bodvar.

Bye, Gussi, said Fru Gudrid.

The man set off along the pathway that leads across the garden from Soleyjargata to the Hringbraut, but after going a few steps he turned and cocked his head to one side.

How big is the house? he said. Shall I ask a man I know whether he'd paint it for you?

Fru Gudrid answered for them both. No, that will be quite unnecessary, she said flatly. We can manage.

IV

Once again a roar filled the sky, nothing like so loud as before, however. A twin-engined aircraft passed rapidly over the garden, touched down, a gleaming mass of metal, on the runway to the south of the Hringbraut, and vanished. Since the sun came out, the garden seemed to have acquired a magnetic force, drawing visitors of all ages to both sides of the Pond. A couple walked past holding their small daughters by the hand, and behind these came a youth wearing a student's cap and carrying a camera. Two brightly clad girls crossed over the newly cut lawn wheeling a stroller and chattering in low voices on Pastor Bodvar's left. Several little boys played on the grass bank above the lawn, wrestling and turning somersaults, while others ran about among the trees. Somebody cried out, You can't get away, you donkey, you *can't* get away!

No indeed, how true it was. And where should one seek refuge? Pastor Bodvar trembled. He that governs his temper excels the conqueror of cities, he thought, as often before. He seized the crumpled-up wrapping paper from his coat pocket and turned toward a green bench beside the pathway.

Here is a trash can, he said, throwing away the paper. This is where it belongs, not in the Pond.

Having said this, he ambled northward along the reddish path at his wife's side, feeling no better, supporting himself on the gift of a vanished congregation, and still trembling like a dry leaf to the strange echo: You can't get away, you donkey, you *can't* get away!

He tried to control his wandering thoughts, or rather, the dark shadow that reached up from some recess of his mind threatening to engulf him. He knew that a long silence had always been effective in restraining that shadow, and a quiet prayer—driving it back into its recess to be forgotten, or seemingly forgotten—but still he could not refrain from remarking, Poor Sveinbjorg!

Yes, answered Fru Gudrid quietly, she is dead.

He wasn't long in finding himself another, said Pastor Bodvar.

No, replied Fru Gudrid in the same quiet tone, apparently not.

A Faroese girl, he said. Twenty-five years old! Then he added, Poor thing!

Fru Gudrid clicked her tongue. I don't see why she should be pitied, she said.

Why she should be pitied? Pastor Bodvar swung his stick, and his head shook. You don't see why she should be pitied—a strange girl in a strange place. Wandered up here from the Faroes looking for work, I daresay, he continued. To fall into the clutches of a man to whom nothing is sacred, nothing is . . .

He checked himself. His head ceased to shake, and he stopped leaning on the gift of a vanished congregation. The old woman was all hunched and knotted by age and infirmity. She had seen him to the door according to custom, half-blind, and bidden that God bless and reward him for his visit. He had walked home from Tangabae in a better mood than for a long time, even humming quietly to himself—a tune, would you believe it, to the words of a poem by an old schoolfellow. Just after five o'clock it was, that Sunday toward the end of September, the sea dead calm, the mayweed fallen, the still air a trifle cool and autumnal. Following the track from Tangabae, he had continued to hum quietly and happily to himself until he reached the strip of shore to the east of the village. Here some distant noises caught his ear: shouts, and peals of laughter. Where the track curved round the sandy potato patches of the Vogshus men, with potato plants withered along the ridges, and ran along the shingle foreshore where they had their sheds, he heard a sharp report from the beach, followed by cries, and a chanted, Right on the jaw! A-a-a-m-e-n!

In the same instant, he saw the idiot, the grandson of the old woman at Tangabae. Lying behind a rock right by the sheds, he was peering ahead, disheveled and ragged as ever.

What was going on?

Who was it who imagined that he was intoning the church service?

What was the blessed half-wit staring at?

Before he was aware of it he found himself making for the drying sheds and the opening above the Vogshus fishing huts, for it was from there that the strange sounds were coming, and in that direction that little Magnus was staring. I have just come from your granny, my lad. Why are you lying here?— that was what he had meant to say, when suddenly the bay, dead calm, the beach, and the huts were exposed to view. Gussi was beside the boat loading a gun, a gleaming rifle, while four other boys were watching him. Two of them, the Vogshus cousins, were newly confirmed; the others, the brothers from Eyri, still to be confirmed. Below the high-water mark a tallish post had been erected between rocks. It had a piece of gray burlap daubed with paint tied round the middle of it, and an ancient receptacle reversed on its top, a pockmarked chamber pot. Gussi kneeled by the stern of the boat, head cocked to one side, and took his time, aiming deliberately, just as though he—a grown-up man well into his nineteenth year—wanted to spin out the silent anticipation of his fellows. There was a report: the chamber pot shook on the post, and the boys shouted, Ha ha ha! He hit the pastor on the ear! Ha ha ha! He hit his ear!

A-a-a-m-e-n! Gussi stood up, released the empty cartridge case from the breech, and whined rather than chanted, A-a-a-m-e-n!

Tryggvi of Vogshus, who had been a well-behaved confirmand and shed tears at his first communion, swore even more violently than his cousin Skuli. Let me have a go, he pleaded between oaths. I shall . . .

Wait! Gussi put his hand in his pocket for another cartridge and reloaded the rifle. He grinned. First I'm going to tickle up the small bobbin below Pastor Bodvar's navel!

Ha ha ha! The small bobbin!

Little Magnus, the poor half-wit, gazed dribbling and smiling at the one who was being insulted, as if there were nothing in the world more natural than for the pastor to stand here, too, and watch this assemblage. Gussi shooting you! he declared with satisfaction, which turned to complaint as he added, I'm not to join in!

At this moment a dead silence descended. They had become aware of his presence; someone had seen him up there on the shingle bank. The brothers from Eyri took to their heels without waiting to hear anything, running eastward along the beach like a pair of whipped curs. The Vogshus cousins seemed shamefaced—avoided looking up at the bank, not taking to their heels exactly but moving off in the same direction as the brothers. But Gussi, oh no, he continued to grin, pretended not to have noticed. He fumbled with the loaded rifle and knelt by the boat as if to take aim at the post.

I'm not to join in! complained little Magnus again. I'm not to join in!

The silence seemed to tremble like a taut string near the breaking point. He turned away without a word, neither answering the half-wit nor waiting for Gussi to pull the trigger, walked briskly on his way down the shingle bank and past the drying sheds. When he had gone some way to the west of the Vogshus boundary fence, to where the track widened, becoming passable to vehicles as it turned toward the village, the game began anew, as he had expected: the cries more subdued and hesitant, it was true, but the chant-

ing of their leader just as prolonged and loaded with malice: A-a-a-m-e-n-!
A-a-a-m-e-n!

What was it all about? What was the meaning of that behavior? Why on
earth did he have to carry on like that, a grown youth nearly nineteen years
old? Was he still at the same immature stage as his comrades there on the
beach, lads newly or not yet confirmed, easily led astray and full of animal
spirits? Or was he driven by some impulse to pay back his pastor—to insult
him in some way in return for his unmerited goodwill and tolerance? Had
he not already begun to show his teeth the previous summer, about their
home for weeks on end, employed to paint the outside of the house, and
part of the inside, too: the dining room, kitchen, and bedroom? Had he not
begun to take advantage toward the end, whistling hymn tunes with comic
exaggeration, grinning his mockery even while having benefits showered
upon him? It was Gudrid who had engaged him to paint for them and who
had come to terms with him about payment. It was she . . .

V

Pastor Bodvar strolled back beside his wife, swinging his stick as though in
anger. The dark shadow reached up yet farther from the innermost recess of
his mind, but instead of resisting it—preparing himself for a period of prayer
and quietness—he could not refrain from breaking silence.

What were you saying? *Our* house?

Fru Gudrid made a sound of interrogation.

Weren't you saying something about *our* house? he asked, his voice shaking. About having the roof painted?

Fru Gudrid nodded. It could do with it, she said. Both the roof and the
window frames.

Our house? Pastor Bodvar brandished his stick, and his head shook. Are
we then the *sole* owners?

It was just my way of speaking, said Fru Gudrid. Don't you suppose I
know as well as you that we aren't the sole owners?

Good! Pastor Bodvar continued to brandish his stick. Then I suppose you
have consulted the couple downstairs. Perhaps they have asked you to deal
with the matter?

I am under no obligation to consult either them or anyone else about things that are self-evident, replied Fru Gudrid in a constrained voice, as if tentatively. I am under no obligation to consult anyone about whether the roof should be allowed to rust or the window frames to rot.

That's strange. I wonder what you would say if they were to behave as though we had no share in the house? Pastor Bodvar caught his breath. Besides, I have heard no mention of the roof rusting up to now . . .

But we were talking about it only a few days ago, retorted Fru Gudrid. Don't say you have forgotten.

Utter nonsense, thought Pastor Bodvar, but he could not exclude the possibility of her being right. He no longer trusted his own memory where recent events were concerned. You are under an obligation to consult the couple downstairs, he said angrily. At least about the roof. You have no business to be rushing off and engaging a man . . .

Was he able to take it on? asked Fru Gudrid.

That has nothing to do with it. You should have consulted them first! Pastor Bodvar pointed his stick, and his head punctuated every word: Engaging a man to paint the roof and window frames as though you owned the whole house!

If he can be called a man! he added. That confounded windbag and weathercock!

But I was thinking about the expense, said Fru Gudrid. I don't know what you think, but I know that I wouldn't want us to have to pay the standard rate, which everybody complains about so much.

Do you really imagine that *he* would make any concessions on our account? Pastor Bodvar caught his breath again. Save me expense! What, that unprincipled, boorish rogue!

What is the matter with you, man? asked Fru Gudrid. What a fuss you are making about nothing.

A lawbreaker and a delinquent from childhood! exclaimed Pastor Bodvar. Always shooting eider ducks! And more than once under suspicion of illicit distilling, to say nothing of poaching!

What a rage you're getting yourself into! Fru Gudrid raised her voice and declared conclusively, I was perfectly free to ask him whether he could paint for us, wasn't I? Didn't we sometimes turn to him back in Adalfirth? Didn't we get him to paint for us then?

Who turned to him? demanded Pastor Bodvar. Did I do so?

It's more than likely that you left it to me, just as you did so many other matters, answered Fru Gudrid. It may also be that Gussi was in the habit of shooting eider duck and that he sometimes took a drop too much, but could you find any fault with his work? Or was he ever unreasonable?

It was the last thing I would have dreamed of, to ask such an unscrupulous fellow to do a hand's turn for me, said Pastor Bodvar, looking at neither the church on the far side of the Pond nor the old bishop's house on the other side of the street. I have never approved of him and his mad . . .

Well, I never! Fru Gudrid seemed more surprised than angry. From what I can remember he was popular back in Adalfirth, she said. He was considered both amusing and clever with his hands.

Is he supposed to have been popular, too? thought Pastor Bodvar. That uneducated lout, that bigmouthed clown! But he said, Well, now, was he popular?

You're no judge, my love; you could never take a joke, said Fru Gudrid.

Is that so? Pastor Bodvar started and straightened himself, brandishing his stick. What kind of a joke?

Ai, I'm tired of this grumbling over nothing, she said. You are welcome to consult with the wretched woman downstairs about the roof and the window frames. You're welcome to find a painter, and you're welcome to pay him the standard rate. I'll be more than happy to be rid of all the fuss and bother for once!

Pastor Bodvar caught his breath but said nothing when it came to the point, was suddenly stricken with dread, as though he were standing on the brink of a sheer precipice. The dark shadow had reached up from the innermost recess of his mind, so far that he had no choice but either to capitulate to it, whatever the consequences, or to strive against it as well as he could—not utter a word, come what might, until he had prayed and recollected himself in privacy.

I'll be more than happy! repeated Fru Gudrid.

He remained silent.

He who knows all things, knows that! she exclaimed. I'm sick and tired of the eternal bother and the eternal grumbling!

He was expecting her to intensify her attack, remind him of the growing inflation, invite him again to pay the standard rate, call him Sigurhans. But when she did nothing of the sort, remaining as silent as he, Pastor Bodvar was little reassured. Why this behavior? What lay behind her restraint?

He shot a glance at her, but in profile her face seemed entirely free from any waxen smile. Just look at that hat, he thought, silently despising the brimless cylinder on her head. What a confounded piece of affectation in a sixty-year-old woman! After that his head shook and he trembled, blaming himself for swearing and frightened at the words on his own tongue. He looked down at his feet, supporting each step with the gift of a vanished congregation. He that brings disorder into his own household inherits wind. He that puts a curb on his mouth and tongue preserves his soul from calamity.

They strolled silently past the baker's at the corner of Tjarnargata and Vonarstraeti, but Pastor Bodvar was unaware of it, nor did he discern any smell to remind him of his school days of long ago, the doughnuts of the late Veiga, or the currant buns of Bernhoft. He was so far away that he scarcely knew where they were walking, before the ornamental iron gate of Gudmund, the company director, with its gilded classical figures, announced the proximity of their house—or rather, the house they owned jointly with the couple downstairs. It occurred to him to have a look at the rust patches on the roof, but just as he was adjusting his spectacles, which had slipped forward on his nose, Fru Gudrid broke the silence.

By the way, she said, we have been invited for coffee this evening.

Where? He was thrown off balance again and began to brandish his stick. Where, I'd like to know?

To Pastor Steindor and Finna.

Is that so?

You may remember, he looked in briefly yesterday and asked us to come this evening.

That is something to look forward to!

Fru Gudrid made a sound of interrogation.

I said that is something to look forward to! Pastor Bodvar wrinkled his nose as if smelling a bad odor. I said that is something to look forward to!

Fru Gudrid shook her head. Fancy you behaving like this, she said quietly.

Behaving like what?

Talking in that way about our old and good friends: your schoolfellow and my cousin.

Pooh! Pastor Bodvar brandished his stick as though engaging an invisible enemy, fencing with a ghost. That . . . , he began, then stopped short, gaining control over his tongue. That tiresome pair! That fat, stupid female! he continued silently. That dull-witted stick of a man with his knack for pushing himself forward and getting one living after another, each better than the last, so that when he was due to retire a few years ago, he was comfortably off! What was that in the paper the other day? The previous weekend, wasn't it? "The well-known clerical personality Pastor Steindor Jonsson preached a brilliant sermon on the duties of a Christian toward the authorities in a democratic society." The well-known clerical personality! Who could have dreamed in early days that Dori, on whom two head students had always found themselves taking pity, would one day earn such a description! The well-known clerical personality! Oh yes, from the beginning of his clerical career he had fulminated in the pulpit as though he were personal adviser to the Holy Trinity, as though he had a detailed plan of the Lord's purposes before him, as though God almighty were some kind of keen businessman ready to make a deal with any rogue if the terms were favorable! His sermons were assiduously loaded with facile optimism and gushing sentimentality or filled with unintelligible verbiage which was supposed to be elevated and poetic. He had used his voice like an actor, contracting and expanding as appropriate, smiled at the congregation when fitting, and forced out his words tearfully and with difficulty when this was expected of him. He had known how to advertise himself and attract attention, had contrived to support the authorities, whether on the left or on the right, had flirted decorously with the unlikeliest of policies and opinions, had even had wit enough not to engage in open propaganda for his spiritualist nonsense while holding a benefice. Dori, the well-known clerical personality—no, he had never had a day's illness, wasn't really retired, in spite of his age. Endlessly holding forth on the radio and scribbling in the papers. The author of a recently published best seller about his old protégé, the spirit raiser. And of course at work on another volume, about mysterious phenomena at the dark séances of some other sorcerer.

Friends! Pooh!

Pastor Bodvar's head shook. He was like a cornered sparrow. He could see neither houses nor gardens in the quiet street near the Catholic church, only a boring evening at the house of a well-known clerical personality, a house crammed full of the gifts of congregations, old and recent—paintings, photographs, silverware of various kinds, china, crystal, pottery, brasswork, as well as a number of carved and molded ornamental articles, such as his desk and chair, the desk lamp with its angel, and the great inkstand that represented the well of Mimir—all bearing witness to a regard for the cleric. The financial gifts made by the parishioners of three wealthy livings to the shepherd of their souls, over and above these, were not visible, however. Dori had long been endowed with a shrewd money sense, had nursed a deep-rooted affection for his purse, even contriving to let it be as empty as the poor box when he expected to be faced with some expenditure. This evening he would begin by discussing national problems, either pacing the room as he talked or throwing himself into a deep armchair, hale and ruddy of face in spite of all his parties, coffee drinkings, and cake eatings, while Finna—that dumpling, that lump of suet—would urge him to tell his guests about the prodigies and marvels of the latest ghost congress, with Haflidi the Second-Sighted or Lauga the Medium. And no sooner would the dumpling have mentioned one or both of these sorcerers than a practiced expression of sanctity would pass over the face of the cleric and his voice would assume a suitable tone: Wonderful testimony, a singularly fruitful connection! Pah!

Pastor Bodvar brandished his stick against such heresy and was on the point of walking past his own house, when Fru Gudrid opened the gate.

Well, she said, we're home.

He queried this with a grunt but quickly recovered his bearings, turned, and followed—not only on account of his rheumatism and shortness of breath but also because he had suddenly remembered his failure to look at the rust patches on the roof. The nameplate outside their apartment augmented his ill humor—that polished brass shield his wife had given him, to be screwed on the door without his approval:

Bodvar S. Gunnlaugsson
pastor emeritus

Of course she had consulted Steindor before having the shield engraved. Whence, otherwise, the Latin *pastor emeritus*? It was typical of Dori, the school dunce, the blockhead, to display the little knowledge he possessed in order to give the impression that he was the most learned of men. It was just like Gudrid, too, to indulge her whim while making a parade of her generosity. Bodvar S. Gunnlaugsson, *pastor emeritus*! The words grinned at him as his wife took the key from her bag to open the door of the apartment. She would be obliged to consult Dori again when his gravestone was on the agenda. She was sure to order an impressive stone for the grave, more than likely with fancy carving—a dove or a pair of clasped hands in marble—so that all might witness her devotion to the earthly remains of her husband. Pastor Bodvar S. Gunnlaugsson would be inscribed at the top, then some dates: born, ordained, died, and finally, the overworked words

REQUIESCAT IN PACE

—Latin from Dori.

Well, remarked Fru Gudrid, putting her bag on the chest of drawers in front of the mirror while she pulled off her white cotton gloves and unbuttoned her coat, I think it's time for a cup of coffee.

Pastor Bodvar closed the door until the latch clicked. In his mind instead of a polished brass shield he saw a tombstone engraved with a dove that in some way reminded him of his wife's preposterous hat: Requiescat in pace!

I think I'll make a few doughnuts, just for the two of us, said Fru Gudrid, removing her hat. She passed a hand over her hair and glanced in the mirror. I'm afraid there isn't much to go with the coffee.

It was as though a whisper came to Pastor Bodvar that she knew how he felt, had a suspicion of his agitation, but also knew that his health was failing. She will be glad of her freedom, whispered the merciless voice. She is younger than you; she has waited for years to be rid of you. Requiescat in pace!

Fru Gudrid put her gloves and scarf in the top drawer of the chest of drawers, opened the cupboard, placed her brimless hat on a shelf with other hats, and hung her coat on a padded coat hanger with a pattern of roses on it.

Somehow you're looking so tired, she said. Are you feeling unwell?

No!

Shall I help you out of your coat?

No!

Pastor Bodvar pulled himself together, shot his stick into the space to the left of the cupboard, threw his hat onto a hook, and shed his coat without too much difficulty. I . . . I don't need your help, he said, his voice shaking. I can manage to unvest myself on my own!

Fru Gudrid shook her head and sighed. It's really shocking to see how bad you are today, my dear.

She did not look again in the mirror but turned her back on it, contrary to her usual habit, and stood motionless beside the chest of drawers, seeming somehow to shrink into herself: It's shocking to see how bad you are . . .

Well, what about it?

Pastor Bodvar reproved himself for his thoughts, touched the cupboard door with his knuckles, and vanished like a fugitive into his retreat, the study, closing the door behind him.

VI

He had not waited for his heartbeat to become normal or the pain in his side to disappear completely before standing up from the chair to look through the window. The paintwork on the outside window frame was admittedly beginning to show signs of wear—cracked and weathered, even flaking to a considerable extent at the sides, though it was by no means a foregone conclusion that the frame was bound to rot unless it was painted this summer. Or was it? Could Gudrid perhaps be right? Was there indeed a danger of deterioration?

Pastor Bodvar turned away from the window without coming to any conclusion. Sitting at the desk, he glanced briefly at the three photographs of his daughter and then at the multicolored backs of his books and finally at his writing materials. When the discomfort in his left side was almost gone, he bowed his head, clasped his hands, and prayed with closed eyes. He repeated an old prayer that he had learned at his confirmation, added a few stumbling words about strength and mercy in adversity, repeated silently two verses which had accompanied him since childhood, and then very slowly recited the Lord's Prayer, moving his lips and rocking a little in his chair. . . . For thine is the kingdom, the power, and the glory, for ever and ever. Amen.

A-a-a-m-e-n!

He was ashamed to be recalling distorted cries when he should have been listening to the voice of charity, and remained for some time without moving, head bowed, eyes closed, and hands clasped. He felt better then, it was true, but the change was less marked—the effect not nearly so profound as on some much slighter occasions. Pray and you shall receive, seek and you shall find, knock and it shall be opened to you . . . He decided to repeat his prayers when he was more fully recovered, but for the moment he had to find something to occupy him, try to do something: read a good book, or perhaps write if that could ease his mind a little. He ran his eye at random over a few sentences at the beginning of the short article which was to appear in the *Church Gazette,* but they seemed so strange to him in spite of the careful work that had gone into their composition that he put the proofs back on the corner of the desk. It had always been enough for him just to turn over the pages of one of his favorite books, such as *The Imitation of Christ,* or the poems of Jonas Hallgrimsson, for him to be borne on their breath to a purer region. Nevertheless, he relinquished the idea of taking any such from its shelf. The letter which he had begun to write before wandering off to the Gardens and getting so depressed lay on the desk in front of him, and his pen was lying on the sheet of paper.

> My dearest daughter,
> God grant that these lines find you and your husband in good health.
> I haven't much news to tell at present, for little of note has happened
> here since I last wrote . . .

Pastor Bodvar suddenly remembered that he had last walked across Posthusstraeti a fortnight ago in the bright sunshine of an early afternoon, on a Friday. On the other hand, he was somehow dissatisfied with the beginning of this letter, so he tore the sheet to pieces and threw the pieces in the wastepaper basket. Then, after a short hesitation, he moved his chair nearer the ancient desk, took his fountain pen, unscrewed the cap, and started a new letter.

My dearest Svava,
God grant that these few lines which I am writing to fill in the time find you in good health, as well as your husband and his folk. Nothing of note has happened here since I wrote to you a fortnight ago, but all the same, some kind of news I must . . .

Pastor Bodvar looked involuntarily at the three pictures of his daughter. She smiled back at him at the age of five, as well as newly confirmed, and twenty years old—dark eyed, black haired, and vivacious. There was a soft, silky sheen on the waves of her hair, although it was scarcely so dark as in the picture in the living room, where she stood in her wedding dress at the side of her husband, James K. Andrews, the civil engineer. News, he had written. What kind of news could he find that would interest a young woman on another continent? Should he tell her about the recent devaluation and the rapidly accelerating rate of inflation, that for a long time he had not been able to afford to buy himself a book or even a box of cigars or a packet of good-quality tobacco? Should he mention, in a letter to be read on the other side of the globe in the world's greatest city of skyscrapers, that her mother was occupied, day in, day out, making ends meet, as she called it, supplementing his pension by sewing little flags and crocheting traditional shawls to sell to foreigners? Should he perhaps admit that he had no cause to complain over a lack of intellectual companions? Pastor Steindor occasionally invited them for evening coffee, either alone or with other guests—for instance, the elderly maiden lady with the slipshod manner of speech who imagined she heard mysterious voices or the old author who believed himself to have discovered a scientific basis for his superstitious ghost hunting and nonsense about omens. Should he devote a few words to her mother's woman friends, all of whom she must know, except Fru Camilla Magnusson, maybe, widow of the late Bjarni Magnusson, the chief clerk, or describe their card evenings, which had hardly become subject to contract and regulations before last winter?

Those old harridans! Those woman friends of Gudrid's! Perhaps it was unfair to include Fru Camilla in the same category, although she bought flags and scarves from Gudrid and dolls in bogus national costume from old Vilborg, who was the most tolerable of the whole bunch, in spite of her nose. Fru Camilla presumably accepted invitations to coffee in order to discuss business, and she neither played cards with them nor returned the invitations—either lacked the time or did not have the inclination, since she moved in wider circles than the others. She owned two shops, in one of which she sold souvenirs.

Nothing of note has happened here since I wrote to you a fortnight ago, but all the same, some kind of news I must . . . find, he added, but could get no further. News? Clear in his memory were the card evenings of the past winter when those same old harridans sat down in the living room and made out that they were playing cards—bridge or whatever it was they called it— though never for a moment did they stop talking about money and again money: their under-the-counter deals, and those of others, trade and prices, vanity and scandal. He could hear the purring and mewing of Sossa, who produced one story after another while shuffling and dealing the cards, eyes half-closed, mouthing the misdeeds, misfortunes, and disasters of total strangers. He could hear the booming laughter of Fru Magnhildur, that coarse, ironhearted, greedy woman, who measured all things in money and could be trusted to try and swindle her own flesh and blood. He could hear the nasal yap of old Vilborg, who was really of an altogether different sort: kindhearted and generous by nature, and besides such a dunce at cards that she lost every bid, whatever cards she was holding and whatever hands there were against her. And some time after ten Gudrid would open the door of the retreat, which was called a kontor in her language, and summon the *pastorem emeritum* to take coffee with them. Old Vilborg could continue with her nasal and harmless yapping, but Sossa and Magnhildur would become reserved, stare at him as though he were some venerable antique, call him Pastor with every other word they addressed to him, assuming, moreover, a kind of churchgoing expression that filled him with disgust. Many times he had demurred at drinking coffee with the bridge party, making one excuse or another, but Gudrid was adamant. Pastor emeritus, the simpleton who had never been able to make head or tail of money matters, the dusty antique who would soon be nothing but dust, was to be exhibited shortly after ten o'clock so that the gossipmonger and the ironhearted should not have occasion to suppose that they were there without the approval of the master of the house.

S.
Requiescat in pace

Pastor Bodvar laid down his fountain pen, unable for the moment to remember any news he could relay to a young woman in a distant metropolis. It occurred to him briefly to seek consolation from Brother Thomas, or read a chapter from the last book given him by poor Indridi: *The Diary of a Country Priest* of Bernanos. At all events the letter was not likely to grow any longer until he had rid himself of the bitterness possessing him since he concluded his appeal to God—until he had been purged of the dark shadow that surely had little in common with the theme of his meditation on the power of prayer.

Indridi . . . oh yes. Indridi dead, and Bogi dead. Steindor, on the other hand, with the best of health. The well-known clerical personality!

Pastor Bodvar raised himself a little on his seat, moved the chair a few inches from the desk, and inserted an old key in the keyhole of the drawer where he kept the manuscript of his memoirs. Removing the crumpled paper cover from the manuscript, he read a short note which he had written in the margin of the last page, and then the words, We were a lighthearted company, my schoolmates and I, and we found many ways of amusing ourselves. Once there was a great to-do in our class, when . . .

He was oppressed by the fear that henceforth he would be able to write scarcely anything of worth, in spite of the literary grant awarded him in the annual finance bill—thanks to whose good offices, he had no idea. Perhaps he would never complete the volume of his memoirs, not even the section on his school years, to say nothing of a further chapter in which he would have the difficult task of tracing a path between events he could relate and others which he would have to take with him to the grave. And though he finished the book and somehow managed to have it published, who would be any the better? What would become of it among all this madness and confusion in this world of armed forces and propaganda, of cars and airplanes, of moneygrubbing and hard drinking? Who would trouble to wade through a tome that did not offer exciting plot, mysterious phenomena, or obscene language? Who, in these days, could be bothered to read the simple memoirs of an old man who had become a pastor not out of a sense of vocation but out of weakness and debt and who had afterward been tormented by doubts for as long as he had a dark hair on his head? Indridi? Yes, Indridi would have read his memoirs, probably the instant they were put on paper. Bogi would have read them, too, and understood, in spite of a difference of viewpoint. But they were dead. Both vanished behind the curtain . . . Indridi and Bogi were dead.

He slipped the manuscript back into its hiding place and locked the drawer. Then he inserted the key in another keyhole and opened a smaller drawer in which he kept various odds and ends, among them two withered flowers in a dainty case, a cigar box containing some pebbles, a certificate from the Latin School, and a large yellow envelope which he had sealed and inscribed faintly, in pencil, Give N.L.

Give the National Library? When had he written that? When had such folly entered his mind? Give the National Library those poems—with instructions that the seal was not to be broken until he had lain for twenty-five years in his grave?

He shook his head, moved his lips slightly, and fingered the envelope with trembling hands, touching the red seals with his fingertips. No, he thought, he would not have any stranger—some clown, maybe, or coarse fellow—pry into his poems after he was dead, speculating over them and filling in the gaps with guesswork. He must take them out of the envelope, tear them to pieces, and throw the pieces away, using an opportunity when he was alone at home. Those about which he was most sensitive no one had been allowed to see. Indridi had read some, and Bogi some, and one autumn evening in a friendly house it had even been proposed that some of them be sung.

Oh yes, that was how it was.

He opened neither the case in which he kept the two withered flowers nor the cigar box containing various odd pebbles but pushed the drawer shut, locked it, and pocketed the key. Then he took off his spectacles and polished them with his handkerchief while the Schubert air sounded in the distance like a broken echo of the past: Leise flehen meine Lieder . . . durch die Nacht . . . zu dir.

He sniffed, lowered his head, and dried his eyes with the handkerchief. After that he replaced the spectacles and answered the fading echo in a whisper: Oh yes. That was how it was.

The bitterness had given way to a sad tranquillity, the itch and sense of disgust faded, the shadow gradually withdrawn into the innermost recess of his mind from which it had reached out. Yet he was something less than fully recovered. For the moment he felt that he had never been so feeble. Besides, he could no longer recall why he had begun opening drawers, for what he had been searching—or had he been searching? For something that he needed urgently?

He pulled out a third drawer. It was not locked. At once his eyes fell upon a letter from his daughter—about two months old if he remembered rightly. In the top left-hand corner of the envelope there stood, From Svava B. Andrews, 505 Woodhaven Blvd., Queens, Long Island, New York, U.S.A. This was the very letter, if he remembered rightly, in which she told him that her civil-engineer husband might be offered a highly paid position with another American corporation, in which case they would be obliged to move to South America in the early fall and stay there for at least two years. Let's see, here it was:

> James still doesn't know whether we would be in Chile or Peru if it comes off. He says that the job is in connection with the corporation's copper mines in both countries. He says that we would have luxury accommodations and plenty of servants.

What did they want with servants, a young, childless couple? And what was to be gained from living in some great barn of a place? Where would he drag her in the end, this blessed James of hers who seemed incapable of thinking about anything but calculations, machinery, and dollars? Would he draw a line at being whipped away to Australia if he were offered a higher salary there? They spread themselves all over the world with their engineers and industrial complexes, these great moneymaking organizations, gaping and swallowing everything up. Chile or Peru—two years in South America?

Pastor Bodvar folded the pages and returned them to their envelope. Where would he be in two years? When was he going to reconcile himself to the idea that he would not see her again this side of the grave? Did it make any difference whether she lived in North America or South America provided she was happy? She had been luckier than had seemed likely for a time, more fortunate than many girls who had left their native land. And without a doubt she was happy after her own fashion. That James of hers was kind to her and gave her all she wanted that money could buy, both necessities and luxuries. They were determined to enjoy life, as it was called, to amuse themselves and see the world while they had the chance. But one day they were bound to have children, God willing, and then their outlook would change. Then they would settle down and accept their responsibilities. Besides, it was quite possible that nothing would come of this idea of theirs about a two-year stay in Chile or Peru. Had Svava made any mention of it in the few lines she sent her mother, about . . . about a couple of weeks ago?

There was rattle of dishes from the kitchen. His wife was busy there, had probably been resting for a while. Pastor Bodvar replaced the envelope in the front of the drawer, where he always kept his daughter's most recent letter so that he should not be obliged to search for it if he wanted to check its date and contents. Svava's other letters, yes, they were there at the back of the drawer, on the right-hand side. There, too, were his favorite presents from her, a few small articles she had brought him when she was small: a handkerchief that was supposed to be embroidered, a watercolor of the church at Adalfirth, a green mechanical pencil, a chest of drawers made out of six matchboxes, a yellow-streaked shell.

Gone. Torn away from him, like so much else.

Pastor Bodvar looked again at the three pictures of his daughter: smiling at him, aged five; newly confirmed; and at twenty with an expression that was full of warmth and a little arch. He suddenly remembered that his grandmother had been dark haired: Katrin, his father's mother, dark of hair and complexion, and from what his father had told him, slender and sprightly. To his constant regret, that kind, generous-hearted woman, who could also improvise verses, had never come near a camera. Nevertheless, his father had talked about her so often, describing her in such detail, that sometimes, before realizing, he began to think of her as though he had known her, had spent his childhood in her company, even been brought up by her. Little Svava undoubtedly took after her, the dear girl, he concluded from his study of the three photographs, nodding his head involuntarily—in appearance, at all events. He had said these same words to himself in private many times before, of course, but now it was as if a new light and warmth went with them. Oh yes, the dear girl. His dear little girl. There was no doubt about it: she took after her Great-Grandmother Katrin, that sensitive, intelligent woman who was ever eager to help others. Both of them dark haired and dark eyed. Both slender and sprightly. There had been a time when he thought dark hair beautiful.

Perhaps she would come this summer if they didn't go rushing off to South America? Perhaps she would come one fine day without warning? They thought nothing of it, nowadays, these young folk, flying from continent to continent, soaring through the air halfway across the globe. Perhaps she would come . . .

Pastor Bodvar took another look at the gifts in the desk drawer: the embroidered handkerchief, the sketch of the church of Adalfirth, the old mechanical pencil, the matchbox chest of drawers, the yellow-streaked shell. Clearly in his mind he saw his daughter's first smile at him as she lay in her cradle, kicking and somehow so enchantingly helpless that words could not describe it. Her hands and feet, how small and soft they had been, and what a world of activity had lain in store for them. He remembered how she prattled and crawled to him with her bib hanging down, how she climbed up into his lap and made him give her a ride on his knee. He picked up the shell and was walking past several houses in Adalfirth, until he stood on the beach to the west of the village and could hear both the calm-weather murmur of the sea on a spring day and the soft voice of a child: You can have it, Papa, you can have it. She had found two shells on the sand and was quite determined to give him the bigger one. The dear girl. His dear little girl—what had he given her in return? Had she received the sincere affection she needed? Had she been adequately equipped to face the journey into a perilous world of atom bombs and space travel?

You can have it, Papa, you can have it.

Pastor Bodvar felt the breeze of that clear spring day on his cheek, strengthening his faith. As the heavens are above the earth, so are my ways above your ways, and my thoughts above your thoughts. The destiny of his daughter, his little girl, was in the hands of God almighty, as was the destiny of every living being. She was in the keeping of that eternal providence just as much to the west of the ocean as to the east, just as much now as when encompassed by the snares of fashion and the quest for pleasure. How often he had reminded a vanished congregation, and himself no less, of the words of Saint John: God is love, and he that dwells in love dwells in God, and God in him. And how often he had preached on the words of Saint Paul in his First Epistle to the Corinthians: And now abideth faith, hope, charity, these three; but the greatest of these is charity.

Yes, the greatest of these is charity, demanding nothing, understanding all things, forgiving all things, knowing no distance, bridging oceans. He who keeps charity in his heart shall never be lonely.

Pastor Bodvar put the shell back in its place and closed the drawer. Then edging his chair a little closer to the desk, he took up his fountain pen and read silently: Nothing of note has happened here since I wrote to you a fortnight ago, but all the same, some kind of news I must find . . . He did not continue at this point but after brief consideration tore the page up and began the letter a third time.

My darling daughter,
God grant that these lines find you and your husband in good health, as also his parents and sister. I am jotting them down, not because I have any special news to tell you but rather by way of a pastime and amusement for myself. I also do it with a surreptitious hope of repayment, for every day I await news of my precious sunbeam and am, I suppose, ever hoping to see her again before too long. You mustn't take my words to mean that I've suddenly started interfering and giving orders in my old age. I've never been dis-

posed to dictate, and the last thing I want is for you and your husband to change your plans in any way on my account—or rather, I should say, on our account. What matters most is that you are happy and prosper in all things. Of your mother and myself there is little news to tell, except that we both enjoy God's priceless gift of reasonably good health. I'm troubled by rheumatism at times, besides other appurtenances of old age, but these are only trifles.

VII

Yes, they were only trifles: the shortness of breath, and the pain in his side which never troubled him for long at a time; also the backache and that unpleasant numbness which sometimes affected his left arm, and even his legs too. He was fine. He suffered no pain, felt no discomfort at present, and bore no marks of his recent distress, or of having seen ludicrous hallucinations that made him fear with every step that his mind was being enclosed in a hell of darkness from which there was no escape this side of the grave. In love there is no fear; rather, perfect love casts out fear, for fear embodies punishment, and he that fears is not perfect in love. He felt that maybe at the back of his mind there was something that he needed to remember, but the nightmare itself was gone, like the pain in his side. Instead of all being lost, everything was as before: serene and tranquil, the presence of the trees plainly felt, the light a little misty, a few midges dozing on the windowpane, and a redwing singing nearby. Also a smell from the kitchen now crept into the study: an agreeable frying smell bearing a promise of hot *lummur* and coffee, for it was time to be taking some light refreshment, probably four o'clock. Gudrid . . .

Pastor Bodvar refrained from looking at the farewell gift of his parishioners: the gold watch he had unconsciously taken from his vest pocket. Fingering the chain, he leaned for a moment against the back of the chair.

Gudrid, oh yes, perhaps she was not too happy, being tied to a Laodicean, neither cold nor hot. Perhaps many things would have been different, both then and now, had he acted in accordance with his own words from the pulpit, overcome the obstacles in himself, made a determined effort to amend and sweeten his marriage. When all was said and done, Gudrid had been a good wife to him, in many respects. She had borne his interests at heart and been concerned for him, in her own way. It was thanks to her that they had been able to buy a half share in the house when they moved south. It was thanks to her that he was able to pursue his interests in his old age, to putter about and indulge his appetite for research more or less unhindered, enjoying peace and relaxation in this study of his. Perhaps it was thanks to her, too, that he obtained the grant for literary work, for someone must have persuaded some person of influence to stir up the awards committee in his behalf. Admittedly he had always assumed that the mind of Gudrid was bounded by their daily bread and material possessions, but how would they have fared if she had been as helpless as he in such matters? Besides, she was by no means more tied to the concerns of the moment than some of his fellow clergy, whose souls were in their stomachs and purses and who devoted all their energies to providing butter for their bread. For instance . . .

Pastor Bodvar stopped fingering his watch chain abruptly. What kind of nonsense was he talking? What person of influence could Gudrid possibly have known who might have pulled strings with the awards committee to get him a grant for literary work? He remembered nobody, unless it could be Pastor Steindor Jonsson. It had to be said to Dori's credit that he was loyal by nature, the poor fellow, and would doubtless feel grateful to him to his dying day for past help, but he would hardly have been responsible for such an act of friendship without bragging about it afterward, even announcing it from the rooftops. Gudrid could never have gone to him, to him of all people, to ask him to use his influence. Or could she? Wasn't Dori's wife, Finna the hulk, closely related to her? Hadn't Dori himself enjoyed the same kind of supplementary benefit in private for a long time, for literary work—on supernatural phenomena?

Pastor Bodvar sighed, leaving his question unanswered, shunned further questions, and struggled to recapture a spirit of charity for the letter to his daughter. He wrote that the weather was very calm and mild, a so-called high-pressure area over the country. Yesterday the sun had been hidden, but today it had broken through in the early afternoon. He predicted dry, still weather for the next day and also mentioned the fact that, according to the radio, the hay crop was well above average in most districts and the haymaking prospects good. Besides this, the trees and shrubs seemed to be flourishing this summer, to judge by these blessed bushes here in the garden.

A strange tremor disturbed the peace of the room, like the ripple of a wave passing under a film of thin ice. Pastor Bodvar continued leaning against the back of his chair, pen between fingers, and listened to the wavering boom as it quickly melted into the distance. He had become such an authority on noises that he recognized the boom and was startled by it no longer. It was no novelty for the American forces to be hurtling over the city and its neighborhood in those aircraft of theirs that some called jets.

Ah yes, he thought, that's how it is.

After that he began to enumerate the points that he had to mention to his daughter in this letter. He was not sure that he would be able to finish it today, and perhaps not even tomorrow either. It would be a long letter. This letter would maybe make up for the manifold neglect and inevitable mistakes of past years. He would tell his daughter about her great-grandmother, the late Katrin, that kindhearted, tenacious woman who wanted to give comfort and happiness to all. He would remind her of the spring morning and summer evenings at Adalfirth when she was little, recall the names of the mountains and creeks, the moors and glaciers, the lakes and rivers. He would ask her to learn by heart some poems about their native land by his favorite poets—Jonas, for instance—and impress upon her one's need in this age of sorcery, whatever happened, not to lose one's soul: one's faith, one's hope, one's charity.

It would be a long letter.

This letter must not be written hastily.

He fumbled with his pen, leaned back in the chair, and enjoyed the peace and tranquillity that prevailed over all. He also enjoyed the odor from the kitchen that reassured him of the prospect of early refreshment provided by his wife: coffee and *lummur*. Perhaps Gudrid had put raisins and ground cinnamon in the mixture, as she sometimes did when she wanted to give him a special treat. He was not so fond of ordinary *lummur*, but hot, with raisins and cinnamon, and a half-melted coating of sugar, they were undeniably the greatest of delicacies, in no way inferior to the currant buns of the late Bernhoft or the doughnuts of poor dead Veiga. He could not suppress a longing for *lummur* of that sort, unable to remember when he had last tasted them. But even if Gudrid had not gone to so much trouble as to sprinkle raisins and cinnamon in the mixture, he still felt the urge to refresh himself with coffee and to light up his pipe.

The letter ... yes.

Pastor Bodvar looked with affection at the three photographs of his daughter. There she was in her sixth year, had perhaps given him the shell that very spring. There she was newly confirmed, holding her hymnbook in her right hand. There she was at the age of twenty, bless her, wearing an elaborate dress, with an unnecessarily low neckline, really, some trinkets dangling from each ear, and a fashionable necklace—a string of multicolored beads—quite hiding the birthmark on her neck, that large, distinctive mark just above the collarbone.

The picture of his daughter at twenty seemed to fall under a spell, the light in the room to acquire a twilight shade, the time to stand still.

Above the collarbone? thought Pastor Bodvar. Above the collarbone?

He blinked. He was pale, and there was a strange expression on his face. He sagged in his chair, and the pen dropped from his fingers without his noticing. He suddenly realized what he had been trying to recall for some time. It was as though a gust blew at a cardhouse balanced on top of another cardhouse, blew again and again, so relentlessly that Pastor Bodvar could no longer keep his seat. His head shook, and clutching at the edge of the desk, he slowly got to his feet, as if he meant to counter this assault by walking about the room, walking round and round in circles until he had overcome it. But the moment he let go of the desk he had a strange surprise. What had happened? Where was he? Where had he strayed? He felt giddy, heard a low humming noise, found himself unable to distinguish anything in front of him but did not have time to support himself on the desk, adjust his spectacles, or look about him before, doubled up by an intolerable agony, he collapsed.

At this moment Fru Gudrid called from the kitchen that coffee was ready. After a short while she called again with a trace of impatience in her voice, but there was no reply.

When she opened the study door, her husband, Pastor Bodvar Gunn-laugsson—or rather, Bodvar S. Gunnlaugsson, pastor emeritus, lay in the middle of the floor motionless.

THE STARS OF CONSTANTINOPLE

I pressed hot lips against the windowpane, blew hard, and did my utmost to melt the film of ice, until a little space surrounded by rime-furred frost flowers appeared in the middle. I saw the mountain and the sky, the frozen marshes beyond the home field, and the snow-covered levels of heath beyond the marshes. Outside it was calm and cold. The Advent dusk deepened swiftly, but the moon had not yet risen, and the stars were somewhere out in space—invisible searching eyes, far away from an impecunious boy who longed for their silver-bright glitter. They will soon be here, I thought. They must surely be coming, as they did yesterday, as they did the day before, as they do always when the weather is clear and bright.

The fact was that the stars above the mountain raced away to a measureless distance when dawn swept the shadows from the glacier in the east and lay diagonally across the marshes beyond the home field. They vanished like a dream of rare delight but appeared again in the evening twilight, arraying themselves in the sky above the mountain, alive and sparkling. I could not quite understand why they made this journey, why they did not remain unmoving above the mountain and let me admire them. Maybe they had to array themselves in the firmament above another mountain out in space. Perhaps some small farm lay under the mountain out there, and some small boy made a bare spot on a windowpane? And perhaps they went all the way to Constantinople and sent their gentle beams through the castle windows there?

Ai, it was really a shame to be so small and not be able to go at once to Constantinople. Three years earlier my sister had been much taller and plumper than I was now, much more capable and clever. I was a runt and a weakling, incapable of gathering loose tufts of wool in the spring and lazy at my work in the winter. I possessed two kronur and fifty aurar in my box, but this substantial sum of money lost all its splendor when compared with my sister's wealth. She had been twice as quick as I was in running up the slopes after wool tufts, and twice as ingenious and lucky at finding them. I was only in my eighth year and terribly small for my age.

Nevertheless I was already beginning to long for variety and delight, to long for some unspeakable bliss that was sure to rock me on downy clouds edged with gold, to rock me hither and thither and make all my wishes come true in a single instant. I dreamed of figs in the night. I had seen a colored postcard at the next farm: it was a picture of Constantinople. Dear God, what palaces, what turrets on the palaces, green and pink, like the forest all around—a wonderful forest of romance where leaves were longer than your arm and broader than pancakes! Night after night I would glide to this distant city, climb the trees, and sing, disporting myself on the domed turrets, stuffing my face with cakes of every description and eating figs out of bottomless paper bags. But sometimes I would lose my balance, shout, and fall. I would wake hungry and frightened in the bed beside my father, pitch-darkness in the badstofa and everybody asleep. No figs for me until the wool was taken to the village, about midsummer, no unforgettable bliss, no forest. The disappointment often brought me intense emotion, but I would console myself with the thought that it was better to snuggle in safety beside Pabbi than to tumble from the domed turrets of Constantinople. When I was older I intended to go there with my parents and my sister—to protect them from robbers, brandishing a sharp scimitar—and lead them through the trees in the palace gardens or ply them with delicious sweetmeats. What a difference there would be! No horrid firewood or sour black pudding in Constantinople, no spindle or hanks of wool, no frosted windowpane with a tiny bare spot on which I had to blow constantly to prevent it from icing over again.

But the stars above the mountain? Were they going to come later than usual this evening? No, wait a minute! The first one appeared all of a sudden over the southernmost peak. I saw it far away, burning in the firmament like a faint, flickering candle, but I knew that soon it would move closer, growing and glowing, and cast a clear ray on the snow, reflecting itself in the ice pools.

There came another, and a third—many, many, maybe newly arrived from Constantinople, having recently glittered perhaps in the windows of the castles. I did not attempt to count them but ran my eyes in grateful pleasure from one to another until I had forgotten the cold and the spindle, forgotten turrets and figs, and bathed my indistinct longings in the growing lights of the sky.

Geiri! Geiri! whispered my sister, tugging me away from the window. Come outside and listen!

There was so much urgency in her voice that I complied without question—snatched my cap and ran after her down the passage. We stood in silence out on the terrace in the calm of the evening, poor and diminutive before the splendor of the heavens: the northern lights flamed above the heath, and a slender edge of moon cast a brazen glimmer on the glacier to the east.

What is it? I asked curiously.

Shh, Shh! Don't talk. Just listen, my sister whispered, and she caught her breath.

I heard sharp reports of the frost in the marshes and a low murmur from the falls in the river to the west, but neither of these sounds seemed to me especially remarkable, so that a demand for some sort of indemnity on the part of my sister for fooling me was on my lips, when I became aware of a strange noise out of the stillness. It was a trilling whistle.

What was that? I asked in wonder, but my sister did not answer.

For a moment we both listened, holding our breath. I stared in the direction of the frozen marshes, for it was from there that the sound seemed to come. But I could see nothing in the dusk and wished with all my heart that the moon would rise more quickly: the brazen edge on the glacier stood quite still. Hush, hush. I distinctly heard the sound of voices. Two loud voices were briefly interwoven. Then they separated: one fell silent, while the other ended in the same trilling whistle. I did not much care for this. I did not like hearing strange noises without being able to explain their origin to myself. It was quite another matter traveling to Constantinople and fighting with robbers in my mind.

Elves? I queried, alarmed.

But my sister, who was three years my elder and more experienced and realistic to boot, dismissed the idea as ridiculous.

Visitors, she whispered. Can't you see them?

No, I said.

Look, there they come, she whispered, and pointed ahead. Two visitors.

I looked in the direction in which she was pointing, and trembled with excitement. Dear God, I could see them both as they strode across the ice of the marshes just beyond the home field, heading toward the farm.

I'm going to slip over to the barn and let Pabbi know, my sister said, and she rushed off. I stood alone on the terrace and watched the mysterious visitors rapidly drawing nearer. Perhaps I was aware of my smallness and insecurity before the strangeness that accompanied these people. Perhaps I was just unwilling to play second fiddle to my sister in reporting news. At all events I turned and ran into the kitchen to tell my mother.

And soon after, I was back at the house door, peeping. My father was on the terrace, shifting from foot to foot and inserting a new plug of tobacco in his mouth preparatory to receiving strangers. But my sister did not stir. She was staring, quiet and resolute, into the Advent dusk, as though this was the most ordinary, everyday occurrence. What courage!

Welcome to the men! said my father, chewing, and hunting for something in his trouser pocket.

Good evening, replied two dissimilar voices: one was deep and solemn, imbued with an admonitory sort of wisdom; the other shrill and piping, over-flowing with gleeful mockery, as though the words escaped through a con-tracted throat striving to suppress peals of rippling laughter.

They both greeted my father and sister, but in spite of my curiosity I shrank bank into the passageway, so that they should not see me. I heard them put down their baggage on the terrace, puffing loudly, as though re-lieved of a heavy load, but I dared not venture forward to see: I was only in my eighth year. They announced their names and inquired about the weather of the past weeks.

The weather has been unusually bad for the time of year, replied my father deliberately. It snowed heavily just before the beginning of Advent. Then one day there was a harmful thaw, and it froze again. Since then it has been calm, very cold, with no clear grazing—a sheet of ice over everything, as you can see, but quite still.

Unusually bad? A blessed calamity, said the deep voice. But its agreement seemed inspired by the weariness and wretchedness of the journey.

Snowed heavily? It certainly did! One day a harmful thaw? Oh yes, that was the way of it! A sheet of ice over everything and no grazing?

One devil of a disaster! said the shrill voice, half laughing, as though meaning to turn the injustice of heaven and earth into a huge joke.

Do the men propose to go on far? inquired my father.

No. Can you put us up?

Yes, replied my father. Here no man is turned away.

I did not wait to hear more but ran ahead of them into the badstofa. They stumbled along the dark passageway with their baggage: bulging strapped bags and brown suitcases. They sat down each on his bed, while my mother lit the badstofa lamp, her hand shaking a little. She was not sure whether these important strangers could eat thin tasteless porridge and pickled blood sausage. I shook hands with lowered eyes, then hid myself in a corner behind my father's bed and furtively appraised them. The deep-voiced one was quite bald and had deep wrinkles in the middle of his forehead, while his eyes were steel blue and sharp, as if they could pierce through one. He had a flattened nose and thick lips, fleshy cheeks, and heavy lines from nose to mouth. His face was composed in an expression of distinction and calm. He leaned back on the bed and sighed wearily.

His companion, on the other hand, was brimming with life, bubbling over with extraordinary energy, rocking himself back and forth on the edge of the bed, glancing with amusement in every direction, and waving his hands as though playing an invisible instrument. His eyes were coal black and burning. Sometimes his forehead was creased in many wrinkles; sometimes it was smooth. His curly hair even fell from time to time to the enormous, fiery beak of a nose. The jaws were lean and narrow, lips paper-thin, mouth sometimes wide and open, sometimes small and pursed—the whole face constantly changing and in constant motion.

Although the visitors had little in common as far as personal appearance was concerned, I felt there was some secret connection between them, and their clothes seemed to confirm my suspicion. They were both wearing ankle-high boots, both had thick jackets with ornamental buttons, both had strapped bags and brown suitcases. I realized suddenly that my father was ragged and dirty. I noticed that his dun-colored jersey had holes in the elbows and was dotted with wisps of hay from the barn. I saw that his trousers were patched and shabby, the bottoms stuffed into his socks, and his skin shoes unspeakably lacking in style beside the laced boots of the gentlefolk. Perhaps he felt the same, for he stroked his forehead in an embarrassed manner, chewed his quid, and discussed the weather with the deep-voiced one.

Hi, young man! called the shrill-voiced one, pointing at me. Come here a minute.

I edged toward him, timid and shy. There was an agreeable aroma about his clothes. He laughed and wriggled all over, put a hand in his jacket pocket and told me to open my mouth. I obeyed as if in a trance. He popped a round ball into my mouth, shaking with merriment. Eat that, young man, young towhead, young genius, young bag-o'-down, he rattled on, patting me all over. The round ball melted at once, filling my mouth with a sour-sweet taste. I no longer felt shy with him. He coaxed me, talked to me as an equal, and quickly made me his confidant.

When I was your age, he whispered roguishly, I once stole a muzzle-loader and potted a cockerel without permission—shot a French cockerel, my lad. And it flew up high in the air when it was dead.

Did it come down again? I asked.

Oh yes, it fell into a cesspool! And the old woman chased me in her drawers, hee-hee! The old woman wanted to wallop me with a six-foot catfish! But I got away, my lad, I escaped!

What old woman? I asked.

The old woman who owned the cockerel, young man, young genius. I once shot a brindled gray tomcat, too. Let loose on him up on a stone wall, where he was gobbling down altar wafers, young towhead, young bag-o'-down. It was the bishop's tomcat, but you mustn't tell anyone. He was of a breed from Mesopotamia, you know!

I shifted from foot to foot before him with a sour-sweet taste in my mouth and was about to ask him what bishop it was who had owned the highborn brindled gray tomcat, when my father spoke, saying, What road are you men taking?

Well, that one there is on the road to God, replied my benefactor, and he pointed to his deep-voiced companion. And I dared not do other than join him, for fear of losing my way, ha ha ha! He has been to America.

The deep-voiced one raised his eyebrows and directed a solemn gaze at my father's chest.

That is correct, he said quietly. I was in America for a time, but not to make money or pursue the vanities of this world, for God redeemed me long before I went there. I was a missionary in America.

It emerged that our overnight guests were both of them representatives of world culture of a kind, but at the same time they tended to entertain people in remote country districts before Christmas. The deep-voiced man confirmed his goodness of heart and strength of faith by selling at a modest price Bibles, colored religious pictures, and various kinds of inexpensive religious tracts. My benefactor, however, claimed to be completely free from positive religious opinions. Admittedly, he had once imbibed three bottles of altar wine and bought the cassock of a drunken clergyman, which he sold in pieces as material for the national costume of the daughter of the prime minister, but he displayed his concern for the spiritual welfare of children by offering them toys of every description: perhaps you good people would like to examine our stock immediately?

I gave my father a quick glance, red-faced and filled with anticipation. But my father had suddenly changed. His expression had hardened and his eyebrows sunk, as they did when the clerk of the parish council demanded the rates.

Well, now, he said stiffly, knotting his quid into a corner of his handkerchief, we have enough religious matter in the house already, and we can't afford to be buying any gewgaws.

My mother put food on the table and in a low voice asked the men to excuse our poverty. The missionary crossed himself hurriedly, then turned to my father and remarked in an admonitory tone, My good man, there can never be too much religious matter.

My father muttered something to himself and again knit his brow.

On the other hand, added the missionary, it is true that these are hard times for the dear countryfolk. Nevertheless I would sooner starve than go short of the gracious fountain of God's word in Scripture, sermons, hymns, and other holy writings. Shall any man live by bread alone?

I daresay you're welcome to show us your stuff after I've watered the cow, said my father after a moment's silence, and I was so happy I wanted to jump up and put my arms round his neck and pat him on the cheek. All the same, he added, I'd have you know that I don't intend to buy anything. Times are not easy just now.

He went outside, while the men bent themselves over the food. The missionary ate slowly, impaling the morsels circumspectly on his fork, appearing even to scrutinize each one before placing it in his mouth, chewing thoroughly, and scarcely looking up from his plate. On the other hand, my benefactor stuffed himself with bread and blood sausage as though engaged in an eating contest. I admired him with a childlike candor: his every motion seemed to have a hypnotic effect on me, and I moved closer until I was standing beside him, staring with open mouth. He must know everything.

What have you got to say, genius, bag-o'-down, towhead? he inquired with a conspiratorial chuckle as he gulped down a whole slice of pickled sausage, making his Adam's apple bob up and down.

Have you been to Constantinople? I asked in a low voice, for my sister was standing in the door staring at me gravely as if meaning to rebuke me for my temerity.

I should say I have! he replied with a peal of laughter. I battled with the heathen Turk day and night, beat the Soldan and whipped the princes, tore open the harem and emptied the wine vats, bankrupted forty shops and stripped all the feathers off the parrots!

I did not care for this. To judge by what he said there was little glory left in that far-off city. It had never entered my head that such a commotion could occur in Constantinople. Moreover it now seemed to me open to question whether I ought to take my sister and parents there. Perhaps I would be overpowered even though I brandished my scimitar to good purpose and was ready for anything.

Are there no figs there? I asked fearfully.

Oh yes, indeed! Figs, dates, raisins, oranges, apples, and peaches, griddle cakes, pancakes, and doughnuts, young friend, young philosopher. Nothing to do but eat and sleep!

I felt a glow of satisfaction. Moving still closer, I asked: But the stars . . . are there stars in Constantinople too?

I should say there are! Full of stars, gold and red, green and blue, oh yes, full of stars of every color!

Do you think I'll ever be able to go there? I whispered very softly.

For heaven's sake, why not? he said nodding, and taking a quill from his waistcoat pocket he began to pick his teeth, quivering with suppressed laughter. You must talk to the sheriff and see if he won't let you go—offer the sheriff pepper for snuff and ask him to write a letter of recommendation to the Soldan for you!

The missionary looked up from his plate, chewing. Gazing accusingly at my benefactor, he said solemnly, It is also a sin to play the fool with the guileless.

I did not understand his words and paid no attention to them. To me there seemed nothing romantic about the missionary. He had never stolen a muzzle-loader. He had never shot a French cockerel nor let loose at a bishop's tomcat that was gobbling down altar wafers on top of a stone wall. He had never been to Constantinople. America? Pooh, that was nothing! I hardly gave him a glance.

Ha ha ha! Laughing, my benefactor popped another ball into my mouth. See now, young bag-o'-down, here comes your Pabbi. And now you shall see all the glory.

The missionary unbuckled his strapped bag and opened the brown suitcase. My parents both leaned on the table watching. My sister leaned up against Mamma and followed the missionary's movements. I prayed silently to God that he would finish his display quickly so that my benefactor might start unveiling the mysteries that must be hidden in his baggage. The Bible? The hymnbook? Involuntarily I recalled the long family prayers when I had to sit still on my bed while my father droned on endlessly. Involuntarily I recalled the two thieves who hung on crosses with nails through hands and feet, recalled the wound in our Savior's side with blood and water pouring forth. Ai, *that* was not what my soul yearned after. I suspected on the other hand that the mysteries in my benefactor's baggage would be in harmony with the indistinct desires of my heart, and I prayed God in heaven to make the missionary hurry up with his display.

No, said my father, shaking his head. We have the Bible and the hymn-book. He pointed to the little shelf above his bed. We've no need to be buying the Bible or the hymnbook.

What a blessed calamity, declared the missionary, and he took yet more material out of his strapbag. A new book of devotional readings? Price: eight kronur.

No, said my father. We have *Jon's Book* and *Petur's Pious Exercises,* and *The Meditations of Sera Pall* besides. Again he pointed to the shelf.

The Hymns on the Passion, with music? Price: two kronur and fifty aurar.

No, said my father a little hesitantly. We have no use for music. We have no harmonium.

What a blessed calamity, exclaimed the missionary. The lines on his brow deepened as though he were hunting for new arguments. Well, who knows but you won't acquire a harmonium one day? he continued, his face lighting up. And then it will come in useful to have the *Hymns on the Passion,* with music.

No, said my father with a cold laugh, there are not the means for har-monium buying at present.

People ought not to be shortsighted and think only of the passing mo-ment, said the missionary, his eyes piercing my father. I happen to know that the price of wool will be going up soon, my good man. Meat will go up too. Maybe we'll have another war, and then you farmers will be enormously better off. Who knows if the little daughter of the house may not become organist in your parish church after a few years? Who knows if the little daughter of the house may not become the most famous organist in the whole shire? Poor child! How she longs to have *The Hymns on the Passion,* with music.

My father looked quite embarrassed and searched in his pocket for a new plug of tobacco, but finding none, satisfied himself with removing the old quid from the corner of his handkerchief.

Very well, he said finally. I suppose we'd better buy it.

God will remember those that honor his word, said the missionary, and he began to dig into the brown suitcase. But one must also have something to hang on the wall to remind one every hour of the Atoner of all our sins. See! Here are some fine biblical pictures . . .

My father interrupted. No, he said, we can't afford them.

What a blessed calamity, sighed the missionary, but nevertheless dangled a couple of pictures in front of my mother, plunging his piercing steel blue glance deep into her breast. One picture was of the Good Shepherd, the other of the crucifixion with the son of the Almighty hanging on the tree, crowned with thorns and liberally spotted with blood.

The Savior, whispered my mother, moved, and she pointed at the picture of the Good Shepherd: Jesus Christ on the mountainside among gentle snow-white lambs. The Savior, she whispered, and looked beseechingly at my father.

You know we can't afford it, Mamma, my father said sternly. You know as well as I do that we can buy nothing unnecessary.

Jesus Christ is never unnecessary, corrected the missionary. He arranged the pictures before my mother's eyes. Price: only one krona fifty each.

Pabbi, said my mother, it can hardly make much difference if we buy one picture of the Savior.

Oh, very well, very well, said my father, sighing deeply. But now there's no point in your showing us any more.

He went to his bed, lifted the pillow, took his purse from under it, and untied the thong that bound the purse, which was old and threadbare. Having removed the thong, he inserted a thumbnail under the brass press stud and peered for a long while into the compartment inside. I noticed that his expression had suddenly become tired and harassed. I wonder if it's quite empty now, I thought in consternation. But in fact it was not quite empty, because he took two coins from it and handed them to the missionary. After that he tied the purse up again and put it back under the pillow, tidied the bedclothes, and pushed the blanket down to the head of the bed. My sister leafed through *The Hymns on the Passion,* with music, while my mother admired the Savior among the gentle snow-white lambs.

God blesses those that do him honor, said the missionary, putting the money away in his pocket.

Yes, I've always done that, said my benefactor, laughing. He seized his strapbag and winked at me, and I shivered with strange anticipation.

THE STARS OF CONSTANTINOPLE

There's no call to be showing us any gewgaws, said my father dryly. You'll have nothing but the trouble for it. We buy no gewgaws, damn it.

Doesn't matter. Not a scrap. Not the least little bit, said my benefactor, squirming in his seat. The children might enjoy looking at my stuff, all the same. You see, I'm something of a magician.

And he unveiled the mysteries.

I was overwhelmed. I stuck my finger in my mouth and stared speechless at the glories of civilization, unable to utter a word. I felt as if I floated on air and had lost all sense of direction, for there in front of my eyes glowed and glittered a whole world of enchantment, as when the first rays of morning kindle the colors of the rainbow in the white valley mist of spring. Splendidly arrayed horsemen of pewter, four-wheeled coaches, jumping jacks in striped trousers and top hats, Yule gnomes with red caps and bags on their backs, twittering birds, many-colored fish, friendly beasts—all these merged in a happy haze filling my heart with delight as well as an inexpressible yearning sadness. I longed to possess all these things but had a profound conviction that I would never possess any of them. Above all else I wanted to flee far away and weep.

Bag-o'-down! exclaimed the magician. See the guns and caps! Young tow-head, young genius, you put the cap in there and pull the trigger. It's quite harmless, but you can scare the wits out of the dog! When I was your age I had a gun like this and would shoot it off at elderly women in the dark! It costs four kronur with a hundred caps.

No, said my father. We have no need for any noxious tools to frighten the animals. And his mother is jittery enough without giving her a shock with some diabolical noise.

Bag-o'-down! cried the magician, jogging my arm, and he displayed a strange apparatus consisting of a disk with little spots on it, and a long tubular spring and small plunger attached to the disk. Here we have the stars of Constantinople!

He pressed the plunger, and in the same instant stars of every color lit up the surface of the disk, the spots on it changing to celestial sparks of light invested with a matchless enchantment.

Price: two kronur and fifty aurar, he announced slyly.

I looked up. Civilization appeared to have no visible effect on my sister.

Besides, she had acquired *The Hymns on the Passion,* with music, and an excellent prospect of becoming the most famous organist in the shire if meat and wool went up in price or a new war broke out and my father became rich. She gazed at the radiant splendor with cold, passionless eyes, as one might observe a beautiful tuft of roseroot stonecrop on a ledge of some unscalable cliff. My father's brow became yet heavier and his facial expression more severe, while my mother held the picture of the Good Shepherd and looked at me affectionately. Maybe she could see that I was fighting back my tears; maybe she suspected the secret yearnings of my heart.

Pabbi, she said pointing at me, he must have something too. He's only just over seven.

My father frowned more heavily still and bent forward. What does this cost? he asked putting a little bird on the palm of his hand.

Thirty-five aurar.

I suppose I'll have to buy this trinket for the boy, he said, and digging the purse from under his pillow once more, he again untied the thong that bound it, again inserted his thumbnail under the brass stud, and finally laid thirty-five aurar on the table.

Flinging my arms about his neck I whispered, May I buy from my wool money now?

No, he replied with annoyance, but then directed his words to the magician: I suggest you put that confounded rubbish back in your bags. Otherwise the children are going to be driven out of their wits.

But that night I was unable to sleep. For a long time I lay awake thinking about the star instrument. I felt that I would be everlastingly unhappy if I was unable to obtain it. What a difference it would make to have a remarkable device like that when gales raged wildly about the roof and snow covered the windows, or when rain beat on the windowpanes and the badstofa was filled with darkness! What a difference it would make to kindle clear sparks during the evening work time, instead of spinning yarn on a spindle. I listened to the strange breathing from the guest bed: the missionary snored, while the magician whistled. Their sleeping sounds were a kind of symbol of the presence of civilization, but at the same time a painful reminder that they would continue on their way early in the morning. I prayed God in heaven to enter the badstofa and help me gain possession of the star apparatus before they disappeared. I clasped my hands together and stared humbly into the winter night hoping for a miracle. Maybe it would be better to address my plea to the Savior, because he was the friend of children. Oh, Jesus, dear Jesus, son of the virgin Mary, conceived by the Holy Ghost, crucified, dead, and buried, oh help me, Jesus. I shall always be good if you help me. I shall never doze during family prayers. Oh please, Jesus, please. In the name of the Father, and of the Son, and of the Holy Ghost.

At last I dropped off to sleep at Pabbi's side with the Savior's name on my lips.

But when I woke in the morning, the visitors were up. They were sitting at the table sipping coffee and eating newly made pancakes. They looked as though they were on the point of leaving. Long, untraveled roads were reflected in their faces; unknown markets conjured a strange bustle into their movements and disrupted commonplace remarks about their immediate destination. I was seized by a hopeless dread: within a short time they would leave us, taking with them the delights of civilization. Perhaps I would never see them again, never again enjoy the raptures that accompanied their presence. I dressed myself in headlong haste and paced restlessly about the floor of the badstofa, not knowing what to do.

My benefactor exclaimed, Hi! Good morning! Good morning! How did you sleep last night, young bag-o'-down, young genius? Did you dream perhaps about the stars of Constantinople? The Soldan? The harem? The parrots? Ha ha! Now we're off, young friend, young towhead. Maybe we'll never come back.

It was as if he were able to read my thoughts. He waved his hands, a mischievous smile played on his lips, and his coal black eyes gleamed, impudent and tantalizing.

Then they both stood up, stretched themselves with grunts, and thanked us for their night's lodging. I was utterly confused, though, and felt the happiness of my whole life at stake. Everything seemed to spin round or stand on its head, leaning forward as though about to collapse on top of me at a moment's notice. I heard the missionary bidding me good-bye. I felt him clasp my right hand briefly. I heard my benefactor say, bag-o'-down, and, genius. And I felt him pat me on the head and shake me all over on parting. And the next moment they had disappeared out onto the terrace with my parents and sister. I was left alone in the badstofa.

All at once I forgot my father's prohibition, forgot my honor and conscience: driven by a strange force, I opened my box in the writing case and poured my wool money into the palm of my hand. There were ten beautiful, shining twenty-five-aurar pieces. I had vied with my sister in gathering tufts of wool on the slopes of the mountain, run long distances to every small hollow, panting as if my heart would burst and weak at the knees as if my legs were about to double up under me. I clenched my fist about my treasure and looked furtively about. Was anyone coming? Rushing out, I ran into my mother in the passage. The overnight guests had started on their way. They were striding westward across the home field, while my father was trudging off in the opposite direction with a haybox on his back. He was on his way to the sheephouse. My sister was standing by the house wall gazing after the strangers.

Where are you going? she called to me.

They forgot, they forgot . . . , I lied in my confusion, and took to my heels.

I caught up with them by the hill, when they were out of sight of the house. They were chattering and laughing, seeming to share a joke, as though their relationship had become much closer and more intimate than it had been the previous evening.

Hi, young friend, what do you want? my benefactor asked in surprise, and he lifted one eyebrow, letting the other sink.

I want to buy the stars of Constantinople, I panted, and I opened my hand to show the money in my palm.

Buy? Buy? I suspected as much, young bag-o'-down, young genius! You're just like I was at your age, hee-hee!

He laughed heartily and hurried to unstrap his bag, while the missionary grinned.

Here they come, brave young fellow, my lad! Twenty-five stars of Constantinople! Twenty-five stars from the Soldan! But have you the money to pay? One krona . . . two kronur . . . and fifty . . . that's right enough. Just speak to the sheriff before you go. Tell the sheriff that the Soldan has sent you an invitation to burn incense in the harem and cut the corns of the madam, the head madam, hee-hee!

He handed me the star apparatus and slipped my wool money into the breast pocket of his jacket, patted me on the head, shook me a little, and smiled. Good-bye, young man, young friend! he said, and whistled strangely. We'll meet again!

Look here, my boy, said the missionary, have you any more money?

No, I replied in a low voice.

Ah well, in that case I won't show you any Bible pictures . . .

They went on their way, while I stood motionless for a while in the cold, frosty air of the winter morning, plunged in a profound happiness tinged with a vague feeling of dread. I examined the magical device as if in a dream, then hid it in my pocket and trotted back to the house. I had to share my happiness with someone and allow someone to enjoy the marvelous beauty of it, so I crept into the cowhouse and slipped into Brownie's stall. Dear Jesus, thank you. Amen, I whispered with ardor, glancing briefly up into the rafters, then took the magical device from my pocket and pressed the plunger. What glory! Blue and red sparks, yellow and green starlight, a whole firmament in my hand, a complete cosmos under my control! On the other hand, Brownie showed little appreciation of the achievements of civilization and displayed no enthusiasm. She only blew moodily, slapped a tongue over her wet muzzle, and swung her tail. Disappointed, I left her and made my way into the badstofa. But I dared not let anyone else into my secret, for I had disobeyed my father's injunction and disregarded time-honored moral principles in spite of my youth. I was only in my eighth year.

And my mother handed me a huge ball of wool, after which she went out into the kitchen.

I perched on the chest at the foot of my bed, tossed the spindle in the air, and tried to spin. My sister was knitting a sock and looked neither to left nor to right. There was silence in the badstofa and a strange empty look about everything, as if the outward appearance of objects had grown darker. But I found it utterly absurd to be spinning yarn this day when I had the stars of Constantinople in my pocket. I had grown enormously in my own eyes, and it was quite out of the question to be making me do dreary household tasks. And suddenly I had a brilliant idea. I turned to my sister, and in whee-dling tones I said, Will you spin for me?

No, lazy, I won't, she replied firmly, and counted the stitches on her needles.

You can have the bird that Pabbi gave me yesterday evening.

I don't want it.

I jumped down from the chest and jogged her arm sharply, just as the magician had jogged my arm, tried to lift one eyebrow and let the other sink, pursed my lips, and whispered, I'll show you something a little bit special if you'll spin for me.

How funny you look, boy! said my sister smiling. Why are you making faces?

I thrust a hand into my pocket and let the plunger of the tubular spring appear. Do you believe me now? I asked.

What's that? She stopped knitting and stared at me curiously.

I'll show you all of it if you spin for me a little bit, I said complacently. But you mustn't tell. You mustn't say a word to Pabbi. Nor to Mamma either. Will you swear, cross your heart?

Yes, said my sister, and she swore, cross her heart.

I took the magical device from my pocket and ignited the stars, while my sister stared wide-eyed with wonder. Where did you get that? she asked, and did her best to hide her envy. Yesterday she had observed civilization as a tuft of roseroot stonecrop on a mountain ledge, or as a distant rainbow which no one could grasp, let alone possess, but when she saw that I had got hold of this magical device, her whole attitude changed.

I bought the stars for my wool money, I whispered. But you have sworn, cross your heart, that you won't tell anyone. Aren't you going to spin?

Yes, my sister replied sullenly. She put down her knitting and took the spindle. She spun for a while but stared all the time at the magical device in my hands, and an expression of cunning and greed crept gradually over her face.

Shall we swap? she asked suddenly.

For what? I asked.

The Hymns on the Passion for the stars?

No, I replied without hesitation, and shook my head.

But they're *with music.*

Makes no difference.

And you'll be organist in church.

I don't want to be.

But if I let you have my rose-patterned insoles too?

Makes no difference, I said haughtily, and juggled the magical device in the palm of my hand, for its value had now increased manifold.

Very well, then, I shall stop spinning, said my sister, and she put the spindle down.

You're breaking your promise, I protested. You promised to spin for a little bit. You swore, cross your heart!

I haven't the slightest intention of spinning any more unless you let me light it like you, she said with a toss of her head.

Very well, I said. Light it, then.

You must let me hold it, too.

All right, if you spin half the ball of wool and swear, cross your heart, to it.

She swore twice over, snatched the magical device, and lit the stars. Enchanted, she gazed at the tiny bright golden sparks, her lower lip drooping slightly as if she were deep in thought. Then she lit them again.

No, I commanded imperiously, you were only to light them once. Give it to me!

My sister gritted her teeth and spun for a while but did not take her eyes off my hands. I lay facedown on my bed and toyed lovingly with my treasure. I was intensely happy. I possessed the stars of Constantinople and did not have to perch on the chest and bother myself with twirling the spindle. I could exploit civilization to make others work for me. I felt a good deal older than seven, much more mature and intelligent than my sister: I could command her, control her, compel her to obey me.

Geiri, she said, how many stars are there?

Twenty-five, I replied proudly.

I shall knit you a cap with a red tassel if you'll do a swap with me.

I don't want to do a swap, I said.

And give you my berry rake, she added.

Makes no difference, I replied, adamant.

Very well, then I shall stop! she said, hurling the spindle into a corner.

But you promised to spin half the ball, I said angrily.

Only if I can light it again, she said ingratiatingly, and held out her hand. I gave her the magical device with reluctance, for I did not care for the tone in her voice. I had never heard that tone before. She snatched the apparatus from me, laughed wildly, and pressed the plunger time after time.

Are you going to ruin my stars? I cried in desperation. *Give it to me!*

No, never, never, she exclaimed, laughing. Something cruel and wicked had appeared in her eyes: a kind of hate-filled, gloating ruthlessness, as if she would stop at nothing.

Do you want me to break it? she asked threateningly, and clenched her fist about the tubular spring.

For an instant I was paralyzed with fear—powerless and irresolute in the face of the inevitable war. Then I leaped forward and struck her in the face, reached for her arm and tried desperately to seize the magical device. She twisted away from me, hit me on the cheek, and attempted to escape into the kitchen. I caught hold of her skirt and tugged with all my might. I was only just over seven years old. For the next few minutes we fought in silent fury, tearing at each other's hair, biting each other, and scratching each other, torn and bleeding. I did not come to my senses before I saw my magical apparatus lying in pieces on the floor: the twenty five stars of the Soldan of Constantinople were scattered, my hard-earned civilization destroyed.

I stared and stared. My sister ran sobbing from the room, but I could not bring myself to touch the broken, twisted fragments. I threw myself on my bed, buried my face in the pillow, and cried. So I lay for a long time, overwhelmed by bitter grief, struck down by a sorrow deeper than words can describe. It was of no avail for my mother to try to comfort me or point out that it was only a wretched mechanical contraption put together with tin, screws, and sulfur. It was of no avail for my father to exempt me from reprimand and punishment, for my heart was overborne by an unspeakable grief and pain long after the stream of tears had dried on my cheeks.

I did not get up until the Advent dusk had insinuated itself into the badstofa through the frost-furred ice flowers on the windowpane. But then it was as though a spell had been broken. I suddenly remembered the stars above the mountain. I knew that after a short while they would return from outer space in countless, countless ranks, ranging themselves in the firmament and bathing in their glittering blue light my poor dream, my indistinct yearnings—and my grief.

BUILDING PYRAMIDS

It was Fridmund Engiljon, the cunningest builder in the world, who unveiled for me the mystery of the pyramids and taught me to understand the most cryptic architectural constructions on earth. He stepped out of the haze of a still July day furnished with every sort of tool and implement, twirled his reddish moustaches in a lordly manner, and lodged with us for more than two months. We had expected him, in fact, much earlier, for he had promised my foster father by letter to come to us about midsummer at the latest to build a new barn and cowhouse. But Midsummer Day went by, the days after it went by, too, until they turned themselves to a week, a fortnight, three weeks, without a word from Fridmund Engiljon. What was the man thinking of? Had he perhaps forgotten his written promise? Had he perhaps given other construction work in other districts priority? My foster father shook his head anxiously and suffered from sleepless nights. He declared that he could make neither head nor tail of such failure to honor one's word, nor could we reckon on this barn's being up before some time in the autumn, to say nothing of the cowhouse. He handled the timber with heavy creases in his brow, circled the turf foundation walls again and again, stared along the road thirty times a day, but all to no avail. Fridmund Engiljon was nowhere to be seen. The foundation walls awaited him, newly laid and neatly trimmed, the posts awaited him, long and thick, as well as the corrugated iron sheets, and tar paper, the window glass, nails, and hinges, but Fridmund Engiljon continued to nail and saw elsewhere, somewhere far away. He was not one to let things make him lose any sleep, that man! He certainly did not seem concerned to honor his word!

BUILDING PYRAMIDS

Then one peaceful Sunday in the middle of haying I was idling about with a rusty barrel hoop by the wall of the house, at the west of the farm. I looked alternately at the bents in the uncut meadows and the first haycocks in the stackyard behind the site of the prospective barn, but the worries of my foster parents banished all enjoyment. In fact I was thinking about Fridmund Engiljon, and not thinking too kindly about him, when suddenly he stepped out of the haze, short, thickset, and bandy-legged, laden with his tools and belongings. He hurried up the track to the farm with a remarkably nimble step, swinging one arm rhythmically and looking to neither left nor right, and approached me rapidly. What an extraordinary piece of luck that I should happen to be outside! What a feather in my cap to be the first to see him! I moved at once, threw down the rusty barrel hoop, shot like a streak of lightning into the badstofa, and proclaimed the news in the middle of the room. Fridmund Engiljon had at last arrived!

Yes, he had really arrived, in the flesh and full of life, nor could I take my eyes off him as he twirled his reddish moustaches, wiped the perspiration from his bald head, and stuffed his bent and burned pipe with yellow-brown tobacco. He brought a new atmosphere into the badstofa—an aroma of sawdust and wood shavings, pipe tobacco and travel, while his hands were a categorical certificate of skill and experience issued by the Creator himself. They were the hands of a craftsman. He seldom laughed outright but chuckled quietly, shaking inwardly, or simply compressed wrinkled lids until the dark blue eyes, clear and piercing, threw beams on all those present. And when he spoke his voice would thread a kind of hairsbreadth path between jest and gravity, while his words took the forms of simile, saw, and riddle that invited comprehension while causing questions to rise to my lips.

He puffed at his pipe and repeatedly apologized for having let us down. I had no good of it, he told us, all that cursed messing around! He had been hammering together a bit of a badstofa in another district where everything was at sixes and sevens and took an eternity to do. The timber turned out to be both of poor quality and lacking in quantity. The cat must have eaten half the nails, for one morning they ran out. There was always something missing, and it was always necessary to be running off to the village to get it. The people huddled together in the sheephouse, a dark, leaky, tumbledown affair that bore no comparison with the corresponding edifice out east in Bethlehem. The babies whimpered, the grandmother shivered, the mistress of the house complained endlessly—and Fridmund Engiljon hadn't the heart to rush away before he had finished the bit of a badstofa. Well, now was no time to be hanging around; now it was necessary to roll up one's sleeves.

Having said this, he began working to some purpose—measured the foundation walls, measured the purlins, the posts, and the rafters, muttered complicated figures under his breath but wrote nothing down, never wrote a thing in his red notebook but committed it all to memory, scratching himself behind the ear and arranging every detail of this complex work in his bald pate.

What a memory! What a pate!

He possessed an array of tools and implements: saws, hammers, bradawls, planes, chisels, pincers, pliers, levels. And his hands performed on all these instruments with a confidence and skill that seemed little short of magic. I shall never forget my pride and delight when my foster parents ordered me to help him—run errands for him and bring him watered buttermilk to drink in the midday heat—since I was too young and weak to be of any help with the haying. I did not need to be told twice, and like a little satellite I orbited round Fridmund Engiljon while summer rode the blue skies on its journey into autumn. I never tired of admiring his movements or of gazing at the bald head gleaming in the sun, the glance of genial eyes, the humorous wrinkles of the face, or the carefully upturned moustaches with sawdust and wood shavings sticking to them. He was always in a good mood and ready to talk with me on the most diverse themes, as though I were a grown-up man. But more often than not his replies and remarks had the character of dark parables or exalted words of wisdom which made me feel either remarkably clever or incredibly stupid. I have often kicked myself for not having taken more advantage of his wisdom or memorized some of his answers and excellent advice, and I am especially ashamed of the brash and idiotic questions with which I first deluged him, before science came into the picture and plans for the pyramid took possession of my mind.

I said, Why do you have such a funny name? Why are you called Fridmund Engiljon?

Many a mishap besets the butter, he replied, shaking his head over the rafter. Now it would be fun to have a four-inch nail, my boy!

I handed him the nail but picked up the thread of my inquiry once more as soon as he had stopped hammering.

Did the pastor maybe think you were an angel? I asked.

A calf can do with a cross mark, he answered. It's good to be a pastor at Paschaltide and an angel in a tempest.

I was silent for a moment and stared at his hairless head until I could contain myself no longer.

Were you dark haired or fair haired? I asked.

Neither, he replied instantly.

Then your hair must have been brown, I said.

No, he said.

What color was it, then?

Probably the color God created it, he said grinning, and made the rafter echo to his blows. It wouldn't surprise me if it was exactly the color God created it, my boy!

I was not altogether satisfied with this treatment of the subject and wanted some indication of the reason for his loss of hair, and whether he did not find it disagreeable to be so bald and skullcappable. He answered me to such effect that later the same day I requested my foster mother to cut my hair short and would not give her any peace until she had done what I wanted. And that was not enough. When I went to bed I huddled under the quilt, clasped my hands together, and prayed the Creator to give me a bald head that very night—a shining, white bald head—that I might become as clever as Fridmund Engiljon, as wise and as skillful. As it happened he had said, A fool is ever well furnished with hair. And glancing briefly up from his work he had gazed somewhere out into the blue and twirled his moustaches in a lordly manner, and I felt his eyes resting on my curly mop and blushed scarlet at the reproach. It was altogether intolerable not to be bald.

The next day we were waiting for the sunshine of the early afternoon. But scarcely had the first rays reached us on the grassy bank by the foundation walls when Fridmund Engiljon laid down his saw and passed a flat palm over his bare head before taking up chisel and hammer.

What's this now? he said, pretending surprise. You've had yourself properly stripped, I do declare, old fellow!

Yes, I said, and tried to make my voice grown-up. It's much better to have one's hair short.

I'll say it is! Nothing like it! He nodded.

It's so comfortable in the heat, I said, stroking the crown of my head with flattened palm.

You couldn't say a truer word—quite exceptionally comfortable! he agreed, shaking all over with internal laughter as he cut a groove for a tie beam in the edge of a rafter. You must be an uncommonly bright lad, I'd say!

I was up in the air and could scarcely contain myself, changed the subject quickly to the barn and cowhouse; shifted from foot to foot—puffed with self-importance—beside him, discussed the building operations back and forth, as if filled to bursting with knowledge and experience. I was bold enough to put forward a number of suggestions and express my opinions in generous measure: it would perhaps be better to have this that way and that the other way, drive the nail at an angle, use the chisel so, have a deeper groove, and hold the handle of the hammer nearer to the head. Fridmund Engiljon listened patiently to my prattle for quite a while, then lit his pipe, puffed at it slowly, and smiled drily. It was the first and last time that he smiled at my words in this way; indeed, I never tried to advise him about the building again.

Here we float with the apples, said the lumps of horse manure! he chuckled. What a great deal of dust can blow up in a calm!

I became suddenly silent and dared not address him until the sun had driven the last clouds from the sky and the air was filled with the strong scent of the drying swaths on the home field. I slipped into the house for watered buttermilk and watched Fridmund Engiljon timidly while he emptied the bowl and sucked the moisture from his moustaches. No, my lot was surely not an enviable one. Here I stood, chastened and ignorant, unable to get a word out, and with no prospect of raising myself to a state of esteem. I wanted to be a great man in a speedy, mysterious, and preferably easy manner, to become gifted, clever, and learned, to let my deeds speak for me, and to bask in praise and admiration. But I could discern no ready road to the satisfaction of this immature yearning. Summer was in its fairest bloom. The grass waved furry tufts, the cotton grass crowded the channels in the marshes, white as

newly washed wool, the people worked hard at the haying, Fridmund Engiljon worked hard at his building. I alone was a pair of useless hands and a
weakling, not fit for anything and capable at the best of making myself a
laughingstock by my bragging and boastfulness. God had even denied me
the boon of a decent bald head!

Galvanized gridirons! What the deuce has become of my foot
rule! muttered Fridmund Engiljon, turning many circles as though at his wits'
end. Now that blessed puppy has carried it off somewhere!

No, I said quickly, it's right there in front of you.

Splendid, he said. Thank you very much. You've got your eyes in the right
place, my lad. So much for my powers of observation! I don't know how I'd
manage without you beside me.

I cheered up considerably at this and seized the occasion to tell him that
I was to start school the next winter. I was to learn from many books at school
and was of course determined to come in first in the examination.

That's what I like to hear, he said with satisfaction, brandishing the foot
rule like a fencer. It's good to teach someone who wants to learn. Have you
got any books now?

I've the catechism and Bible stories.

Nothing else?

Yes, a geography book, I said.

That's something, he said. Do you know how many continents there are?

Five, I said uncertainly, and hurriedly added, There's a picture of pyramids in my geography book.

I might have known it—pyramids! he said, and searching for a stub of
pencil, he drew a line on a purlin and began to saw.

There seemed to me something significant in this, so I asked hesitantly,
Have you ever built pyramids, Fridmund?

He stopped sawing for a moment and winked at me, eyes sparkling with
glee. Wouldn't that be a bit of luck, though, my lad! he said, and laughed
aloud, contrary to his usual custom. I dare say you know the answer to that
question.

Is it terribly difficult? I asked, impressed and burning with curiosity.

Difficult? he repeated, continuing to saw. Some are inclined to the view that it's the most difficult thing there is. But I've never found it difficult. Not a bit difficult. It's not a job for the fainthearted, though, building a pyramid, my friend. A good thing too!

Have you built any big ones? I asked in excitement, moving closer.

Big and small, he answered darkly. The trouble was that they would collapse rather fast.

I have no clear recollection of how it happened, but shortly after this we reached an agreement to build a pyramid together as soon as Fridmund Engiljon finished the barn and cowhouse. I seem to remember that the suggestion was mine, for I thought it a splendid idea to raise one on the home field, where I sometimes played tag with myself or with the first snowflakes of autumn. We decided on the spot that our pyramid should excel all other pyramids on earth. It was to tower up to the sky, blue and gold, with apex pointed as a needle, sharp edges, and majestic appearance. It was true that on further consideration it occurred to me that we might be lacking financial means, material, and manpower to handle such a massive undertaking. And there were times when I was half-afraid that the project would come to nothing.

But Fridmund Engiljon took a different view. He sawed vigorously, self-assured and smiling, as though he anticipated no trouble in dealing with such trifles.

Materials? he said confidently. It's easy enough to get material for a pyramid.

How? I asked.

You leave that to me, he said. I wasn't born yesterday, my friend. But don't you mention it to a living soul, mind you! You promise me that?

Yes, I whispered solemnly.

It's just between the two of us, he said, not to go any further.

Just between the two of us, not to go any further, I echoed—and I orbited round him twice as submissive as ever. Thus in a flash I had risen to a state of esteem. Thus in a flash fortune had embraced me. I had become the comrade and confidant of Fridmund Engiljon. We possessed a common secret: we were resolved to build a pyramid before autumn came.

It will be a long time before I forget the passing of that summer. It passed like an expectant dream which continues to reverberate in one's breast long after one has awakened. It rode the blue skies, mild and glittering. But gradually a deeper hue spread through the grass, the sedge withered, and the cotton grass let the wind scatter its wool, soft and white. Finally the potato plants flowered and the evenings became dark and serene, until a red-gold moon and faintly twinkling stars reappeared in the firmament. I was filled with uneasy presentiment. I dreamed most nights of the pyramid, and always in such a way that I was haunted with fear that we would not have time to build it before the winter came. Sometimes when the people were sitting over their food, I would take out my geography book and look up Egypt and stare as though mesmerized at the picture of those ancient monuments, which suggested at one and the same time science and magic. Repeatedly I touched on the subject with Fridmund Engiljon, asking whether he didn't think we ought to start work, but he always brushed it aside, telling me to have patience until the barn and cowhouse were finished: those that wait go with the wind; those that won't must row against it. Then he added, Now the rafters are ready, the frame shipshape, and the purlins longing to lie as flat as prunes in a pudding. If you would be so good as to hand me that packet of nails there—no, not that one, the other!

I handed him the packet of nails and listened in silence to the strokes of his hammer, sharp and resolute. It was clear that Fridmund Engiljon had set his mind to speeding up with work to the utmost of his ability. He tore himself out of bed in the small hours, worked furiously into the dusk, and allowed himself no time for discussing heaven and earth with me—except very occasionally, when he was absolutely compelled to twirl his moustaches. And yet I felt that there was little progress. There were five stacks of hay in the yard, five giant stacks which my foster father intended to move into the barn when it was finished. The haying in the meadows was almost over, the green of the marshes was rapidly being replaced by sallow colors, the meadowsweet had lost its fragrance, the bloom had departed from the dandelion and cinquefoil. I sensed autumn lurking behind the clouds in the west, and behind autumn lay winter. And still we had not started on the pyramid, had not even ordered for it nor discussed the mode of operation, material, and tools any further The time would soon be gone. Eventually, though, the day arrived when Fridmund Engiljon had delivered the final touches to both barn and cowhouse. What a barn! What a cowhouse! He also smoked one pipe after another, puffing blue clouds into the frosty morning air, puttied the windows carefully, and inquired with a kindly look whether I was not looking forward to the roundup, for tomorrow was the day of the roundup.

Ye-e-s, I answered slowly, and glanced in turn at the trowel in his hand and the half-fallen potato plants in the kitchen garden. Fridmund, I said in a low voice, when are we going to begin on the pyramid?

There you go again with that confounded pyramid! he chuckled blithely, shaking with internal laughter. Well, now we've nothing to wait for. Maybe we'll begin tomorrow!

Tomorrow? I said doubtfully, hearing the sound of bleating in the distance. We have no material.

What balderdash, he said, and pointed at the mountain. We'll get the material up there!

The rocks! I exclaimed, astonished. Do you mean the rocks?

Of course, he said. Of course I mean the rocks. We'll dispense with all inessentials such as putty and windowpanes, for example. There are no windows in a pyramid, my boy. No windows!

I did not much like this. I thought I could see clearly that it would take a long time for us to tear rocks out of the mountainside and move them down to the home field, to say nothing of hewing them into shape and fitting them together into a pyramid. I shook my cropped head incredulously and scratched myself behind the ear, was conscious of a strange constriction in my chest, and felt uncomfortable.

Fridmund Engiljon was also deep in thought. More haste, less speed, he said. Nothing can be considered too carefully. I shall have to make a trip down south before we begin.

Do you think you'll be gone long? I whispered.

No, he chuckled, I shan't be gone long. The devil take me if I'll be away long. I only need to get some soldiers and whips.

I was so dumbfounded that I could not utter a word, gaped in astonishment, not knowing how to take this. What was afoot? What had the man in mind? Was he maybe intending to extricate himself from our common undertaking?

It's no easy matter building a pyramid, he continued. And then he explained his plan to me. He said that we were absolutely obliged to have foreign soldiers to round up all the people of the district, all the horses and wagons of the district, while after that we would have to enslave the men and women—even the children—without mercy or consideration, make them labor and sweat from dawn to dusk, let the soldiers lash them with whips, strip off their clothes, and flog them at Sunday service if they showed any signs of insubordination. He said that we must not soften though the backs of the men were bloody, the women weak and sick, and the children emaciated and constantly whimpering. No, we would have to drive ahead with a firm hand, cursing and swearing, until the work was done—after ten or fifteen years, maybe, if there were no obstacles. Believe me, it wasn't like putting out your tongue, building a pyramid!

I stared at Fridmund Engiljon while he held forth, stared at his mouth and moustaches, his hands and feet. But when I had convinced myself that he was not joking, I was filled with such horror and distress that I could feel the blood draining from my veins.

What do you think of that, my lad? asked Fridmund Engiljon. What do you think of that?

I was unable to answer.

It's too late to say Amen when all the deacons are silent, he muttered in a reproving tone, and gave me a sidelong look. I'll buy you a first-class whip with a strong handle and a long lash . . .

I don't want one, I said in a shaky voice, shrinking into myself.

What's this I hear? chuckled Fridmund Engiljon. Are you getting soft?

I don't want to build a pyramid.

You don't want to build a pyramid? he repeated, imitating me, and grimaced fearfully, pursing his lips. Galvanized gridirons! If I remember rightly you were the one who suggested it!

I don't want to anymore, I said.

Shockingly confusing you can be! he said irritably. One thing one day, another the next—that's the way of it. No stability. No endurance. But I'm not certain you're going to get away with that so easily, my lad. At any rate it's better to keep your word.

He applied the putty more deliberately along the edge of the pane, then took his pipe out of his pocket, stuffed a large plug of tobacco into its burned bowl, lighted it, and once again puffed pale blue clouds into the frosty morning air.

What is the barn for? he asked.

The barn? I replied foolishly. It's for the hay.

Then what is the cowhouse for? The new cowhouse?

The cowhouse? I answered. It's for the cows.

Absolutely right, he said. Absolutely plumb right! But what is a pyramid for, old fellow? I'd like to know that!

I shredded an old wood shaving, red-faced with embarrassment, and sniffed violently, feeling a kind of quivering in my knee joints. I remained as silent as one accused.

Ah well, he said drawling the words, you're at a loss for a reply, it seems. In fact there's a fly in the ointment and dirt in the corner of the meal bag. Pyramids are for Death, old man. Pyramids are the temples of Death, full of bones and bodies, skeletons and skulls. Full to overflowing!

I was so horrified that I could no longer hide my emotions. I dropped the wood shaving, looked in distraction down at my feet, and said with a sob in my throat that I had given it all up. I didn't want a whip. Didn't want to build a pyramid.

Fridmund Engiljon laid down the putty and trowel, laughed out loud, and gave me a friendly pat on the shoulder, his eyes emitting a warm, kindly sparkle.

Well, well, well, he said playfully, let's drop the subject then and mention it no more. I have never built a pyramid except in my head, old man. Never, except up here in the top story! He pointed at his bald crown, puffing at his pipe. That was a kind of pyramid quite different from those in your geography book, he added. A much better kind than in your geography book.

After that he left. Vanished into the mysterious distance out of which he had come, leaving behind a scent of pipe tobacco in the badstofa and a bright, intriguing memory. Our summer was over. It had ridden the blue skies and sunk into the arms of autumn, the arms of eternity. I happened to be sitting at the window and struggling on with my geography when the first snow-flakes came flying out of space, falling on the frozen earth, on the broad smooth home field where we had planned to build a pyramid. Heavens above! We had come perilously near to enslaving every living soul in the district and getting armed soldiers and knotted whips to raise a temple to Death, a temple for bodies and bones, skeletons and skulls. I blushed with shame and was suddenly filled with such gratitude toward my friend Fridmund Engiljon that I shut the book and ran out of the house to play tag with myself and the first snowflakes across the home field.

INTERRUPTION

His mother was hanging laundry on the line: a checked shirt, some little dresses, and a blue striped apron. His sister stood beside her and watched the clothes flap. He hung about in front of the farm door, wielding his great church spire, and whistled. It was Sunday, the weather hot and sunny. He wet his dry lips and whistled again, but neither of them looked at his church spire.

Well, he said, unable to waste any more time by the old clothesline, I'm off!

Bee-bee, said his sister, pointing to a small bird, a wagtail. Bee-bee!

His mother took a clothespin out of her mouth.

Where did you get that stick, Bjossi? she asked.

Stick? She called his green church spire a stick!

I found it, he replied shortly, and moved away, one step, two steps. I'm off!

Where are you going? his mother asked.

Down to the bay.

What are you going to do there?

Build, he replied.

Don't be long, Bjossi, she called after him. Be careful!

He strode whistling along the path across the home field and swung the green church spire. Then he stopped whistling and walked thoughtfully over the low hill between the home field and the bay. A man who is going to build a new village all on his own has to think carefully about a number of things. He looked at the fjord, at the gulls over the fjord, and at the village on the far side of the fjord. When he had decided, several days earlier, to build a jetty and a fish-freezing plant all by himself, there had been a choice of two sites: the sandy bay on this side of the home field, and the gravel landing place to the south where his father and Gvendur of Ness had joint shares in a two-man boat, a net for lumpsucker fishing, and an old shed. Gvendur of Ness sometimes called him a shrimp and grinned at him. Gvendur of Ness was always predicting storm and disaster. It seemed unlikely that such a man would be able to appreciate his achievements, so he had chosen the sandy bay, where no one talked about shrimp, or grinned.

Seldom had the bay been as blue as it was today! He forgot Gvendur of Ness and began to contemplate his handiwork: the long jetty, the massive fish-freezing plant, the cooperative store, the primary school, the church, and the pastor. The pastor lay all in black in the middle of the church, waiting for the spire.

Pastor Ludvig, said the boy.

Silence.

It's green, said the boy, and he wedged the spire between two stones, poured sand round it, and stepped back a few paces to inspect it, shutting one eye and putting his head to one side.

Now you can intone, he said, and he lifted Pastor Ludvig up into the pulpit, but the pastor remained silent, silent as a piece of tar paper. He refused to intone without an organ.

An organ? Well, that would have to wait until he had more time. The boy could not afford to be asking for subscriptions for an organ until he had finished the village. There were still boats to be made, even trawlers, dozens of houses to be built, roads and streets to be laid, and people and cars to be moved in. The cooperative store had begun to collapse, so he filled up the hole in its wall and at the same time altered the shop, adding a new department, its counter and shelves groaning with chocolate and candy. He also changed the manager, taking out his penknife and slicing off his big belly: the manager of the cooperative on this side of the fjord didn't have to be the same as the one on the other side. Then he enlarged the playground in front of the primary school and, going into the freezing plant, switched on the current, so that the giant machines all began to turn and roar. At the same time he saw a boat sailing into the bay loaded to the gunnels: Chugga-chugg, chugga-chugg! He ran down to the jetty and inspected the catch: yellowish gray cod and fat haddock. The loud-voiced fishermen stood in the middle of the heap of fish in jackets and crotch-high seaboots, shoveling the catch into baskets and spitting.

The boy spit, too.

Heave away! one shouted.

Where are the trucks? asked another.

The boy was just on the verge of dashing home for the trucks when the boat vanished, the girls in the freezing plant stopped chattering, and the roar of the engines ceased. A tern hovered above the bay and dived twice just beyond the end of the jetty. Then it flew away with a small fish in its beak, and the boy again reminded himself that he had determined to finish the village that day. For a while he worked energetically, making various roads, some straight and some crooked, arranging small stones in rows, and shoveling sand. Then he was stuck, and stood for a long time gazing across at the village on the far side of the fjord. It was child's play building gray houses and one or two light-colored ones. And if he wanted the roofs to be green, like the spire of the church, there wasn't much trouble in covering them with grass or moss. But red houses? How on earth was he going to get material for building red houses? Red houses were beautiful, he thought.

The sunshine was as bright as ever, and the warm land breeze came in gusts, sometimes almost dying away altogether. The boy stood by the lighthouse, a long, narrow can he had found on the shore, and listened absently to the gentle murmur of the waves. Just a moment, though; he had noticed some reddish-colored stones over on the ridge last year when he went berry picking with his cousin and saw the cars shooting along the road in the dip beyond the rise. He wet his lips with the tip of his tongue and strode off, whistling, to examine these red stones.

The lower part of the ridge was covered with heather, though higher up it was bare and stony. In some places the unripe berries were beginning to darken, especially on the slope where his cousin had picked most the previous year, humming loudest while she picked. The boy put a handful of green berries in his mouth but spit them out again. In three weeks, his mother had said yesterday, in three weeks' time we can go berry-picking. He couldn't be bothered to try to imagine how long three weeks would be but walked faster, humming like his cousin, and looked about him for red stones.

He had almost reached the crest of the ridge when at last he found some stones that would do for houses in his new village. True, they were nothing like as red as he had imagined, but in a pinch they would do, and he would be able to finish the village today if he worked hard.

He began to pick out the best of them and had just put two houses into his pocket when he happened to look up.

A strange girl was standing quite near him, between the rocks on the crest of the ridge. She was thin and lanky and was wearing a white jumper and blue slacks. Hallo! she said, walking toward him. What are you doing?

The boy was so startled that he dropped the house he was holding in his hand. For a time he couldn't say a word but stared in astonishment at this strange girl who seemed to have sprung up from the ground or out of the rocks. She was bareheaded, and her hair was fair, and he noticed that her shoes were almost as white as her jumper.

Finally he pulled himself together and held out a hand in greeting. How do you do, he said shyly.

Hallo! The girl moved her mouth as if she was chewing. What are you doing! she asked again.

The boy looked down at his feet. Collecting houses, was on the tip of his tongue, but instead he replied, Collecting stones.

Oh, she said, what for?

I'm building, he said.

There was no doubt about it; she had something in her mouth. She chewed steadily, stared at him vacantly, and pushed her hands into a little pocket in the front of her slacks. Building what? she said. Are you playing?

The boy couldn't bring himself to tell her everything. I'm building over there, he replied in confusion, pointing toward the sandy bay. But when she took no notice and looked past him, still chewing, first at the headland and then at the village on the other side of the fjord, he ventured to ask who she was and where she came from.

Her name was Freyja, and she lived in Reykjavik. We nearly went off the road, she said. We had a blowout.

A what? said the boy.

A flat tire, said the girl. Pabbi is changing the tire.

At the same moment there was a fearful yell: Yippee!

The boy looked up, alarmed, but the girl shrugged her shoulders and took no further notice. A strange figure, somewhat small in stature, was standing by the rock beside them, shouting. The face could hardly be seen for a wide-brimmed hat. The figure was dressed in long yellow trousers and a many-colored jacket with tassels and fringe, with a broad belt round the waist embossed with metal studs and a leather holster attached at each hip. The boy was about to greet this strange fellow when he pushed the hat back onto his neck and fixed him with a piercing stare. Then sticking out his chin with a determined expression, as if ready for anything, he spread his fingers and crouched like a cat. Quite suddenly two gleaming pistols were whipped from the leather holsters at his hips and he leaped toward the boy, yelling, Yippee!

The boy retreated, not understanding these gestures, only realizing belatedly that he was in danger.

Don't move! shouted the little man, pointing the pistols. Hands up!

What? said the boy.

Put your hands up, stupid!

The boy thought of running away, but the little man jumped closer, watching him all the time.

Hey-ey-ey! Up with your hands!

The boy obeyed, reaching his hands into the air, fearful and hardly daring to draw breath.

Your money or your life! roared the little man. Your money or your life!

I . . . I don't have any money, stammered the boy.

Behave yourself, child, said the girl.

Then I'm going to kill you! roared the little man, rolling his eyes. Your money or your life!

I . . . I don't have any money, the boy stammered again, staring in consternation at the pistols.

I'll shoot you! cried the little man, and puffing out his cheeks he pulled the trigger of one of the pistols, at the same time shouting, Bang-Bang! Then he aimed the other and fired again: Bang-bang! After this he stared triumphantly at the boy, stuck both pistols back in their holsters and announced, You're dead!

Behave yourself, Ingi! said the girl, turning something over in her mouth. You are always behaving like an idiot! she added more sharply.

The boy discovered that he was not dead, not even wounded. He could feel no pain anywhere. He could hear and see as well as before. It was true that his heart was beating rather too fast, but the strength had come back to his knees. He realized that this unexpected attack had only been a game. The face of the little fellow was no longer twisted into a hideous grimace but was smiling and friendly and, above all, rather proud, as though he felt he had proved what he could do.

You had a devil of a scare! he remarked.

The boy said nothing.

The little man sat down on a moss-grown rock, took his hat off with a sigh, and stuck his thumbs in his belt.

What's your name? he asked.

At last the boy found his tongue. Bjorn Gislason, he replied. Usually called Bjossi.

Where do you live?

At Strond, he said, pointing at the farm.

What have you got in your pockets?

Nothing, said the boy. Just stones.

The little man put his head to one side. Haven't you any money?

No.

And no gun?

The boy looked embarrassed. No, he had no gun.

What a poor wretch you are! said the little man. Have you never played cops and robbers?

At that moment a remarkable phenomenon occurred. Something pink suddenly emerged from the half-open mouth of the girl, expanded like a balloon, and burst. The boy was rendered speechless at this wonder. The little man shifted uneasily on the rock and searched his pockets, but the girl continued to gaze vacantly into space as though nothing had happened. No sooner had the first balloon burst than a second, smaller one appeared between her lips, vanishing again and reappearing with the next breath. It gleamed pink in the sunshine, swelled, and burst. The boy waited, fascinated, for a third balloon to emerge, but the girl shifted whatever it was that she had in her mouth and remarked, How horrid it is here.

The little man stopped searching in his pockets. Freyja, he said, give me some bubble gum.

The girl shook her head. Finished, she said. You've got plenty yourself.

Not *bubble* gum, though, said the little man. He tore the silver paper off two strange-looking strips of something, put one of them in his mouth, and handed the other to the boy. Here you are. Have some.

The boy thanked him and nibbled politely at the strip. The taste in his mouth was agreeable, both sweet and acid at the same time, reminding him of the white peppermints with red stripes which his cousin always had with her when she came to stay in the summer.

The little man was watching him. Hey, he said, why don't you put all of it in your mouth?

What? said the boy.

Haven't you ever had chewing gum before?

No.

The little man assumed the air of an instructor. You shouldn't bite it into pieces, he said, and you shouldn't suck it. You should chew it, as I do. You can chew it all day, and tomorrow too, if you keep it tonight.

You mustn't swallow it, said the girl in a friendly tone. If you swallow it, you may get a pain in your tummy.

The boy did as he was told. He put the whole strip into his mouth and began to chew. The knowledge that this sweet-sour taste would last him till evening, and even tomorrow, drove the last traces of fear and suspicion from his mind. He gazed with gratitude and respect at the broad-brimmed hat of the little man, and then at the little man himself—or rather at his long yellow trousers, his many-colored jacket with tassels and fringe, the wonderful belt, the metal studs, the leather holsters, and the pistols.

What's your name? he asked.

The little man replied without hesitation: Roy, he said, squirming all over on the rock. Roy the cowboy.

Don't you believe him, said the girl. He's my brother. His name is Ingolfur Jensson, and he's called Ingi.

It's a lie! cried the little man. My name is Roy the cowboy!

Stop behaving like an idiot! said the girl.

The little man jumped to his feet with a grimace, pulled a pistol from its leather holster, and aimed at a bird. It was a curlew. Bang! he cried. Bang-bang! The curlew flew on its way uttering a high-pitched call, while the cowboy stuck the pistol back in its holster and announced, It's dead!

They continued to chew in silence for a while. At some time or other the boy had heard his parents say that Gvendur of Ness was surly and awkward with guests. He began to fidget, not wanting to be like Gvendur of Ness, longing to tell these guests some news but half-afraid that nothing he might say would be interesting enough. Should he tell them that he was building a village? That his father had gone to a meeting and wouldn't be home before evening? That the berries here on the ridge would be ripe in three weeks? That his cousin always hummed when she was picking berries? For a moment he thought of inviting them to come and look at the village down in the sandy bay, but instead he swallowed his sweet-sour mouth water and remarked in as grown-up a manner as he could, It's warm today.

Neither of them answered him. The little man continued to chew vigorously, gazing intently at the hill and the fjord, while yet another pink balloon shone between the lips of the girl, swelled up, and burst.

How dreadfully boring it is here! she said.

The little man snapped his fingers. I sneaked down to the harbor the other day and caught four flounder, he said. Do you have any tackle?

Yes, replied the boy.

Have you ever caught a flounder?

Last summer I caught a sea scorpion.

What did you use for bait?

Lumpfish liver.

How big was it?

The boy hesitated, at a loss, then spaced his hands to indicate the size of the sea scorpion, but somehow the gap between them grew bigger than he intended. His hands recorded a sea scorpion different from the one in his mind.

Li-like this, he stammered.

It would be damned good fun to go fishing, said the little man.

The boy suddenly grew unusually bold. Pabbi has a boat, he said, not mentioning Gvendur of Ness. I'm sometimes allowed to go out with him to look at the lumpfish nets.

The little man stopped chewing. Is it a good boat? he asked. Do you know how to work the engine?

It doesn't have any engine, said the boy. It's a two-man rowboat.

Where is it? asked the little man.

At the landing, said the boy, pointing in the direction of the farmstead. On the south side of the home field, he added.

The girl sucked an exploded balloon back into her mouth and brushed a lock of hair from her forehead. Come on, Ingi, she said.

The little man did not answer her but put his hat on and stared under its brim at the fjord, bright in the sunshine. I say, are you game? he said.

Eh? said the boy.

Shall we take the boat out?

The boy hesitated. The fact of the matter was that they owned the boat jointly, his father and Gvendur of Ness. Gvendur of Ness would see them from his window and he would be furious. He would chase them away and call them confounded shrimp. He never went to meetings.

The little man pushed the hat onto the back of his head. Are you game?

The boy looked uncomfortable. I don't know if we *can* have the boat, he said.

We'll steal it! said the little man eagerly, apparently ready to run off at once. We'll row out to sea and catch some flounder!

The girl caught him by the arm. Don't behave like a fool, she said sharply. Come on, idiot!

The little man broke away from her. Shut up! he said. Idiot yourself!

At the same moment they both looked up toward the crest of the ridge. A woman's voice was calling in the distance: Children, children! Ingi, Freyja!

Mother's calling us, said the girl. It's up to you if you want to be left behind!

With these words she ran off without saying good-bye to the boy, while the little man, Ingolfur Jensson, alias Roy the cowboy, gazed after her until she disappeared behind the rocks.

What an infernal bore! he said. Pabbi must have finished changing the tire on the old crate!

He shifted from foot to foot for a moment, as if undecided, started chewing again, tugged at the brim of his hat, stuck the thumb of his left hand into his belt, and contemplated the sun-bright fjord.

What an infernal bore, he said. We might have caught some flounder!

The boy said nothing.

Ingi, Ingi! a man's deep voice called from the far side of the ridge. Come along, boy! Come . . .

The little man started off as if he had been jerked by a string. 'Bye! he called to the boy over his shoulder. 'Bye, Bjossi!

He could be seen running between the rocks in his yellow trousers, the metal studs glittering and the fringe of his many-colored jacket like feathers. Just as his hat appeared against the sky, he emitted a yell, brandished one of his pistols, and fired at a curlew: Bang-bang! Then he vanished.

The boy stopped thinking about the boat and Gvendur of Ness. He stood for a moment on the same spot, confused, and then suddenly remembered some important news that he could have told these visitors. He could have told them that he had found a nest that spring. That he had been stung on the palm of his hand by a horsefly. That he could whistle a tune, turn a somersault, and hop like a flea. The visitors had gone; now it was too late to tell them this news and show them the small lump on his palm. But all the same he walked up the ridge, making for the mossy hillock where the little man's hat had appeared against the sky.

He had no sooner got to the hillock than he saw their car gleaming in the hollow below, pale blue and white, with silver in front and behind, like the car belonging to the manager of the cooperative in the village on the other side of the fjord. He saw the little man and the girl enter this magnificent vehicle, together with a man in shirt sleeves and two women wearing dark brown slacks. He heard a low hum from the engine and smelled a faint whiff of exhaust. Then the car started moving, slowly at first and then gradually faster, until its gleaming shape vanished behind a rise, leaving a tall column of dust behind it. Finally the exhaust smell went and the cloud of dust faded away.

The boy pulled himself together and swallowed. Then he began to look for red stones once more. But now he found that he could no longer get a sharp-sweet taste from the gum in his mouth, however hard he chewed, and what was more, the stones seemed to have changed during the past few minutes. Now they were about as unlike houses as anything could be, and even their color seemed to have faded. He continued searching for a while and kept one or two pebbles, though he was not at all sure that he could use them. On the way back down the ridge, he went over in his mind every word that the visitors had spoken. He had a vivid picture of the balloons made by the girl, of the little man's many-colored jacket and long trousers, of his broad-brimmed hat, and above all, of his belt with the leather holsters and the pistols. An unaccountable tremor passed through him: if he had some pistols—just one, even—what a scare he would give Gvendur of Ness!

Once more he stood by the blue bay and stared with surprise at the village he had been building. He was angry. He no longer saw the fish-freezing plant with its roaring machines, the church with its green spire, the brand-new school, the cooperative store with its shelves packed with goods, the long jetty covered with fish scales from the heaped-up catch, the towering lighthouse. He only saw childish piles of sand scattered here and there, rows of pebbles, a few pieces of wood, two figures cut out of tar paper, and a rusty can.

That was no village!

Some shrimp had been at work here—wearing shorts, what was more!

He took the reddish-colored stones out of his pocket, felt ashamed of them, and threw them away, one after the other, as though they had never been intended for houses. He looked at the church where the pastor was leaning out of the pulpit, refusing to intone without an organ. He felt a sudden wave of fury at such a cleric, called Pastor Ludvig a miserable wretch, and took his revenge on him, tearing him in two and throwing the pieces away. He treated the other paper man, the manager of the cooperative, as roughly as the pastor. He seized the lighthouse, the pride of the place, and flung it out into the bay. Then, kicking at the stones and piles of sand, he leveled his village with the earth. No one should see that a shrimp had been at work here. No one should . . .

Something cracked under his foot. He had knocked down the green church spire, with which he had no quarrel, stepped on it, and snapped it in two. His anger suddenly evaporated. Instead of picking the green sticks out of the ruins of the church and throwing them into the water, he took out his pocketknife and began to whittle at one of them, surrendering himself completely to a new idea. Chips flew from him and fell on the sand. He hacked and whittled for a while, but his knife was so blunt and the wood so tough that his progress was slow. Finally he stopped, the job only half done, and walked briskly homeward with his incomplete handiwork made out of half a church spire. He was going to sharpen his knife, or ask his mother to lend him a sharper one.

The sun shone over the moor, while flowers and cattail grass swayed ceaselessly in the warm land breeze. The boy strode homeward along the path across the home field, not pausing to look at the fjord, which seemed bluer than ever, or at the village on the other side of it, whose roofs and windowpanes shone above the stone gray harbor wall. His sister was alone outside. She was sitting on the grass slope in front of the house playing with her toys, while the laundry flapped its various colors on the line and a wagtail strutted along the wall of the cabbage garden. Nothing had changed, nothing had happened while he was away. He had intended to go straight to the storeroom, find a whetstone to sharpen his knife on, and continue whittling, but he was suddenly seized by trembling of a kind he had never felt before, and in the same instant was in a strange world of mystery and violence. He stopped, adjusted the gum in his mouth, and clenched his hand around the rough piece of stick. Aiming it at the wagtail, he took a deep breath, then shouted at the top of his voice, Bang-bang!

The wagtail took fright and flew away, while his sister looked up astonished. Then she saw him and smiled.

Bjothi! she said. Bjothi!

The boy ignored this style of address. Sticking out his chin, he crouched like a cat.

Yippee! he shouted, launching himself forward in a wild rush across the slope, and waved his gun. Hey-ey-ey! Up with your hands!

Bjothi . . .

His sister stared at his grim, distorted face, and the smile suddenly faded from her lips, took fright and flew like the wagtail. Her eyes no longer reflected astonishment but fear. Her world had changed. She dropped her toys, jumped to her feet, and was about to escape into the farmhouse, but the boy forbade her to move, leaping in front of her and threatening her with his pistol.

Don't move, he shouted. Hands up!

The corners of her mouth began to droop, but she ventured to look at him again, as if wanting to make sure, before starting to cry, whether the expression on his face was as fearful as she had thought. The boy exerted himself to dispel any doubts as to the purpose of his attack. Crouching low, he slowly approached her, glaring.

Hands up, you idiot! he commanded. Your money or your life!

His sister retreated and began to cry. Then she fell backward on the slope and cried still louder. Finally she got to her feet and, making no further attempt to save herself, began to howl and whimper as if she were being tortured. The boy faltered. Such wailings had no place in the mysterious and exciting world where hats towered, metal studs flashed, and balloons exploded. He was just about to shoot her, tell her that she was dead, and then comfort her and wipe the tears from her cheeks, when his mother came out the door and called to him.

Bjossi, what are you doing? she asked. Don't tell me you're teasing the child!

Teasing? What had that to do with it? She hadn't even asked him what he was building when he set out for the sandy bay! She had scarcely looked at him! She had called his church spire a stick! She hadn't wanted to make him a pair of long trousers this spring! Overcome by a new wave of trembling, he turned against his mother and pointed at her with the unfinished pistol made from half a church spire.

Your money or your life! he heard himself shout. Your money or your life!

Who taught you that? asked his mother. Do you know what you are saying?

She was neither frightened nor angry, but stared at him in astonishment as he scowled in her face and ordered her to put her hands up.

What's the matter with you, Bjossi? she asked, and gripped him by the shoulder. Have you gone out of your mind?

The boy gasped for breath. The tone of her voice confused him. Why wasn't she angry? Why wasn't she frightened? Why did she look at him like that? Something in his chest seemed to be released. His eyes shifted uncertainly. His hold on the pistol relaxed.

Bjossi . . .

Suddenly he was no longer living in a world of mystery and excitement. He heard his sister crying and saw the laundry on the line flapping its various colors in the sunshine. At the same moment he broke away from his mother, threw down the piece of wood, and took to his heels. He ran and hid himself—ran into the cow shed and hid in a dark corner behind an empty water barrel. Gvendur of Ness had predicted storm and famine, grinned at him, and called him a shrimp. The little man had called him a poor wretch because he had neither a gun nor money. His sister had begun to howl when he pretended he was going to shoot her. And his mother had looked at him as if he were a changeling. Nobody understood him. Nobody was on his side. Perhaps he would be thrashed when his father came home that evening.

He thought of the village he had begun to build beside the sandy bay. He made up his mind to stay where he was, in this dark corner, until he died, and he kicked ruefully at the empty barrel, sobbing and chewing. The taste in his mouth was now neither sweet nor sour. The gum which was to have lasted him all day, and even tomorrow as well—if he kept it overnight and was careful not to swallow it—oh, it had become so tasteless that he no longer enjoyed it.

Nevertheless, he continued chewing.

An Old Narrative

I t was an early spring morning several decades ago when I drank fresh milk from a rose-patterned mug, which my foster mother had given me for Christmas, and ran half-dressed out onto the terrace, forgetting to wipe my mouth.

I am not going to try to describe how the glacier appeared to me that morning, outlined against the sky far away to the east, nor the clouds, white and soft above the glacier, nor our mountain, snow-free, with patches of green moss and dark blue rocks. Even the pale meadows, the shrub-covered knolls, and the river were a vision that caused me to hold my breath for a long while, captivated by the novelty of earth and heaven.

God had passed his hand over the world during the night and transformed it, though the chasm, in the western slope of the mountain, was as dark and ominous as ever. I had always been scared of the chasm, having fallen over its edge in dreams and started up out of my sleep in a cold sweat. It was rather strange that God should not have changed this too while people slept.

While I stood there on the paved terrace and was about to count the dandelions and buttercups that had sprung up on the edge of the home field since the previous day, I heard a sudden rush of pinions and a trumpeting call overhead. Two whooper swans were heading northward, brighter than the clouds above the glacier, gracefully swimming through the bluish calm-weather mist like winged suns, conversing in song on their morning flight to distant lakes deep in the wilderness. I gazed after them, completely rapt, until they vanished behind the ridges and crests on the far side of the river. They were different from any other swans I had seen: God had passed his hand over them in the night—as he passed his hand over me at that moment. In fact I felt suddenly changed, or on the point of changing. I was an instrument on which invisible fingers were playing a strange music which I tried my utmost to understand. I closed my eyes in the hope that the message of this strange music might become clearer to me. Then I was no longer in any doubt: it resounded and rang throughout my whole being that I was to become famous, to perform some notable deed. But how I was to do this the instrumentalist did not specify. Instantly I hurled myself at the tethering stone, but I could not even budge it. I rushed at an old barrel and rolled it a few feet. I jumped up on the wall, flapped my arms, and tried time and again to fly but always fell to the ground and ended up by grazing the palm of my hand. I made an attempt to jump the wall of the cabbage patch at its highest point but missed my footing and popped a button. Just then I was called from indoors. Steini, Steini, cried my foster mother, you must put your jersey on!

I gazed at the sky, the glacier, and the mountain, then went inside to Fostra.

Wipe your mouth, boy, she said.

I shifted from foot to foot beside her and asked her to sew on my button. But when she asked how I had pulled it off, I did not tell her the truth: that God had waked in the night and changed the earth, touching me in the process and playing strange music on me. I simply said that I had been trying to jump over the wall of the cabbage patch.

Just like you, she said. How did you graze the palm of your hand?

I was trying to fly. Fostra threaded her needle and laughed. Just like you, she said again. Bless the child!

She sewed on my button and bandaged my hand, but in my mind I continued to turn over ways of achieving fame.

What can I do? I said. I want to do something.

Just like you, said Fostra. Have you mucked out the cow barn?

No, I said, I want to do something big.

Bless the child, said Fostra. You'll soon be driving the cows out every morning.

For the first time in my life I was conscious of time, or rather a portion of its law. The clock ticked unremittingly; a long while had elapsed since God had played a message in music on me, and still I had not achieved anything—only attempted to fly, wrestled with a stone, rolled a barrel, jumped, and fallen down. I determined to seek the advice of my foster father and rushed outside. But while I was looking for him, it suddenly occurred to me: I knew what I could do to become famous.

Fostri, I said breathlessly, I'm going to climb the mountain!

My foster father helped himself to some snuff and smiled. Ah, he said, and what business might you have up there?

I am going to build a cairn, I said.

Well, well, old man, said my foster father. Why are you going to build a cairn?

I was at loss to reply. I was not sure whether this resolution of mine was to the glory of God or of myself—or maybe of both of us.

There are no ways up that mountain in winter, said Fostri. And not in the autumn, either, when it's dark. But when you are bigger you can smarten up those cairns across the heath to the west. Your uncle lost himself up there one Advent and was found dead.

But I was not to be put off, in spite of my uncle's tragic fate. The heath was lower than the mountain: an endless expanse of bare sandy wasteland with pale patches of moss. I wanted above all things to build a cairn close to the sky, so that it could be seen by both God and men. Up there, I said, pointing at the summit. I'm going to do it at once!

My foster father gazed for a time at the chasm and then at me. What nonsense, he said, speaking more deliberately. I forbid you to go up the mountain alone.

I knew the tone of voice too well to make any protest. Besides, I'm inclined to the opinion that I would never have dared go up the mountain alone. I had fallen over the edge of the gully in my dreams, waking in bed beside my foster mother paralyzed with fear. A few days later, however, I happened to meet my friend from the neighboring farm. Her name was Una, and she was about my age. I still remember how dark her hair was, how red her jumper, and how green her stockings. She seemed to be growing out of the ground. Also she had a birthmark on her neck which I thought so extraordinarily attractive. I met her in the sunshine beyond the home-field fence and turned a somersault, but she was not impressed.

I can imitate a snipe, I said.

How? she asked, incredulous.

I neighed.

That's wonderful! she said, laughing and clapping her hands. Do it again!

I expanded my chest and neighed several times. Then looking down at my feet, I said hesitantly, Will you come up the mountain with me?

Yes, she said.

And with that we set off.

It was bright over the glacier, and the day was warm. We threaded a winding path for a while, then walked straight up across the heather-covered ridges and grassy hollows where everything was coming to life. I led my friend by the hand and did my best to amuse her. This is the voice of the redwing, this of the whimbrel, this of the brook. In return she told me of the rag doll she had made that winter—a little scrap of a thing she called her baby and put to sleep every evening. It was a delightful journey, and we found it the most marvelous fun to be alive and chatter about little things. But when we reached the foot of the mountain I fell silent, for the slope was considerably steeper than I had expected. My friend looked to the west.

Shouldn't we explore the chasm? she asked.

I was startled. Are you crazy? I said.

My friend did not understand why I was so set against exploring the gully. She had dreamed about wandering along its bottom, discovering multi-colored rocks, and strange plants—soft flowers on thick stalks not unlike angelica.

I hurried to dissuade her. No, Una, it's too dangerous, I said. People have fallen into the chasm.

Then imitate the snipe, she said.

But I was no longer in the mood for such vanities. Instead I started up the steep slope, for I was determined to get to the top as soon as possible and carry out my purpose of building a cairn. Besides this, I was constantly thinking about the world beneath us—how it grew in size as our farms dwindled, how the great river lengthened and unfamiliar pools glittered in the distance, some like glass and some like silver. Every time I looked back over my shoulder and saw that ever-growing view, I was filled with wonder and delight, but at the same time I felt a kind of trembling in my chest. It became clear to me that I would have to build a much bigger cairn than I had proposed—or it would be unworthy of the grandeur of this world.

Shall we have a rest? asked my friend.

No, I said, we'll go on.

Where the moss came to an end the crests of the high fells of the wilderness could be seen to the north, incredibly blue and numerous. We were standing by a low rock wall where the actual summit began, the hardest part of the climb. Now my friend would obey me no longer but sat down on the highest clump of moss and gazed at her hands.

I'm tired, she said. I'm not going any farther.

Come up to the top, I said. We'll build a cairn.

I want to go home, she said. I'm hungry.

I felt uneasy. I had asked her to come up the mountain with me, had invited her to take part in performing variations on the theme which God had played on me after a night of waking. But neither her expression nor her tone of voice made any secret of her disappointment. She declared that she was hungry, but I had no food to give her. I had left home without leave— what was more, had forgotten to muck out the cow barn. Just then a cloud covered the sun—only for a moment, it was true, for it was no bigger than a fair-sized tuft of wool—but all of a sudden I was of two minds as to whether I ought to give up my plan or tackle the hardest climb alone. I gazed at the glacier and the high fells until the sun came out again and a warm breeze brought me a redolence of rock so distinct that I shut my eyes for an instant and speculated on its source. Then I asked Una if she would wait for me while I slipped up to the top and built a cairn.

My friend uprooted a handful of moss but did not look up.

I won't be long.

She remained silent.

I'll pick some flowers for you this summer.

What kind of flowers?

White ones, I said. Cotton grass.

That's not a flower, it's grass, she said, continuing to uproot moss.

I'll give you my rose-patterned mug, too.

All right, she said. But be quick.

It was by no means without discomfort that I left her. In fact I remember little about my journey up to the summit. I only remember that it was fearfully steep and stony. But when I stood at last on the very top and looked out at the world, I felt so close to the sky that for a time I stood as though in a happy trance. The one thing lacking was to have my friend standing beside me enjoying this silent glory to the east and the west and above all to the north, where the high peaks of the wilderness rose and fell in marvelous mirage. Then the sun went in, and dark shadows passed over the landscape, the scent of rock faded, and the quivering dance of the high peaks was stilled. A dread of solitude crept over me; I could speak with none, except maybe the sky, the summit, and myself. Una is waiting, I said aloud, and began to carry out my intention, to build a cairn. Una is waiting, I sang time after time while struggling with the stones, but my words fell emptily into the mountain silence and were dispersed like lost birds somewhere in space.

To this day it is a mystery to me how I managed to build that cairn, halffearful, feeble, and unhandy as I was. Many of the most suitable stones were beyond my strength however hard I gritted my teeth, while others were so small or misshapen that I was almost reduced to tears. Nevertheless, a small cairn rose there, admittedly much smaller than I would have wished and ungainly in every respect but still a cairn, and a little taller than myself if I remember rightly. When I had laid the last stone in position, I appraised it, both hands scratched and bruised, not knowing whether to weep or exult over my achievement. I chose the latter course, and hurried down from the summit to meet Una. Darkness was beginning to fall, the heavens were heaped with rain clouds, and the breeze was chilly. When I saw that Una was no longer waiting for me on the clump of moss, I suddenly thought of trolls and elves, but a moment later I saw her along the slope to the west, a short way from the chasm.

Una! I shouted. Una, wait!

She did not look back but moved on with pauses until I caught up with her and offered to take her hand.

No, you're a bad boy! she said. Why were you such a long time?

I built a cairn, I said proudly, pointing to the summit. There it is!

But my friend still did not look back. You never saw what I saw in the gully, she said. I went right up to the edge.

I was shocked. You're telling stories! I said. You mustn't go there! . . . What did you see?

But my friend would not confide in me any more. You're a bad boy! she kept repeating. You trick me into going up the mountain, and then you run away!

I began to get angry, thinking I deserved better than this, having just built a cairn. It never occurred to her to look at my hands, all skinned and bruised from the stones. I told her haughtily that I was too big to be imitating snipe, she need not expect any cotton grass from me this summer, and I had changed my mind about giving her my rose-patterned mug.

I don't care, she said. The roses on your mug aren't pretty.

They're prettier than the birthmark on your neck! I said.

You should be ashamed of yourself, she replied, half crying. You're a wicked boy!

Just then it began to rain. We hurried homeward, wet and hungry, not speaking a word to each other and parting unreconciled at the home-field fence. My foster father had been on the point of setting out to search for me, fearing the worst, and reprimanded me sternly, but my foster mother made him stop scolding the poor child, brought me food, and put herbal ointment on my hands. You must never run off like that again, child; will you promise me? I heard her say as if from a great distance. I don't remember what my reply was, if I replied at all. I was utterly exhausted and fell fast asleep fully dressed, not waking before the sun shone in my face the following morning.

The cairn, I thought to myself, and hurried to dress. I rushed outside, rubbing the sleep from my eyes. Where was the cairn? Could it possibly have collapsed in a single night? Or was it so insignificant as to be invisible from here? I felt a lump in my throat but refused to acknowledge it, and stared and stared, until I thought I could make out a tiny point in the middle of the summit, scarcely larger than a wart on one's finger. There was no mistake about it: I had located my cairn at last. There it was, in spite of everything; there it stood against the sky. Praise be to God, I thought, greatly relieved. It hadn't collapsed overnight, after all.

But now a strange thing happened. That tiny point began gradually to grow bigger and taller—or rather, my sight became keener day by day. It was soon evident to me that I had built a cairn for which I had no cause to be ashamed. Later I saw that the cairn was really a most impressive achievement, in addition to being an ornament to the summit and indeed to the whole mountain. Eventually, when I became convinced that it was not smaller than our parish church and just about as noble in appearance, I could not resist remarking to some visitors that I had a notable achievement to my credit. I did not mention Una, but simply said, I climbed the mountain and built a cairn.

Really? said the visitors looking at me with astonishment, So you built a cairn, did you?

There it is, I said pointing to the summit.

Well, now, said the visitors smiling, to think he could do that!

I smiled too, shifted from one foot to the other, hands in pockets, unspeakably happy, spit manfully, and remarked that I had been obliged to use very poor building material, uneven stones for the most part.

Admirable fellow!

Every time these words were used to me, or when I repeated them to myself in private, the cairn grew in size, sometimes by a few inches, sometimes by several feet. In the end it seemed to have been built out of great rocks and boulders as it towered there on the summit, dark red in the sunset, blue after showers of rain. It had become a monument to rare powers and expert craftsmanship, tapering like the pyramid in an illustration to my foster mother's New Testament. I have probably never been in such a euphoric state as I was that summer, for the consciousness of the cairn never left me, asleep or waking. Flowers, birds, and butterflies seemed to contribute to this triumphant euphoria. The brook chanted a never-ending ode in honor of my achievement in building such a cairn, alone and unvictualed. The wind blew my praises; even the calm weather acquired a voice. Nor did I intend to hold it against my friend that she had failed to understand the performance of divine music and had called me a bad boy. I felt that I could afford to be magnanimous, so often had people said, Admirable fellow! to me. But on the day when I was going to present her with a bunch of cotton grass and as good as promise her my rose-patterned mug if she would tell me what she had seen in the gully, a new visitor came galloping up the track: the parish officer's outrider.

It was a Sunday. The sky was covered with white clouds, and the visibility was good. The parish officer's outrider was a youth from the capital, a person of unquestioned importance, curly haired, round faced, and freckled, in his early teens. He said he had been sent for horseshoes which my foster father had promised his master, and while he stopped for refreshment he showed me some of his accomplishments, patting me on the head in a friendly manner as though I were his little protégé.

He began with various gymnastics on the beam of the badstofa: removing his jacket while hanging by the feet, turning a circle, and swinging back and forth on one hand. Next he caught a bluebottle in the window and put it in his mouth, whistled tunes I had never heard before, blew the fly out alive, and said, Respects to the lady! And when Fostra brought him coffee, he took the cup, balanced it on his nose, and walked round the room with it, then poured the coffee into the saucer and lifted it steaming on one finger. I offered to imitate a snipe, but he would not listen and instead imitated a brass band with blaring and thumping until Fostra suggested that we go outside. Finally he stood on his head on the terrace and did a standing jump over the wall of the cabbage patch.

I said, trying to be as casual as I could, I climbed the mountain this spring and built a cairn.

Ha? he queried, staring in all directions. What mountain?

The mountain, I repeated, and pointed at the peak. The cairn is up there.

Ha? he exclaimed in wonder amounting almost to pity. Do you call *that* a mountain?

I could give no answer. The cairn had completely vanished. Not a trace of my cairn was to be seen. The mountain had shrunk like a slug in dry weather; the peak dwindled rapidly until it was like a hat without a brim, its slopes all sinking and flattening out, apart from a small area to the west where the chasm cleft the rock face, just as gloomy and sinister as ever.

I cannot deny that it was painful to me thus to lose in a single instant so special a cairn, the pride of the world and the crowning peak of a majestic mountain that I had climbed with such difficulty. All the same it never entered my mind that God might have played strange music on me in a spirit of mere trifling. The parish officer's outrider had scarcely ridden away when a new solution to the riddle presented itself to me like a flash of light. I became quiet and restless, surrendered myself to the power of a secret resolution, forgetting several small matters such as, for instance, cotton-grass flowers for Una. The high fells of the wilderness stood clearly in my mind, but especially the clear lake that was bound to lie hidden behind them, deeper and bluer than any other lake, to which the whoopers had flown in the spring.

Those whoopers . . . no, let me call them swans, as if I were composing an epitaph. In brief, I never saw those swans again by daylight. I had a glimpse of them in the moonlight of the wilderness, long after the news of my friend's death was brought to me—that Una's body, disfigured by ravens, had been carried back from the chasm. Somehow I had become separated from my companions and walked past many pools, some silver, some incredibly blue. Now I sat under a mossy rock in the late evening of the first week of autumn, while the moon climbed from layers of cloud and cast its light upon pale wastes, mountains, and glaciers. I listened intently, but the silence was total— not a murmur of water or birdsong to break it. Memories came to me: I began to think of the vanished years—how they had passed, sometimes like landmarks on an instructive journey, sometimes like scattered leaves in a wood. I stared into the palms of my hands and told myself that I must continue my search, but I still sat motionless, recalling one thing after another that had befallen me. And then suddenly I heard a rush of wings overhead. I looked up and saw two swans flying in the moonlight. I knew then for certain that their beauty had become ruthless, like the beauty of the wilderness, their wingbeats in some way fearful and the rush of their pinions cruel. They had been heading south, but unexpectedly wheeled around and turned their songless flight straight for the high fells and the glaciers, as if a voice had called them and forbidden them to leave.

I knew very well that they were both doomed, however deep and blue the lake which they might find for a mirror. Here flying in the moonlight were swans with only a short while left to live, those same swans at which I had gazed enchanted several decades ago.

The knowledge of their doom struck me in my weariness, making me tremble. It was clear that I had still not understood the strange music that sounded in my breast so long ago, when I discovered the spring and the world. I remembered my foster parents. I remembered Una. I remembered solitary days and long night journeys. And yet all was not over for me: there was a glimmer of light, and in its glow I saw half-fallen cairns by frequented heath tracks, howling snowstorms, harassed human beings.

I stood up with my burden and walked in the moonlight toward the abodes of men as briskly as I could, as though a great deal depended on it.

THE PADLOCK

I had no premonition of the misfortune that awaited me on the other side of a few unborn hours as I stood newly dressed on the farmhouse terrace and gazed across the faded meadows, which were wet and dreary after the previous day's downpour. I was wondering whether the sun would manage to penetrate the thin gray cloud layer that covered the unchanging autumn sky, when my father, speaking unusually fast, said, Put on your best clothes, boy! His urgency was due to a sudden decision to send me to the village for some farrier's nails, a stick of ground chicory, and twenty pounds of flour. The fact was that the second horse had to be shod for the sheep roundup and pancakes made for the mustering pens, so my father tore the last blank page out of my old exercise book, sat down at the writing desk, dipped the pen in the half-dried inkwell, and wrote an urgent missive to the merchant: Honored Sir, I wonder whether you would be so good as to add to my account one packet of farrier's nails, one stick of chicory (it should be Ludvik David), and twenty pounds of flour . . .

Don't forget the spool of thread, said Mamma.

A spool of thread? exclaimed my father, looking up in surprise. Do you mean to tell me that all the thread I bought on the wool journey last summer is finished?

Yes, replied Mamma, I need a spool of black thread.

And white, too, added sister.

God help us all! What for, may I ask?

To mend the sheets and pillowcases.

What a load of infernal vanity! said my father, shocked. As if black thread wouldn't do just as well for pillowcases!

But when, knitting his brow yet deeper, he had added both spools to the list, together with half a length of plug tobacco, it transpired that the sailmaker's thread was almost exhausted. See, there's nothing left now but this little bit—less than a couple of yards of it! And how was one to stitch shoes for the roundup without sailmaker's thread? And how was the kitchen range to be lit in the mornings without matches? Just look at the box: it's nearly empty! Besides this, the rock sugar was on the point of running out, and the last ball of laundry bluing was used up the other day, and the green soap wouldn't last to the weekend.

With a profound sigh my father tightened his grip on the pen and complained loudly, declaring that he could not for the life of him understand this ruinous extravagance that would end up by landing us all on the parish. He voiced his conviction that the merchant would be furious at such a shameless accumulation of debt. He would probably utter dire threats and send me home empty-handed. Moreover my father expressed his confidence in my getting confused by all this mountain of purchases, forgetting half the goods, and spoiling the remainder, while I was certain to let some scoundrel steal the saddle, bridle, and maybe the horse as well, and at all events would run into some major trouble or disaster, returning home very much the worse for wear, and then only by a merciful dispensation of providence.

While this was going on, I hurriedly changed into my best clothes, washed myself, and combed my hair, then fumbling surreptitiously in my box at the head of my bed, I knotted my worldly wealth—a golden two-krona piece—in the corner of my Sunday-best handkerchief with the picture of three kittens on it. I was shaking all over with travel fright and apprehension but tried not to show it. My father pushed the cork stopper into the inkwell, carefully folded his letter to the merchant, put it in the breast pocket of my jacket, and demanded two safety pins to preclude the eventuality of its being jerked out on the way. I was then clad in my eldest brother's yellow waterproof, a loose, awkward garment, my mother rolling up the sleeves and presenting me with newly knit patterned gloves which she had really intended to keep until the day of the mustering. We now went outside to the edge of the field, where Blesi was waiting, harnessed and ready. He looked me dispiritedly in the eye, as though suspecting that I would not be equal to the hazards of the journey. No, a ride to the village was surely not without perils! Here in the saddlebag there was a small food packet—I was to eat the contents before returning home—besides sacks for the goods. I was to wrap the flour up well and carry it on the pommel of the saddle but put the other purchases in the saddlebag. I was to dismount when I came to the bridge over the river, and walk across, looking neither to right nor left, nor, least of all, down into the water that flowed beneath. I was to lead old Blesi straight into the stable by the store, close the door carefully, and look out the window from time to time while shopping to make sure that nobody stole the blessed creature. I was to unbutton my waterproof and take the letter out of my pocket, ask for the merchant himself, shake him by the hand, and say politely, Pabbi sends his kind regards and asked me to give you this letter . . .

Yes, and you mustn't forget to address him formally, in the plural; he pretends not to understand if people address him familiarly.

In short: Pabbi sends his kind regards and asked me to give you this letter. Then I was to wait until I was served, quietly and patiently, but watch the clerk and make sure that I got everything that the merchant entered into the account. Last, but not least, I was on no account to speak to strangers but was to leave them well alone, for no one could tell what might be hidden under a friendly exterior in a village: there were all kinds of sheep in every flock, and it was best to be on the safe side.

And don't hang about! said my father.

And don't forget the thread and the bluing! said my sister.

And be careful of the motorcars! said my mother.

And after that I rode off. All these words of admonition and advice had brought me to the verge of a state of real alarm. For the first time in my life I was aware of a heavy burden of responsibility resting on my shoulders and of the many perils that lay in ambush for me in a strange place. But hardly had I left the farm track when warm sunshine flooded through the blue gaps in the thin cirrus, turning the level waters of the great river to a gleaming mirror and throwing a golden mist over the newly faded meadows. In a moment I had forgotten all worries and apprehensions and was urging old Blesi on, speeding my journey along the puddled cart track at the foot of the mountain. I even unbuttoned my waterproof, thrusting my hand into my pocket and complacently fingering my two-krona piece in its pictured hand-kerchief. I was so happy that I wanted to wave my arms and legs, sing, laugh, shout, yell, say good morning to the sheep on the grass flats, and call out to the golden plovers that flew in large flocks across the autumnal landscape. But instead of doing all this, I tried to maintain a grave, grown-up composure, tried to restrain the sheer joy of anticipation and turn my mind to other matters—urgent and weighty ones. I had not yet decided whether my exercise book was to have brown covers or green, the pencil to be in one color or many. Nor had I made up my mind whether to buy candy or figs with the rest of the money, to gladden the hearts of my sister and parents. It never entered my head that my father might scold me for this foolhardy extravagance since I had neglected to ask his permission. But the fact was that I had a great secret which justified my breach of the laws of economy and indigence, strict and rigorous and sternly opposed to all indulgence as they were. This secret had been revealed to me on the first evening of summer the year before last, when I was in my tenth year—revealed unexpectedly, to vibrate in my breast ever since. I remembered it clearly. It had rained without a pause for the previous two days, and the waters of the thaw foamed and flooded. And on that April day the skies were veiled in a soft white haze, the grass slopes clear of snow, the moss green, while a strange murmur in the air addressed the earth without cease. I had been under the spell of this sound from early morning, and when I stood on the rise of the home field in the evening, the sunset had kindled a dull red glow in the west, transforming the clouds into mighty harps with long silent strings. I stared as though in a trance, having never seen anything like the beauty of these instruments. But after a short while the glow faded, the strings were broken, and the harps drooped forlorn in the firmament, finally vanishing into the deepening blue of twilight. I was filled with a strange kind of yearning and went silently into the badstofa. I told no one of it, for instinctively I realized that no one would understand what had happened to me. But when I came to myself I was sitting in a corner with an oil lamp and had written three pages about the harps in the sunset in my exercise book.

Thus my fate was decided.

Since that day I often sat by myself in a corner with a dim oil lamp, writing about everything in heaven and earth; unfortunately, though, I was obliged to economize on paper and make everything shorter and more laconic than I would have chosen. In the summer I had scarcely put pencil to paper on account of the haymaking, and besides, my old exercise book was almost full and now my father had torn the last blank page out of it! Dear Lord, there was so much I needed to write about! For instance, I had never mentioned the brook down there, nor the deep pool that had formed up here in the hollow below the cluster of hummocks. And yet I had sometimes lain full-length on the bank and trailed my hook for the parr that darted among the undulating growth of the stream bed—yes, once caught five in succession, so that the pool certainly deserved a mention! Nor had I attempted to describe how the river glided past on a still evening, or how the colors changed in the woods on the far bank. And I had forgotten to give an account of the herbs and flowers in the dew of the spring night, forgotten to convey the sunshine on the meadows into my exercise book, forgotten to compose a verse about the little, bright, soft, and swiftly moving flocks of cloud that played tag above the mountain in the warm breezes of early summer. No, it was more than a little that remained to be written about. It was really the whole world: life on earth in the light of sun, moon, and stars; the joy of life and its wonderful beauty. And the longer I thought about this, the more evident it became to me that one exercise book would not suffice. I would have to buy two. And I began to calculate, to add and subtract: they probably cost thirty-five aurar, and twice thirty-five is seventy. Last autumn pencils had cost ten aurar, and I supposed they had neither gone up nor come down. Total eighty. And then, let's see, there'd be ... yes, there'd be one krona twenty left over for figs or boiled sweets. Good Lord, yes! I had money enough for two exercise books in which to confide the secrets of my heart. And wouldn't I just make good use of my free time during autumn and winter!

While I was immersed in these meditations, the cart track came to an end and the highway took over, broad and surfaced with gravel. I saw no motorcars, but the rainbow glitter of oil patches on puddles in the wheel ruts augmented my feeling of unfettered adventure. I continued along the highway for some time, scanning the view on all sides and absorbing its novelty: stretches of yellow marshland, strange farms, and an ash gray glacial outflow rushing along shallow depressions. I felt unfettered and venturous, and jerked the rein to make old Blesi canter for quite a stretch. I was just considering whether it might not be advisable to have three exercise books when my eye was caught by the figure of a man stooped over the road a short way ahead of me. I make no secret of the fact that my heart began to beat a little faster, for I at once recalled my father's words of warning and the various crimes that had been committed against innocent wayfarers in both former and recent times. But as it was, this turned out to be the most ordinary roadworker leveling the surface gravel in a leisurely way. He asked me quizzically where I was bound for.

The village, I replied grandly.

The village, he repeated with the ghost of a grin, and leaning on his shovel he sucked his discolored front teeth and spit in a long curving trajectory right across the road. And what do you intend to do in the village, pal?

Buy a number of oddments for the muster, I answered.

The muster? Aha, he said. Right enough. And when is the muster to be?

Next Wednesday.

And things will be lively then, I daresay?

Yes, I said a little uncertainly. I did not understand the tone in his voice.

I say, do the lads in your parish do much distilling, d'you know? Do they sell hooch?

No, I replied, shocked. No one in my parish does that.

Aha, he said, and began smoothing the surface gravel again. Just asked for fun. No harm in asking, pal.

In my embarrassment I remained silent, while old Blesi mouthed his bit and laid back his ears, impatient to go on.

You'll see the village from the top of the rise there, said the man. You just turn down to the bridge at the intersection on the far side.

Thank you, I said. But what house is that up on the hill?

That's not a house, he said. It's a broken-down rusty old stone crusher. Our camp is beyond it, he added.

Thank you, I repeated, and took leave of him courteously as old Blesi dragged the rein from my hand and started off at a trot.

I say! the man called after me. Give my love to the girls down there!

I would in all likelihood have turned back for more information about the unspecified girls had not a truck loaded with steel gray stone chips come roaring toward me at that moment. I hastily pulled Blesi to the side of the road, so that he would not shy at the racket of the engine, and exhaust fumes were borne to me, tickling my nostrils. From time to time I looked back over my shoulder, while the truck driver dumped his load and turned the vehicle, but when he had driven past me a second time, I stood up in my stirrups and pressed on up the rise. There was the stone crusher. And there was the camp. And there, in a quarry below the hill, some men were shoveling gravel into the truck, talking together in loud voices and not bothering so much as to glance in my direction! A short distance ahead I saw the intersection, and beyond the dwindling marshes and the foaming glacial river appeared the village: a huddle of houses of varying shapes and sizes above a level of bare shingle, bathed in the golden red gleam of an autumn sun that was pouring enchantment over it through a gradually shrinking gap in the clouds. I was no longer in any doubt regarding the need for three exercise books, even though it meant a proportional reduction in boiled sweets or figs. I felt in myself that there would be no peace for me before I had written a long account and composed several poems on this remarkable journey. The oil slicks on the puddles, the exhaust fumes from the truck, the broken-down, rusty stone crusher, the man on the road with discolored front teeth who had called me pal—all this flooded my consciousness and demanded detailed treatment on a quiet evening beside a dim oil lamp. And besides, there was still the village to come, the heart of novelty. And when I caught sight of the white suspension bridge, with its towering metal structure on massive concrete foundations, its thick supporting cables, mighty iron bars, and substantial railings, it was too much for me: if I was to undertake a description of this magnificent sight, I could hardly manage with fewer than *four* exercise books and *two* pencils.

I dismounted, stroked old Blesi on the nose, and then led him carefully out onto the bridge, awe and curiosity competing with nervous apprehension in me. Every now and then I edged close to the rail to glance down into the turbid, raging glacial water that lashed the pillars and hurled itself about in vicious eddies. A kind of eager trembling passed through me, as if I had myself played a part in the construction of the bridge and even formally opened it in some indistinct and forgotten dream. I felt myself more of a man than before, so strong, determined, and experienced that the apprehension vanished for a while.

And now, here I was at last in the village!

I saw houses with many windows, all of which seemed to stare at me like eyes, saw people walking in their best clothes among the houses, saw high telephone poles, with white porcelain mushrooms on them and posters stuck to them, saw a red fuel pump and two gleaming cars outside the store, while strange fumes, probably of some foreign fuel, filled my nostrils and reminded me of my father's advice. I was fortunate enough to come across a bearded, friendly fellow with blurred speech who directed me immediately to the stable. It was quiet and dark in the stable, and while I unstrapped the saddlebag and took the letter to the merchant from the safety-pinned breast pocket of my jacket, a sense of the responsibility of my mission came heavily upon me. I forgot to pat old Blesi on leaving him, took the saddlebag under one arm, walked out of the stable, and closed the ponderous doors behind me. And before entering the store, I glanced about me suspiciously. But I could see no thieves or criminals, only smartly dressed, smiling people hurrying between the houses on various mysterious and intriguing errands. Then I was standing before the shop counter, breathing the spice-laden air and staring in embarrassment at several young fellows who held long-necked beer bottles in one hand and lighted cigarettes in the other and looked as devil-may-care as any range rider in a story of high adventure. Their presence at once made me feel fearfully uncouth and insignificant. I glanced involuntarily down at my brother's waterproof, so wide and worn, and blood rushed to my cheeks, while my eyelids began to quiver. I was roused when the clerk, a plump, fair-haired youth about twenty, turned to me, chewing, and said, Wassit?

Ca-can I speak to the merchant? I asked, my voice trembling.

Wadyerwantwithm?

I have a letter for him.

He swung round and called out in the direction of the door of the office: There's a boy here with a letter for you, Dad!

A moment later the merchant appeared. I extended my hand to him across the counter, trying my utmost to be both casual and courteous. How do you do, I said, using the familiar second-person singular. Pabbi sends you his kind regards and . . . But I got no further. I suddenly remembered that I was to use the polite form of address, swallowed in confusion, and changed step halfway through the sentence. Pabbi sends you his kind regards, sir, and . . . and here is the letter, I stammered, blushing furiously.

To my surprise, he thanked me, asked kindly where I was from, then unfolded the letter, adjusted his spectacles, and began to read. I leaned against the counter, swallowed with difficulty, and watched him out of the corner of my eye. It was as though I were standing before a judge. What was I to do if he blankly refused to add anything to my father's account? What was I to do if he were to take exception to the spools of thread and the laundry bluing? Or the rock sugar and plug tobacco? Or the sailmaker's thread and the green soap? Dear God, what should I do if he were to give me a piercing look and say sharply, I can't for the life of me understand this extraordinary extravagance of you people! I felt that I would hardly be able to get a word out, let alone prove man enough to explain our poverty and thrift—no, I would simply shrink into myself inside the waterproof, small and wretched, seize my saddlebag, and flee out the door. His expression gave nothing away. It was a closed expression but not unkindly—quite benevolent. He seemed a long time getting through the letter. At last, however, he pushed his spectacles farther up his nose, handed his son the scribbled sheet, and said, in a tone so ordinary and unemphatic that it astonished me, Serve the boy. And with that he walked to his office and shut the door behind him.

The merchant's son set to work busily, handling paper bags and weights, alternately writing and weighing, while the youths put their empty beer bottles on the counter and wandered through the door one after another, until all were gone. I was still in a state of some emotion and had scarcely awakened to the fact that the merchant had agreed to add to my father's debt without comment. Nevertheless, I felt no elation. I was sunk in a state of total and painful confusion that brought a lump to my throat and made my hands sweat. And the more I gazed round the store, the harder it became for me to fight against a mood of helpless depression and melancholy. A short while before, I had been the richest of mortals, but now there was no one in the world more indigent. During the summer my mother had often remarked that she had no best apron to put on when visitors called, and here in front of me shelf after shelf was heaped with stout bales of varicolored and attractive cloth just waiting to be cut up for Sunday dresses and best aprons. My sister had repeatedly mentioned a flowered silk head scarf and curved hair comb, for she had reached the age of wanting to coil her braids into a bun at the back of her head, especially on Sundays, and there hung silk scarves by the score, while hair combs gleamed prominently on enormous cards embellished with colored pictures of foreign women. And wouldn't it be a change for my father to smoke one of those lordly looking pipes instead of chewing venomous plug tobacco and spitting in all directions! Wouldn't it be a change for my brothers to wear splendid caps like those, and throw away the worn and many-times-washed, shapeless objects they wore that made them look so odd and sheepish! Or the boots and the shirts! Or the leather belts, brown and black, with glittering buckles! Or the zip-up windbreakers and the knickerbockers! What glory! I stuck a moist hand in my pocket and clutched my coin in its pictured handkerchief, shifted hesitantly from foot to foot before the counter, and felt the lump in my throat growing bigger and more painful. I gazed at beautiful writing materials—bottles of ink, pencils, envelopes, and exercise books—but was quite unable to make up my mind. I gazed at the slabs of chocolate and the various assortment of candy in sticks, jars, and boxes, but the weight on my breast became ever heavier and more painful. I gazed and gazed, at a complete loss, and did not come to myself until the merchant's son asked me whether I had anything to carry the goods in with me.

Yes, I said, here in the saddlebag.

Fine, he said. Two sacks. Splendid. But what's this?

Only my food packet, I said.

All right, he said, and continued to chew.

I explained with some difficulty that I was to carry the flour in front of me but put the other goods into the saddlebag, and would he please be so good as to pack everything well, especially the green soap, so that it didn't get into the rock sugar. He assented absently, nodding his head, but all his movements were brisk and confident, his slender, dexterous hands adept at the manipulations of commerce and cold accounting. Before I was aware, he had planted the saddlebag and the tied sacks before the counter, handed me a slip of paper, and announced, Here's the invoice.

THE PADLOCK

I folded the paper, put it in the breast pocket of my jacket, which I fastened with the safety pins, as my father had done that morning. After that, red-faced and foolish, I shifted my weight from one foot to the other on the tile floor, crumpled the pictured handkerchief in my sweating palm, and tried repeatedly to clear my throat. I think I have never felt worse. It was as if I were preparing to leap across a chasm.

Anything else? asked the merchant's son, and he stared at me questioningly.

No, I replied, hesitant.

Did you perhaps forget something?

No, I repeated, and I supported myself against the counter, covered with confusion and unable for the life of me to see my way out of the impasse.

The merchant's son puttered around for quite a while over his books and bills, put something in his mouth, moistened his thin lips with his tongue, whistled a fragment of tune, tapped his fountain pen several times against the knuckles of his left hand, and wrinkled his brow, as though deep in thought. I felt that he was watching me all the time and did not care for my hanging around there with a funereal expression, since my business was concluded.

You're waiting, he remarked impatiently.

Yes, I agreed foolishly.

What are you waiting for?

I . . . I don't know.

Are you alone?

Yes, I replied.

Well, then! he said with a note of query, and pulling the lid off a half-full jar of boiled sweets, he thrust it toward me and invited me to have some with my lunch. Take a couple.

I felt something seethe and boil inside me at this, as if I had been struck on the cheek. He obviously thought I was scrounging, that I was a beggar. It is still not clear to me how I happened to point at the padlocks, though I distinctly remember pretending not to notice the jar of sweets. I straightened myself so that the unbuttoned waterproof creaked, took a deep breath, lifted my hand, and spoke out loudly and categorically: How much are those over there?

Do you mean the padlocks? he asked.

Yes, I replied firmly, without displaying any hesitation, although I had never seen a padlock before and still less had any thought of buying such an article.

The prices vary, he said indifferently. This one here costs two kronur . . .

I'll take it, I said, interrupting him.

Shall I put it on your dad's account?

No! I exclaimed with bravado, and snatching the handkerchief from my pocket I hurriedly untied the knot and laid the two-krona piece on the counter.

Very well, he said, half whistling, and packed the article in a small paper bag. It's a first-rate padlock.

Just at that moment somebody came into the store and stumbled against my parcels on the tiled floor. I thrust the padlock into my pocket, snatched up the saddlebag and sacks, and forgetting to say good-bye, rushed out the door like an escaped prisoner, hearing the merchant's son saying, Wassit? as the door slammed behind me. I hurried to the stable, suddenly remembering that I had neglected to glance out the window and make sure that nobody stole the blessed creature. What would I do if he had vanished? My knees went weak, and I gritted my teeth, hardly daring to open the stable door. My hand was shaking as I jerked at the iron catch, and I was surprised when I saw old Blesi standing before me in the half-light with a sad, dejected look in his eyes, as though he knew all. Not a word did I say to him but strapped the bag to the saddle, slung the sacks over one shoulder, and led him straight out toward the bridge. I looked neither to left nor to right, sickened by everything, was aware of houses, windows, people, telephone poles, and the red fuel pump as a sleepwalker fleeing from enemies. It was of vital importance for me to get out of this village without delay! I had no desire to go to the rail of the bridge and look down at the boisterous eddies, and the mighty supports and massive steel cables moved me to neither exultation nor reckless resolution. I no longer entertained the idea of having played a part in the construction of this feat of engineering in some vanished and forgotten dream—no, when I had crossed to the opposite bank, I never gave it a glance but moved off the highway to find a convenient mounting hummock. And as I buttoned up the waterproof and briefly fingered the padlock, I seemed to detect a mournful compassion in the eyes of the horse, while even the lion-head fittings on the bridle watched my feeble, fitful movements.

Stand still, you stupid jackass, stand still! I shouted furiously, though old Blesi had not stirred. What kind of crazy wild behavior is this, eh? Do you think you can rule me? And no sooner was I mounted than I jerked viciously at the rein, kicked the stirrups against his sides, and did not relent until I had worked him into a fast, offended gallop along the road.

After that, I was no longer angry, and I reined in, rocked myself slowly in the saddle, and took care to look straight ahead, never back. It had become overcast, the clouds thickening ominously, and a chill gust blew in my face. To this day I remember how pale and withered the marshes were, what a distressful note there was in the glacial river, and how the promise of the highway had flown off into an unknown distance. I was returning home. I had ventured out into the world and been defeated. But instead of acknowledging my defeat, I did my very best to deny it and forget it—perhaps because it was so ludicrous, so wretchedly pointless and absurd. I had no thoughts at all, refused to think, just hung stooped over old Blesi's withers, one hand clutching the rein and the other holding the bound sacks. And yet all the time I was looking desperately for some expedient, some hope of escaping from my predicament before I reached home, something to save me from shame and disgrace. It could not be that every avenue was closed against me, that happiness had abandoned me irrevocably this day. Perhaps I should turn back, walk boldly into the store, throw the padlock on the counter, and convince the merchant's son that it had all been an unfortunate misunderstanding, that it had never been my intention to buy a padlock but four exercise books, two pencils, and some candy with the remainder, or possibly figs. But I only had to glance briefly over my shoulder to realize that it was impossible to turn back. I could not do it. In fact I continued on my way, feeling more palpably and painfully how different the road home was from the road out, how quickly the world changed. The oil patches on the puddles, the men in the gravel pit, the gloomy, rusty, broken-down stone crusher, the racket made by the truck, and the exhaust fumes from its engine—all these were out of harmony with my emotions and different from what they had been that morning. Even the man on the road, the leveler, was different.

Back already? he remarked, and leaning on his shovel, appraising me, he spit through decayed front teeth. But his voice was surly and there was a kind of dull resentment in his expression. Back already?

Yes, I replied.

And what's the news?

I don't know.

You're a bright one! Been to the village and haven't any news to tell! He snorted scornfully. What did the girls have to say? I suppose you gave them my message?

I didn't see any girls.

You didn't see any girls? he repeated, and stared at me narrowly, his mouth open, as if I was not in my right mind. Why didn't you see any girls?

There weren't any girls around, I said vaguely.

Rubbish! he said, shoveling gravel deliberately. They are always around when I go down to the village—though it may well be that they'd sooner chat with me than with others. Yes, it wouldn't surprise me at all, pal, if they found one hell of a big difference in chatting with me sometimes!

Would you like to buy a padlock? I asked, at the same time wondering at my daring. It only costs two kronur.

He regarded me narrowly. Look here, he said, how old are you?

I'll soon be twelve, I replied, not following his drift.

Soon to be twelve? And who taught you to get fresh with strangers? he demanded, adopting a preaching tone, and prepared to be offended. When I was your age I didn't speak out of turn like you. I knew the whole Bible from cover to cover, and was so bright and well mannered and well educated that I always answered for myself in pure Scripture. And you watch out, he continued—and laughed loudly at his own wit—you watch out for the car!

I suppose I misunderstood the harmless nonsense of this buffoon, gave it a more serious meaning than was justified. At all events I smarted from his reproaches for a long time after I had left him out of sight. It was really remarkable how different from the outward trip the road home could be! Here I was swinging along on old Blesi beneath a heaped-up, threatening sky, blue nosed, cold cheeked, and famished into the bargain—for of course I had left my food packet behind in the store. What was worse, though, I had left behind all my hope, my joy, and my freedom. I had a padlock in my

pocket! I had ventured out into the world to buy a padlock? Dear God, how
in the name of heaven had this happened? Was I out of my mind? What did I
propose to do with this padlock? What was I going to tell my parents when
they started asking why I bought a padlock? No, I could expect neither understanding nor forgiveness on their part, for it was beyond my power to understand myself or excuse my folly. It was like a bad dream when I put my hand
in my pocket and felt this hideously expensive, ridiculous, and unnecessary
object. It tyrannized over me. It tormented me and mocked me without
mercy. It reminded me constantly of a heartfelt resolution which had belittled
itself before the world, burst and evaporated in face of the world's wealth like
a useless soap bubble. I had not proved myself more steadfast than that, for
all my bluster. I had not shown more stability, in spite of the secrets which
the harps of sunset had sent trembling through my breast. So precipitate and
unresisting had my surrender been, I had failed the harps of sunset, failed
my parents, failed all in life that I loved or longed for. I had a padlock in my
pocket.

Old Blesi mended his pace, for he knew that beyond the next ridges the
cart track to our farm wound gently from the broad highway. I made no
attempt to hold him back, for there was nothing to wait for, my pending
misfortune not to be escaped. And I was on the point of collapse when I
came upon a heavily laden truck that had broken down en route to the east.
I cannot say why I should have suddenly felt lighter and my heart beat faster
than before. It may have occurred to me that here was a last chance of re-
deeming my blunder, for all at once I was filled with an impudent boldness,
drew up, and bade the truck driver good-day.

He looked up from the open engine, high shouldered and with oily
hands, threw down a wrench and seized a pair of pliers instead, curtly acknowledged my greeting, and carried on with his repair work without interruption. I knew the man slightly—had seen him before at one time or another—for he was well known and a popular figure in the district. He lived
a long way off and for the previous two years had handled all the major
transportation for the district, the local school, and the hotel—his willing-
ness and efficiency being a byword. I was sure that he hadn't recognized me,
ignored his coldness, and grew bolder.

Is it a bad breakdown? I asked.

He did not answer me but swore angrily at the pliers, tightened one nut, loosened another, and sighed heavily as though all this effort was to little purpose.

Do you want a padlock? I asked hopefully. I can sell you a splendid padlock.

He behaved as though he hadn't heard my words, but a thoughtful expression came over his face, as if he might be considering them. Also, he employed the pliers more deliberately than before and fingered a number of wires and leads with circumspection.

It's a new padlock, I said. It only costs two kronur.

Where have you come from? he asked without looking up.

The village, I replied.

And where do you live?

Before realizing it, I had recourse to a falsehood and named a farm in the next parish. I had never been to this farm, never even set eyes on it. On the other hand, I had heard various accounts of a famous ghost that had taken up residence there two years before and tormented the occupants so relentlessly that there was talk of their moving away. It seemed to me self-evident that the man would sympathize with a boy who lived in such awful circumstances. But when he suddenly looked at me with suspicion and astonishment, my courage drained away and I drooped, guilty and dejected.

Well, now, is that so? he said, drawling the syllables. Laying down the pliers, he wiped his hands on the legs of his trousers. I happen to be going there, too, so perhaps I'll be seeing you. It's odd, though, that I've never run into you before, old man, if it's a fact that you're my cousin's son!

He gathered his tools together and after a short silence added, If I were you, I'd hurry home, old man. Push off home. And I'd try and get out of the habit of tricks of that kind in the future—because truth is always the best policy. What do you think? Don't you agree?

I could give him no answer. I just shook the rein and let old Blesi trot on along the highway and, soon after, pick his way home by our stony, puddled cart track. The sky grew heavy, and clouds piled up over the rim of the mountain, while the marshes mourned the golden mists of morning and the gusty breeze had long since broken the mirrors of the river. I crouched in my saddle and wept in silence, for no tears could wash away my misery and humiliation. I was wicked, utterly wicked, disgraced and devoid of honor, robbed of joy and hope. I had ignored the advice of my parents, lost my bearings totally in the outside world, lied to strangers, and betrayed the harps of sunset. Nevermore would I sit in a corner by the dim light of an oil lamp and try to transfer the sunshine in the meadows to my exercise book nor tell of the flowers and blades of grass in the dew of a spring night nor compose verses on the little, bright, soft, and swiftly moving tufts of cloud that played tag with one another in the warm breeze of early summer. Nevermore would I want to describe the call of the whooper swans on a still evening nor the swirling current of the river nor the woods beyond it, for I was no longer pure enough to serve beauty. If ever I took pencil in hand again, it would only be to record the darkness of sorrow, cold and silent.

I forced old Blesi off the cart track and rode up to the bank above the pool in the hollow below the cluster of hummocks, where I had sometimes lain stretched out in fine weather and fished for parr, happy and carefree. Unbuttoning the waterproof, I took the padlock from my pocket and flung it into the water. Through my tears I saw it glitter and gleam until it vanished among the pale green and brown undulating growth of the stream bed. But as it vanished, I suddenly remembered that I was deprived even of the possibility of recording the darkness of sorrow, since I had no paper.

CRYING ON AN AUTUMN MORNING

Today I have been thinking about some crying that I heard many years ago. It was strange crying. I heard it on a still autumn morning, when the sky was overcast and a profound, melancholy peacefulness hung over the land and all was fading and withering, taking leave and dying. I remember still how certain I felt that I would preserve that autumn morning in my memory and retain its sadness in my heart to my last hour, for I myself seemed abandoned to some kind of a fading and withering as we waited for the country bus and had nothing to give each other at parting. I thought that I should never see another happy day nor ever forget how we looked alternately down at the ground before our feet and across the heather on the moor or at the thickets on the ridges beyond, where the colors of transience were like a dull, expiring fire, on the point of extinction. I thought that my feelings beside the silent, provocative highway would never become clouded with the mist of time, still less merged with the past like a leaf with mold, giving place to other feelings, other experiences. I was so young and sensitive. Or to be more exact, so immature. Today, on the other hand, I am convinced that I would have long ago forgotten that autumn morning, forgotten the parting with my friend by the highway, forgotten the colors of transience in the heather and thickets, if an old woman had not crouched on the ground and begun crying.

We had walked in silence along winding trackways, where the night frost, bluish in its transparency, had not yet thawed in the deepest and clearest hoofprints. He walked in front, I behind him. The weather was neither warm nor cold, but every now and then we detected a cool fragrance in the air, especially when the track cut through areas of closely growing bush or thicket, where the leaves tumbled, faded, onto the moss and the branches were left half-naked and dripping. Every time I drank in that cool autumn smell I dreaded the return journey alone, back over those long, winding tracks, when I had finished saying good-bye to my friend and had to turn homeward. My friend was going away. He was not turning back, in spite of the words of ill omen and remonstrances of some of his relatives, but was going to seek his fortune in a strange place and try to become a great man, while I was just seeing him on his way, going a little beyond the home field so that I could talk with him in private and wish him good luck on his journey. He was leaving empty-handed, but I felt quite sure that he would become a great man.

You have come much too far, he said in a stiff, colorless voice when we had been following the trackways for an hour and had only a short distance to go to reach the road. It's a shame to drag you all this way.

No, I said in a voice like his. It isn't every day that I come up here with you.

Perhaps we shall be seeing each other soon down south, he said cautiously, and glanced over his shoulder as if to comfort me. Who knows whether I won't be able to find you something to do down south?

Now, in the slump? I asked hesitantly, and tried once again to repel the certainty that I would never be able to run away from my obligations, if, as seemed most unlikely, he should happen to find me a job down south.

There won't always be a slump, he said. One must look on the bright side.

He had said these same words many times before, always looking at me with a smile as if to give me courage and teach me to defy all obstacles, but this time they sounded to me strange and hollow in the clear stillness that seemed waiting for just one sharp, wintry downpour to extinguish the last flame in the bushes. I could not avoid the suspicion that he was no longer encouraging me but answering the clouds that lay over the land or the red leaves that tumbled down onto the moss, for he neither smiled to me nor stepped out of the narrow track so that I could walk beside him and talk to him about the future. In reality he had already taken leave of me and those dreams that had linked us together since childhood and circumscribed our world within a single horizon. He had broken out of all his bonds and determined to set out into uncertainty, with no support but his own belief in himself and his plans: he was going to become a great man.

Later we stood by the main road, chewing cattail that had lost all juice and flavor. We waited for the country bus, and we both found that we had nothing to give each other at parting. It was as though the stillness around us became heavy with this dismal knowledge and strictly forbade us to say a word. We just looked alternately down at the ground before our feet and across the heather on the moor, or at the thickets on the ridges beyond, where the colors of transience clustered and melted one into another. I remember that before we parted I thought something after the fashion that I should never see another happy day or forget my feelings at that time when our horizon cleaved in two.

At last he broke the silence, pointed to the north and said, Here comes the bus!

I took the withered cattail from my mouth and stared to the north too, until I caught sight of the light gray country bus in the far distance, where it tore along the highway with fateful speed, vanished into shallow declivities only to reappear on long, convex ridges, raced though the fading bushes with cold, merciless singleness of purpose, increased in size and distinctness, and drew steadily nearer to us friends, who no longer had the same horizon, the same world.

Well, I said awkwardly, now you'll be going.

Yes, he said, and nodded. I shall be in Reykjavik this evening.

Are you looking forward to it? I asked.

Of course, he replied, and did not take his eyes off the bus. Of course I am looking forward to it.

You are sure to be able to find some sort of work down south, I continued. This slump can't last forever.

No, he said, one must look on the bright side.

I got myself another cattail, chopped it apart between my teeth, and at once spit out the tasteless stalk. The bus had drawn so near that we could hear the hum of the engine when it drove up out of the dips between the ridges, where the leaves tumbled from the thickets and left the branches half-naked and dripping. I myself seemed abandoned to some kind of fading and withering.

You ought to have come too, my friend said in an unnaturally loud voice, and snatched his bundle up from a grass hummock to be sure not to forget it. You ought just to have torn yourself away.

It's not possible, I answered dully. I can't now.

But when do you expect to come? he asked, and shifted the bundle to the pit of his arm.

I don't know, I replied. Perhaps you'll send me a line soon?

Yes, he said readily, and prepared to wave to the bus, which was filling the morning peace with an ever-increasing roar and rattle. I shall write you a long letter when I have got myself fixed up.

And do you think you will be able to find me a job?

Definitely, he replied.

I had intended to confide something to him on parting, but found it difficult to put it into words on the spur of the moment and, what was more, had no chance to think about it. The country bus had barely stopped when an old woman half fell out of it and staggered to the side of the road as though she was blind. A young woman of about thirty with a painted mouth and shining clips in her hair followed after her and said, It will be better for you to sit down here on the grass, Mamma.

Oh, dear Lord, moaned the old woman, and was sick where she stood. Dear Lord, she repeated between retches and groped in the air with her hands. Hold my forehead, Sigridur, I am falling.

She collapsed on the side of the road after bringing up all the food she had eaten before starting her journey. I saw that she had eaten wheat cake and had not had time to chew it properly, for some of the lumps were the size of a five-aurar piece. She took a white handkerchief from her skirt pocket and clutched it in her blue, trembling hand but had no mind to wipe her mouth.

You'll get all muddy, Mamma, said her daughter. Try to sit on the grass here off the road.

I can't, said the old woman. I'm so dizzy.

Of course you can, said her daughter. I shall support you.

But when she had sat down on the grass she began once more to retch and asked for water to drink. I got a rusty can from the driver, ran to a nearby brook, filled the can, and hurried to the old woman. She wiped the rim with her handkerchief and then raised it to her sunken, toothless mouth and drank a few drafts. There was a moldy smell about her worn, threadbare country dress, and in addition the mud of the road had spotted her skirt and dirtied her sleeves below the elbows. I ought never to have come, Sigridur, she moaned reproachfully. They can't do anything for me down south.

Don't carry on so, Mamma, her daughter said, and she looked in turn at us and at the driver, as if asking us to pay no attention. You'll soon be better.

She arranged the clips in her hair, smiled awkwardly, and sniffed. Try and stand up Mamma, she said, bending over her. We must not make the driver wait any longer for us.

They can't do anything for me down south, whispered the old woman. I want to go home.

Don't be so tiresome, Mamma, her daughter said. Can't you see that the men are waiting for us?

I want to go home, whispered the old woman again and again, and then she lay on the ground, huddled herself together, and began crying. She cried softly and weakly and tried to hide her face in blue, trembling hands, and in the agony in her movements was a fragment of the defeat of a whole generation. I had never heard such crying before. It was as if all autumn mornings, with their heavy clouds and uncertain clearness, had united in it or chosen it for an accompaniment to the colors of transience and the soft, dying leaf that frees itself from the branch and falls silently down onto the moss. It was as though she were telling us the story of her life in her crying and showing us that her travels were over long ago, that they had never really been travels at all, that it was all just a misunderstanding and foolishness, no one could do anything for her anywhere on earth, it was best for her to go home. We stood over her in silence for a good while and listened to her crying, but when she had told us her life story to the end and did not have any tears left for the withered grass, we supported her to the bus and lifted her carefully to her seat. I didn't remember that I had forgotten to wish my friend a good journey until the bus had vanished in the distance. I found it so strange that he should be traveling with that old woman.

CRYING ON AN AUTUMN MORNING

Today I have been recalling all this, as so many times before. And it never enters my mind to reproach my friend, though he hasn't troubled to send the letter which I have been awaiting for many years and which I still have not given up all hope of getting some time in the future, when he has become a great man. But perhaps his negligence about writing is due to the effect of the company in which he launched out into life, of the company of that generation which had done with all its travels and knew that they could do nothing for it down south.

The Hand

Upstairs, in the attic, there lived an old woman, though I did not know her name. If I woke early, I heard her footsteps as she crept downstairs. They were quiet, humble footsteps, so I concluded that her philosophy of life consisted mainly in not causing too much noise in the world. Also I occasionally met her on the staircase when she was coming home in the evening. The stairs were both steep and narrow, and she was always the one who drew aside, shrinking against the wall and trying to make herself as small as possible. In this she succeeded remarkably well: I hardly saw her. In fact she appeared to have had considerable practice in drawing aside.

Once, for my own amusement, I drew aside on the stairs for her. I stood still, waiting for her to continue. But the old woman stood still too. She did not move but waited as I did.

Aren't you coming? I asked, impatient.

But she shook her head, this novel courtesy being beyond her comprehension.

She was small and bent. When she looked up—which did not happen often—I saw an infinite weariness in her dark eyes. Her face was expressionless and impersonal, her complexion gray, her hair thin and wispy. She had no characteristics that assigned her to any particular group. She was one of those many persons to be found everywhere on earth. In fact her existence seemed to me of no significance. I had no idea where she came from, what she did, or whether she had lived up there in the attic all her life. But somebody told me that she had a son, a fine lad, who was at sea.

Then something happened that brought us closer together—something

THE HAND

which was the occasion, many years later, of my composing several pieces which I called "Songs of the Old Woman."

During the first few weeks of my lodging in that house, everything went well. I managed to make ends meet, I was feeling at my best, I surveyed the road ahead with optimistic eyes. But alas, the favorable breeze did not hold for long. My money gradually ran out, my friends gradually ran out, my prospects became doubtful, so that I often had trouble sleeping at night. I would pace the floor, back and forth. The night was still. The empty silence swallowed up every thought, every breath.

To sit by the window and watch what was happening in a house on the other side of the street became my favorite pastime. In the mornings I saw a portly housewife busy in the kitchen. She handled plates and pans with complete confidence, smiled at her amusing thoughts, and waddled into the dining room from time to time. She was herself a sort of dining room. But in the evenings my chief interest was focused on a ground-floor window. Here there lived a young man who seemed determined to enjoy life. He did not go to bed early, I am glad to say, but what was more important to me, I could never tell when he was going to turn out the light. There were even occasions when he did not turn it out at all and it burned all through the night.

I resolved to count up to five thousand, and made a wager with myself that my neighbor would switch off his light before I reached that figure. I shut my eyes and began counting. I divided myself in two: one to count, the other to watch and make sure that the rules were observed.

But when the count was getting close to four thousand, I could not refrain from opening my eyes a fraction, just to see if the light was still on. If it was, I counted more slowly, until I got to four thousand five hundred. Then I opened my eyes for a split second, so that the umpire should not see, and after that added three hundred, counting the last tens very slowly, determined to win.

But my neighbor on the far side of the street had in all likelihood no idea of his importance to me. Either he had been very badly brought up or his landlady was very intolerant, for one fine day I saw a new face at the ground-floor window. This was a middle-aged old maid, dried and wrinkled. She switched the light off punctually at ten o'clock every evening.

After this I began to take more notice of the old woman. I noticed in particular that she was bolder and more cheerful when the weather was calm and fine, but on stormy nights she would often chant to herself the night through. I crept closer to her door and eavesdropped furtively. She did not sing any particular tune with any particular text but snatches of many tunes and snatches of many texts. There was a strangely mournful tone to her voice, with a strain of profound yearning and vague dread. I felt convinced she was unhappy, but in spite of this felt no sympathy for her. I had too many troubles of my own.

What? A knock at the door, and past midnight?

Before I have time to say, Come in, the door is pushed open . . . and a hand appears. In its palm there is a small piece of chocolate, and a shy voice whispers, Please take this. I take the piece of chocolate automatically, forgetting to say thank-you. I am unable to get a word out, so astonished am I.

The hand vanishes, the door is closed, and soft, humble footsteps are heard outside on the landing. Then all is silent.

After this, whenever I was feeling at my worst, when insomnia, loneliness, and poverty were almost overwhelming me, without fail there would be a knock at the door—three taps—and the hand would appear. In its palm there was always something to please me. The old woman seemed to sense the times when my need for sympathy was greatest. But she took good care to shut the door before I could shake her hand in gratitude. I cannot remember ever having thanked her.

It is affirmed in many world-famous novels, and is also the belief of many world-famous people, that the eye is the window of the soul. But this is not altogether correct. It is much easier to see people's innermost nature if you take careful note of their hands. Some have fine white hands with long slender fingers, and perhaps painted nails. But closer consideration of the movement of the thumb, or the relationship between the middle finger and the rest, may sometimes lead you to conclude that they are miserly hands, selfish and grasping hands that will never try to help you in your direst need.

The old woman's hand was not a fine one. It was a misshapen hand, red and swollen from hot wash water. The world had been boiling it for many years—five fingers that bore witness to an unlimited resignation to life, ready to give its last mite, in its poverty to bestow all that it had.

During the week before Christmas there was a violent storm, the wind howled fiercely, and iron sheets flew from the roofs of houses. That night there was a knock at my door on three occasions. Three times the hand brought me a gift. It was shaking. I had acquired a remarkable aptitude for understanding the state of mind of the old woman: I could see from her hand how she was feeling. This night I knew that she was unusually upset. I knew that clumsy words of consolation would have no power to cure her sleeplessness, so I said nothing.

And Christmas Eve arrived. The skies were inscrutable: dark clouds sailing a curved course. I had cherished hopes that a little composition at which I had been working for some time might please certain people and ease my struggle for existence. But those hopes were disappointed. I wandered home, gloomy and dispirited. For some time I had been unable to pay the electricity bill, and the current had been disconnected. It was cold in my room. In addition, the evening was not moonlit and glittering with frost as all Christmas Eves should be; instead, small drops of rain fell constantly on the windowpanes, and the distant sound of breakers could be heard. After a while the wind would begin to rise.

I lay on my couch and listened as though in a trance to the peals of bells that solemnly penetrated the raw winter air: dong-ding, dong-ding. I did my best to take this Christmas with composure, invented two talkative characters to recall my most amusing and cherished memories. But that did not work. The characters soon fused into one and fell silent. The darkness became even darker.

Then something happened that I shall long remember: the hand appeared at the door. It was holding a flaming blue Christmas candle, and shaking. But when I got to my feet, the old woman came in herself, set the candle on the table, and handed me a neat package. She waited, looking shyly about her, and finally perched herself on my apology for a chair. The candle flame cast a flickering glow on her face and hair, reddening the room with its light.

I began to fumble with the package. There was a little card attached to it, and on this was scrawled in a hand that bore witness to a life without schooling, Happy Christmas, dear Nonni, from Mamma. I read this several times over before realizing that the old woman must have made a mistake: the package was not for me. I looked at her in wonder and the question, Why? was on my lips. But the old woman who seemed not to notice anything must have read my thoughts. The corners of her mouth began to quiver. Turning away, she huddled in the shadows, covered her face with her hands, and wept soundlessly in the silence.

There was no need for me to ask the question. I understood why.

THE BLIND BOY

M y friend had asked me to compose the tune within a week. Now ten days had gone by since he gave me the words of the hymn, but I had not been able to make anything of it. It is hard to be an unsuccessful composer and have nothing but an ancient, inadequate harmonium that has sounded quite out of tune from the very start. I am inclined to believe that no lot on earth can be harder.

My friend was a schoolteacher in his fifties, bald, shortsighted, and punily built. He had written a Christmas carol that commenced with the memorable words

> Hear the church bells ringing
> For the holy season.

He possessed unlimited faith in me, covered me with praise, asked me to compose a tune to the carol, and promised me twenty kronur in payment. He added, moreover, that the tune should be ready in five or six days, a week at the most, but now the time was up. I had proved no more equal to the task than was usually the case; I had given up. The fact was that my friend intended to let the schoolchildren sing the carol on Christmas Eve, and perhaps a prominent person would be present, an influential and distinguished official who had an appreciation for the fine arts. Did I know that the post of headmaster was vacant? The headmaster had died a fortnight ago.

Good heavens, I said to myself, and paced the floor feverishly. Twenty kronur at stake—and still you can't composes a little tune for a little hymn! I ran my eyes over the unfinished symphonies that littered my table like flotsam, tried to screw up my courage, and thought something after this fashion: that I ought surely not to be at a loss to compose a little tune for a simple little carol when I had already scored rough drafts for all these complicated and unfinished symphonies.

But there were so many things to distract me. I was always looking out the window and wishing that the view were a little more beautiful and more imposing. I was convinced that the tune would have been born in my soul a long time ago if I had been able to see the mountains across the bay. But I saw only a gray sky, a gray gable end, and a gray yard. It is true that the sky was sometimes blue and the shadows under the gable assumed many and various shapes, but the yard was consistently ugly and depressing, full of filth and rubbish from the neighbors, a chosen dwelling place for rats and bacteria. Sometimes weedy children played in the yard, but their games seemed to be robbed of all joy among the dirt and rubbish. They began with frolics and laughter, soon changed to taking sides and disagreement, and always ended in fighting, sobbing, and screaming.

I turned from the window, stretched myself out on the couch, and thought about the carol. But my thoughts would not stick to the subject. I suddenly remembered that I had once again promised my cousin to pay off part of a considerable debt. I might expect him at any time. What was more, the mother of the blind boy had followed my advice and taken her son to the new eye specialist who had arrived here the previous autumn from a long course of study abroad and at once become famous for his knowledge and endowments. They probably now sat in his waiting room holding hands and huddling against each other, silent and solemn. Probably both their hearts beat with the hope that I had so thoughtlessly awakened. What a mad suggestion! Why had I interfered in their affairs? Why had I not left them in peace? I would have done better to have concentrated on the tune which I had promised the schoolteacher!

The blind boy's mother lived in the next room. I had often heard her voice through the thin partition when she talked to her son, I had met her in the passage or on the terrace outside the house, I knew that she was a widow, that she managed by sewing and taking in laundry, but I hardly knew her— and I had no right to concern myself with her life or the blind boy's life, for

THE BLIND BOY

I was only an unsuccessful composer. In her son's hearing, I had asked her whether she had let the new eye specialist examine him: perhaps the blindness was only due to some trifling film, perhaps the film could be removed by an operation, who knew but the boy might yet see the light of day and the skies again. At all events she should go to the new eye specialist and find out whether he considered there to be any possibility of her boy's getting the sight which God had forgotten to give him.

I repeated this several times without realizing what an effect my suggestion produced on the mother and son, especially the son. But when I decided finally to let the matter drop it was too late, for the mother had made up her mind to speak to the new eye specialist. They had determined to go yesterday, but had shrunk from going out in the wind and rain. Perhaps the weather would be better tomorrow, the mother said when they went to bed the night before. We'll slip over and see him tomorrow, God willing.

I wished heartily that I had never mentioned this famous new doctor, and to tell the truth, I didn't feel too good when they left the room half an hour ago, for I knew where they were going. I had never been so conscious of how wretched a composer I was as when they went out.

Yes, perhaps I could have managed to compose a tune for the schoolteacher's carol and earned some money for Christmas if I had lived in some other house, preferably in a tower where I could see across to the mountains on the other side of the bay and be inspired by all kinds of flights of imagination instead of bothering my head about a blind boy and a miserably poor widow of forty-five, large boned and weary, who took in laundry and knitted and sewed for strangers. Perhaps life would have been easier and happier for me if I had been endowed with those qualities that steel men against all the effects of a gray, shadowy, and distasteful yard where weedy children range themselves into hostile parties and end their games in screams and tears. For instance, I am sure that I shall never forget my strange emotion when I saw the blind boy for the first time. He stood outside in the doorway in the pale autumn sunshine, moved his lips as though talking to himself, stepped away hesitantly from the threshold, and felt his way beside the house until the wall ended. Then he turned, felt his way back to the door, paused on the threshold, groping out into the pale autumn sunshine, and then vanished into his mother's room, to wait there alone in the darkness until she returned from her washing and toiling. Never before had I seen such a solitary and helpless child. He was only twelve years old, small and thin, with dark brown, shining hair, pale, clear features, and little, delicate hands that seemed made to pick flowers. His every movement was like a question. I listened often when he talked about the world with his mother, for I could hear every word through the partition. He had very strange ideas about the world, different from the ideas of one who can see. He thought that the sun was always directly in front of people, and could not perfectly understand why it did not shine at night.

Mamma, he said, does the sun have to sleep like we do?

Yes, answered his mother. Certainly it has to sleep.

He thought that the stars were only a short way above the earth; perhaps it was possible to grasp them in the palm of one's hand if one climbed to the rooftop and stretched on tiptoe. He thought that the earth was all soft and sweet scented in the summer like the buttercups and dandelions he had stroked with the tips of his fingers in a patch of field somewhere the year before last. He could find no adequate words to express his thoughts, but he was quite sure that the world must be unspeakably beautiful and that as a consequence all men must be unspeakably good and kind. His mother made no attempt to give him a more realistic picture of the world and mankind but assented to his words without remark. That was how it was, she said, just like that. And it seemed very strange to me.

At that moment someone knocked at the door. My cousin limped into the room, bent and weary with age, perched himself on the creaking chair with his stick between his knees, indicating his distress with a long sigh, and shook his head.

Well, my boy, he said, what have you got in hand now?

I give organ lessons twice a week, I replied.

Do you make anything from that? he asked.

Very little, I replied. Very little.

You surely work more than two hours a week, you a man of thirty-two?

I stood up and showed him my unfinished symphonies, but he hardly looked at them.

Does this dabbling bring anything in for you? he inquired dryly.

I was going to explain to him that one day these unfinished symphonies might be considered of some value, but then he noticed the schoolteacher's

Christmas carol. He snatched up the paper and peered for a while at the writing, frowning irritably.

And what might this be? he asked after a short silence, pointing to the paper with a knotted, quivering forefinger.

It's a Christmas carol. I was asked to write a tune for it.

Will you get anything for that? Will you be paid for it?

Twenty kronur, I hurried to reply.

Twenty kronur! repeated my cousin and quickly put the carol back on the table. I suppose you have finished the tune?

No, I answered, looking at my feet, and I moved into a corner. There is a blind boy in the house here.

Eh . . . what? asked my cousin.

I have been thinking about this blind boy, I muttered. And I have been thinking, too, about you . . . Do you have a kitten?

A kitten! exclaimed my cousin, quite at a loss. Have you gone raving mad, boy?

I do so want to give him a kitten, I said tearfully. I know that he would like to have a kitten.

There is no helping you, he groaned, and he stood up, clasped the knob of his stick with a trembling hand, and made ready to leave. I can see that you are not exactly rich at present. I shall look in after the new year.

And he was gone. He had demanded no money, used no hard words, nor given me to understand that I would never be anything but a useless idler, a vexation both to myself and to others. I blessed him in my heart and seized the schoolteacher's carol, read it carefully from beginning to end, and racked my brains furiously for some melody to fit the lifeless, clumsy words. But my mind was all at sixes and sevens and could by no conceivable means discover a tune for the schoolteacher. I am sure that he would like to have a kitten, I said aloud, and put down my pen after crossing out the scrawl on the music sheet. I am sure that he wouldn't find it so lonely in the darkness if he had a kitten beside him. A kitten—one can cuddle it, stroke it, feel its softness. One can forget pain and grief by holding a kitten against one's cheek.

Suddenly I remembered afresh that they had gone to the eye specialist on my advice. One evening a fortnight ago I had been pacing up and down thinking, or rather humming something for my own amusement and recalling various treasured memories. I had forgotten to light the lamp and put off drawing the curtains. I saw clear stars glittering above the gable, and a bright silver moonbeam fell across my table, onto my unfinished symphonies. A thin white layer of snow covered the yard, and all was so still and quiet and friendly that I could not resist playing the harmonium in the dusk. I played one piece after another and did not notice that I was no longer alone in the room. But when at last I perceived the little dark shadow at my side, I sprang to my feet and struck a light.

The dark shadow was none other than my neighbor, the blind boy. He stood there with his arms crossed, staring silently into his own world and smiling. He had been sitting in the darkness like myself, for he had not needed to light any lamp, and his mother was out somewhere knitting, sewing, or washing for strangers.

I cleared my throat several times, and the blind boy motioned with his hand and said:

I beg your pardon. I heard you playing . . .

He spoke like a grown-up and inclined his head courteously. I knocked on the door, but you probably did not hear me. You were playing . . .

That's all right, that's all right, I mumbled.

He stretched out a white, semitransparent hand that seemed made to pick flowers. It was so beautiful, he said. Where are you?

He made his way forward slowly in the darkness and again asked where I was, but I was so overcome with emotion that I lost all power of speech.

Here you are, he said when at last he found me, and he stroked my face, stroked my shoulders, fumbling and searching, until I took his thin, weak hand.

Thank you, he said. It was so beautiful . . . Good night.

Then he felt his way out of the room like a living shadow. But when his mother returned home shortly afterward I went in to them and asked her, in her son's hearing, whether she had let the new eye specialist examine him. It was not unthinkable that he might get his sight; for example I had read in a foreign paper that a blind man of sixty had been completely cured by a comparatively simple process. So stupid and thoughtless I was that I repeated this to her two or three times, until they decided to follow my advice. And somehow I suspected that they had both turned to God and prayed to him for mercy and help before setting out.

There was a knock at the door.

My friend the schoolteacher bustled into the room, bald and short-sighted, brandished his handkerchief, and wiped the mist from his spectacles—unable to decide whether he should sit or stand—and quite forgot to greet me.

Have you finished the music? he asked between hope and fear. I told him the position: that I had not managed to do it yet in spite of repeated attempts. Besides the words were stiff and awkward beyond all measure:

> Hear the church bells ringing
> For the holy season.

The meter was far too cold and abrupt. How on earth did he imagine that I could compose music for a carol with such a ragged opening? It would be another matter if he could change the meter to something along these lines:

> Hear how the church bells are ringing
> The holy season in . . .

No, no, out of the question, he interrupted, shaking the spectacles on his nose. I suspected really that you would not get this done. But I have something else for you! Look here!

He plunged his hand into his coat and drew out an immense document. It was a New Year's hymn that he had composed the previous day, a hymn of staggering length and prolixity. He said that the Christmas carol would not be sung this time since I had let him down over the music and there was no time left, no time to rehearse the children for Christmas Eve, but if I could produce a good tune for the New Year's hymn by the next morning he would pay me generously, he would give me twenty-five kronur. He even took out his purse and fingered some worn banknotes to confirm his words.

Did you write this yourself? I inquired solemnly.

Of course! he replied quickly, and he shook his spectacles again, arched his back, and touched his yellow skull. Of course!

I brightened considerably, pretended not to see his purse, and hastened to assure him that my inspiration had taken a new lease on life. I should certainly have no difficulty in composing a tune for such an exquisite New Year's hymn:

> Hear, the New Year's bells are ringing!
> Come, my children, all are singing
> With Hosanna here and there . . .

What a genius! I rushed to the harmonium and played a few bars to convince him that I was instantly filled with the spirit. The music could begin like this, for example, I said with a flourish of the hands.

Indeed it could! he said, delighted, and added that it would be a real pleasure to him to pay me the twenty-five kronur now. He would just slip in the next morning to get the music.

Then he handed me the notes without a moment's hesitation and, lowering his voice, asked whether it would be the same to me if my name were not associated with this unborn composition.

Good heavens! I replied, you can have the tune! You are very welcome to say that you composed it yourself!

He thanked me heartily, winked, and gave me a roguish look in which foolishness was united with cunning. He intended to make the children sing the hymn at three o'clock on New Year's Day, and perhaps a prominent person would be present, an influential and distinguished official who could appreciate the fine arts. Had he told me that the post of headmaster was vacant? The headmaster had died about three weeks ago . . .

When he had taken leave of me I paced the floor excitedly, as full of self-confidence as a millionaire. Never had such honor been shown me before! Never before had anyone displayed such a blind faith in my capabilities! He had payed me twenty-five kronur in advance! I was a plutocrat; I was the richest man in the world! And I should certainly take great pains with the music for the New Year's hymn. He would certainly not be disappointed a

The Blind Boy

second time. It was going to be exceptional music, a contrapuntal pattern of clear, crystalline tones, like a hundred silver bells ringing in the moonlight.

But as the evening light was fading outside my window and dusk beginning to fill the sky, just as the music for the schoolteacher's New Year's hymn was on the point of taking shape, I heard the sound of movement on the other side of the partition.

The mother and son had returned from the eye specialist.

I heard her ask him if he wouldn't like a fruit drop: these fruit drops were uncommonly good and sweet. Besides she had bought him a little mouth organ at the shop on the corner; it was a gilt mouth organ in a red case. And I wished with all my heart that she had not mentioned the color either of the mouth organ or the case, for the tone of her voice indicated that the visit to the eye specialist had been without success: the blind boy was never to see the light of day and the world. I could no longer bear to be in my room—I felt responsible for their disappointment—so I snatched my coat from its peg and crept silently out of the house.

Could I not possibly find a kitten to give him?

A kitten can bring comfort to a childish, sorrowful heart.

A kitten can help one forget the world's injustice for a while.

A kitten can ease one's anguish and turn the mind from that darkness which makes life so unspeakably cruel and merciless.

I was on the move from one acquaintance to another late into the night, but none of them had a cat, let alone a kitten, and none appeared to understand why I, an unsuccessful composer, should be so much concerned about some blind wretch who was in no way related to me. I returned home empty-handed when it was approaching midnight, crept carefully into my room, and closed the door. I had no peace in which to think about the schoolteacher's music, for on the other side of the wall the blind boy was crying, locked in endless darkness. His mother was trying to calm and comfort him, but his sobs were so bitter, his grief so profound, that her words had no power to console. Her words seemed to be lost in the ocean of his disappointment and sorrow.

She said, You haven't tried to play your mouth organ yet.

He answered, I shall always be blind.

She said, You haven't tasted the fruit drops I bought for you.

And he answered, I shall never be like other people.

They went on like this for some time. I heard the mother stop her sewing machine and go to him, comfort him, remind him that Christmas would be here in two days, tell him of the spring that would descend over the earth after four months and revive the flowers which died in the autumn, revive the buttercups and dandelions until the grass patches became soft and sweet-smelling once more. I shall pick some flowers for you to put in a vase, she said cheerfully. But her son went on crying.

Soon Mamma and her boy are going to bed. Soon Mamma is going to stop sewing.

I shall always be blind, answered her son.

Perhaps I might try and get us a kitten, she said suddenly. You loved so to stroke the kitten we had the year before last.

No, he answered. I don't want to have a kitten. I shall never be like other people.

After that he could say no more for sobbing. It affected me so strangely that I did not know what to do. I felt that I had been the cause of his disappointment and crying by urging them to talk to the new eye specialist. I felt that I should try to comfort him this evening and make him forget the darkness that closed around him, cruel and endless. I thanked God for the good fortune that I had not managed to find a kitten for him, but I had no idea what I ought to give him instead of the kitten. I had only five kronur of the schoolteacher's money left, for during the course of the evening I had run into two of my friends who had demanded something in the way of repayment. And it was clear to me that the blind boy would not be comforted though I gave him the five kronur that were left. He would undoubtedly go on crying even though I gave him a whole horseload of banknotes.

Suddenly I made a decision. I walked out of the room, knocked at the widow's door, and asked the blind boy whether he wouldn't like to listen to a few tunes. I should try my very best and play only the most beautiful tunes I knew.

He did not reply but tried to check his sobs. He put his head in the crook of his arm and turned in the bed with his face to the wall.

Yes, said his mother, and she stroked a tired palm over the eiderdown. He always likes it so much when the man plays the harmonium.

THE BLIND BOY

I hurried into my room and left both doors open so that the sound should reach him unmuffled. I sat at the harmonium and first played a few pieces by a dead master whom I have loved and worshiped many years. But this evening these pieces did not satisfy the pounding of my heart. I felt somehow that I would be giving away a treasure that was not mine to give if I continued to play them. And before I knew what I was doing I had started to play something extempore. I had started to play something for the blind boy here on earth. A thousand themes ran through me like clear water in sunshine; I was utterly at the mercy of these themes and palpitated with a strange, deep joy that was completely at odds with the consciousness that I was an unsuccessful composer. My old harmonium seemed reborn, for its tones were no longer queer and out of tune but throbbing with a hot, red life that had nothing in common with a gray sky, a gray gable end, or a gray yard. I gave the blind boy from the most hidden and secret resources of my heart, so that he might see a dreamworld, a world of flowers and birds, of roaring waters and blooming forests where the sunshine streamed down at its brightest, gladdest, and most peaceful. I strained every effort to make him see white, soft dream clouds moving across the sky, the water races flashing blue-green, swirling between slippery, moss-covered rocks on a still, warm spring day, see the grass on home field and meadow, wet with dew, veiled in a semitransparent vapor in the early hours of a morning late in June, when the mountains draw one's thoughts to eternity and every stream seems to send a message to the drooping flowers in the plain. Sunset in leaves, sunrise over sleeping waters, the dull red glow of evening on the warm, fertile, scented land—and my blood grew hot and swelled, mingling with the music, melting into the music as I tried with all my might to show him in a dream that world which he had been denied from the beginning.

Thus I continued to play on my harmonium, until I noticed that the blind boy's mother was standing in the door. She stepped forward, looked at me a little curiously, and said in a low voice, It is past one! He went to sleep a long time ago!

I came to myself, supported myself on the harmonium, trembling with emotion, and asked her to excuse me. Perhaps I had been keeping her awake?

No, that was all right, she replied courteously, and explained how her boy had been comforted at once, when he heard the first pieces I had played, the pieces by the master; then he had dropped off to sleep in his bed, in a sudden and deep sleep. Thank you for your thoughtfulness, sir, she said, and nodded to me. Good night.

Good night, I mumbled, confused, and I moved over to the table where my unfinished symphonies lay scattered like flotsam. My eye at once fell on the New Year's hymn of the schoolteacher:

> Hear, the New Year bells are ringing!
> Come, my children, all are singing
> With Hosanna here and there . . .

Dear God! I had promised to write the music for him tonight, he was going to pick it up early the next morning, he had paid me twenty-five kronur in advance!

Suddenly it became clear to me that I would not be able to write music for that hymn tonight, tomorrow, or the day after, though my life had depended on it. I was so tired, so infinitely weary and miserable. I had tried to do my duty toward the blind boy here on earth, but at the same time had destroyed the last vestige of confidence that the world had shown in me, the poor, timid, and unsuccessful composer.

JOURNEY HOME

I

On a chill morning of late February a long-distance bus drove out of a tarmac yard in Reykjavik. There were eight passengers. Four were going east beyond the mountain: a sweet young thing with fair hair sitting by the driver, a dark-browed man in a leather jacket and knickerbockers, a middle-aged farmer with a bushy moustache, and a naïve-looking youth in his early twenties. Behind these sat four skiers who planned to spend the weekend up at the hotel.

The man in the leather jacket lighted a pipe and looked about him. No more passengers? he asked, puffing.

One to come, replied the driver.

Is he going east?

I don't know.

Can we get up to the Sand Flats in this vehicle?

I don't know, replied the driver. Managed to make it yesterday, but it's both snowed and drifted since.

I've got to get over to Olfus by not later than six this evening. Otherwise it's a wasted journey.

The driver did not volunteer any answer to this, so the man in the leather jacket continued, Do you suppose we'll have to wait long for the snowplow? That could be a problem.

I don't know, said the driver. We didn't have to wait long yesterday.

I hope we don't have to wait long now either, said the man in the leather jacket. I have to get over to Olfus by six o'clock this evening.

Some distance along Hverfisgata the bus stopped beside an old, mottled wooden house from whose basement there emerged a disheveled-looking woman, bareheaded and wearing a loose-fitting garment, followed by two children with their fingers in their mouths. A moment later, at their heels, an older woman dressed in a threadbare man's belted overcoat appeared. She was carrying a worn saddlebag in one hand and a paper-wrapped parcel in the other.

Come along now, Mamma, hurry! said the bareheaded one in a shrill voice. Hurry up! Then turning to the driver: You'll see that she gets east beyond the mountain, won't you? She's a bit frightened about traveling, but you'll see that she gets there, won't you?

Before he had time to reply, she had pushed the old woman into the bus, stowed her beside the farmer, and given her a sharp peck on the cheek. Good-bye, Mamma. Have a good trip!

I haven't said good-bye to the children, said the old woman obstinately, and she tried to stand up, but her daughter pushed her back with a frown.

There's no time for that, you know! The bus is leaving, don't you see? Good-bye, Mamma. Have a good trip!

She slammed the door of the bus to prevent any further argument and drove the children before her down the cellar steps. The old woman sagged back in her seat, wrapping her woolen shawl more closely around her head so that little could be seen of her face but a thin, long nose, high cheekbones, and hopeless staring, slightly moist eyes. She sniffed twice as the bus started off.

The man in the leather jacket sighed. Well, he said, and looked at the driver. There are no more passengers, I guess?

No.

And you're going east beyond the mountain, I understand, he remarked to the old woman.

She was silent.

Aren't you going east beyond the mountain?

I'm going home, she said.

Home where?

I've been here for treatment and have got no better. I don't want to go to the hospital, and Jonina can't have me anymore. I'm going home.

The man in the leather jacket shook his head, emptied his pipe, and began to fill it again, while the four skiers all lighted cigarettes. After a short time there was a thick haze of smoke in the bus and the old woman began coughing.

Ai, I can't bear this, she mumbled. I'll be ill if you smoke so much.

The skiers looked at each other half-scowling. There's nothing here that says smoking is forbidden, said one of them.

Put out your weed. We can smoke up at the hotel, said another.

We haven't got there yet, said the third, while the fourth added in a whisper, I don't know what these old women are doing, wandering about in midwinter.

All the same they stopped smoking, and the man in the leather jacket refrained from lighting his newly filled pipe and put it in his pocket.

II

Later on, the country bus reached the valley bottom. Here the wind was fierce, blowing the snow in drifts, and more snow was falling. On one of the inclines the engine stalled, and when started up again, the bus dug itself into the snow, wheels spinning, and stuck fast. The driver jumped out and examined the road ahead, walked some distance along the roadside, then turned back and went to the rear of the vehicle. Finally he got in again and sat at the wheel.

Blocked ahead, he said. We can't go any farther.

Really, it's too bad, said the man in the leather jacket. Shall we get out and give the old heap a push?

There's a deep drift, said the driver. We'll get no farther.

There are enough able-bodied men here, said the man in the leather jacket. Shouldn't we try and shove the old heap up the hill?

The driver smiled sardonically. I'm afraid it wouldn't do much good.

Well, I've got to get across to the east of the mountain by six o'clock, come hell or high water.

The old woman had been sitting in silence beside the farmer, gazing into her hands. Suddenly she gave a start and looked shakily at her companion. What is the man saying? she cried. Jonina can't have me anymore. I have to get home.

The skiers snickered, but the driver was the one who answered. There's no point in trying to struggle on any farther, he said. I think it would be a good idea to go back to the valley and wait there for the snowplow.

Nobody made any reply to this. It was becoming colder in the bus, the mist on the windows getting denser. The skiers fumbled with the zippers of their jackets.

It makes little difference whether the snowplow picks you up here or down in the valley, said the driver.

Turn around, of course, said the skiers. We'll have coffee while we wait.

Is the snowplow expected soon? asked the man in the leather jacket.

It could be delayed with weather like this.

Devil take it all!

The driver bent forward half out of the open door, and the bus jerked, moved slowly backward, and turned on a patch of level ground at the foot of the slope.

In the valley they halted outside a two-story building. It was a restaurant and bore the well-known name of Logberg. The passengers hurried from the bus, first the skiers, then the sweet young thing and the naïve-looking youth. Then the farmer got up from his seat, stroking his moustache in an offhand manner, and climbed across the old woman without remark. The man in the leather jacket, on the other hand, asked her to let him past, but when she ignored his polite request, he did the same as the farmer.

Won't you come inside where it's warm, like the others? asked the driver. You'll be cold if you don't.

I'm used to the cold, mumbled the old woman.

You might catch a chill, said the driver. Why don't you come in where it's warm?

I'm not moving a foot from the bus. I'm not going to be left behind, answered the old woman. I've told you many times that Jonina can't have me anymore.

Oh, very well, said the driver, shrugging his shoulder, and he made no further attempt to persuade her.

One o'clock came, then two. Still there was no sign of the snowplow. The man in the leather jacket paced restlessly around the floor, then turned abruptly to the driver and asked again what was going on.

I don't know, replied the driver. I've just phoned the hotel.

Well?

It's over an hour since he left. He's bound to come any minute now.

Could he have broken down?

It has been known to happen.

The devil it has! exclaimed the man in the leather jacket.

Three o'clock came. Then half past. And finally the long-awaited vehicle appeared, coated with ice and snow. The luggage in the bus was hurriedly transferred to the roof of the snowplow and inside it. The old woman clambered out of the bus and stood silent and trembling beside the strange mechanical monster that was to prevail over the weather and the obstructions of winter to deliver her at the eastern margin of the pass. The worn belted overcoat gaped at her breast, so that she tried to wrap the shawl more tightly, with blue, numbed fingers. Then she bent down, picked up her saddlebag and paper-wrapped parcel from the snow, and waited.

The passengers vanished one by one into the windowless belly of the snowplow and perched side by side on sacks and boxes—all but the sweet young thing, who had already secured herself a place in front beside the driver.

Where am I supposed to sit? asked the old woman.

There was some whispering, and at last the man in the leather jacket spoke in reply. It would be the most sensible thing, my dear, he said in a kindly voice, if you went back to Reykjavik with the bus.

That's right, said one of the skiers. There's no sense in her setting out in weather of this sort.

I've got to get home. Jonina can't have me anymore, said the old woman in a tremulous voice.

What'll become of you if the snowplow breaks down on the way?

You couldn't stand being stuck out in this.

The old woman hesitated for a moment, as though considering their words, then, seeming to have made up her mind, climbed up into the snowplow and asked where she was to sit.

Make room for her, called the driver.

There is no room, damn it, someone replied.

Then let her sit on somebody's lap, called the driver.

The man in the leather jacket suddenly hit on an acceptable solution to the problem. Could the young lady not snuggle up with us here and let the old woman sit in front? he asked.

But the sweet young thing with the fair hair was determined at all costs to stay where she was. Heavens, she said, I shall be carsick at once if I sit in the back.

So that was that. The people crowded close together until they managed to squeeze the old woman into a small slot at the back of the vehicle.

I'm quite comfortable, she answered the driver, arranging the haversack and paper bag on her lap. All right, he said, and slammed the door to.

III

The newfangled vehicle moves to and fro across the white wilderness, crawling on its tracks farther and farther into the swirling blanket of snow, tilting from side to side, but never giving up, though the going is slow. The engine whines and growls, the wiper swings wildly and inexorably across the windshield, clanks and thumps accompany every pitch and roll. A small electric bulb casts a dim light on the faces of the passengers, who seem to have lost their personal characteristics, acquiring an expression of insecurity, even apprehension—a few samples of the human species crammed closely together. Why had they set out on this journey? Why hadn't they stayed in Reykjavik and amused themselves by counting up to 15,728 until nature saw fit to change its crystals into water? They could have eaten Danish pastry, too, and drunk coffee to pass the time, occasionally looking out the window and saying, It'll thaw tomorrow.

The devil take it all, said the man in the leather jacket. It was a matter of the utmost urgency for me to get over to Olfus by six o'clock.

The farmer began to try and draw him out. That's how things are, he said. Some errands are urgent ones.

I should say they are, said the man in the leather jacket.

Can't afford any delay?

Hardly.

A contract, maybe.

Urgent business, said the man in the leather jacket shortly. Urgent business.

The skiers suddenly became noisy. Damn annoying, forgetting it, said one of them.

It doesn't matter, said the second. We can get some up there.

Are you sure?

More or less.

But shark? Do you suppose we can get shark there? asked the third.

Not the best quality, in any case.

You're no judge of that. You're too fussy. You just see if I can't get good shark if I set my mind to it.

Where? Are you going to sniff around in their pantry?

The naïve-looking youth who was going east beyond the mountain could not refrain from putting in a word here. You won't get shark at the hotel, he said. Nor at the ski hut either.

Was anyone talking to you, my lad? inquired one of the skiers. Was anyone asking you for shark? The naïve-looking youth was abashed but tried to treat this as a joke. Luckily, at that moment the sweet young thing with fair hair began crooning a popular song, moreover knowing the Danish words. The farmer glanced occasionally out of the corner of his eye at the man in the leather jacket, solemn and a trifle knowing, as at a purse with many compartments. Perhaps he was thinking to himself that this was an important person, a man of means. En Dag er ikke levet uden Kaerlighed, crooned the sweet young thing once again. The snowplow was filled with fumes, and it was rather cold. Nevertheless, the old woman had stopped shivering now. Her gaunt, emaciated body swayed constantly back and forth. Her half-closed eyes seemed not to be focused on anything in particular. There was no longer any need for her fear that she might be left behind. She was on her way home.

Where are we now? called the man in the leather jacket.

We are coming up to the Sand Flats, answered the driver. It's not easy to see the road, but now it's clearing a little.

IV

It was past six when the snowplow clattered into the forecourt of the hotel at Kolvidarholl. The skiers had now reached their destination and demanded their effects from under the snow-beaten tarpaulin on the roof of the vehicle.

The other passengers hurried inside to gulp down coffee while the fuel tank was filled up and a new driver got himself ready to take over. The naïve-looking youth turned at the entrance to the hotel, ran back to the ice-clad vehicle, and pulled open the door.

Aren't you coming inside to have some coffee?

The old woman was slow in answering. No, she whispered at last.

Are you quite sure?

I don't feel like having anything.

All the same, come inside, where it's warm.

I mustn't be left behind.

There's no danger of that.

I'm not moving, whispered the old woman, somewhat louder. I've got to get home.

Very well, said the simple-looking youth, and he urged her no more.

Ten minutes went by, twenty minutes went by before the sweet young thing with fair hair reappeared and perched herself up in front. The three men who were going east clambered in, one after the other, together with a brisk fellow who was going to assist the new driver if need be. The new driver sat at the wheel, slammed the door shut, started the engine, switched on the headlights, and looked back over his shoulder: All right?

Yes.

The snowplow jerked and started off into the blanket of white, bearing a few samples of the human species in its belly. There was more room inside now: three people fewer, no need to be crammed together. The man in the leather jacket stuffed his pipe with tobacco and addressed the old woman.

You had no coffee at the hotel, he said. You're not spending more than you have to when you travel!

He received no reply beyond an unintelligible murmur.

Do you mind if I smoke? he asked, having already lighted a match.

The old woman was silent. Her face was half hidden by the shawl, and her body seemed to offer no resistance to the jolting and rocking of the vehicle.

I think she's on the point of dropping off, said the man in the leather jacket with a grin. Then, glancing at his wristwatch: Five to seven. Daresay the journey's all for nothing.

What an infernal shame, said the farmer sympathetically. Is that quite certain?

The man in the leather jacket nodded, but then half closed his eyes and sucked at his pipe, as though his thoughts were elsewhere.

They are expensive, these, I daresay, the farmer remarked after a short pause, and he poked the leather jacket with his index finger.

The man seemed not to notice, half closed his eyes and sucked at his pipe as before.

The farmer shifted himself and poked at the leather jacket again. They cost a fair price, these, I daresay, he declared solemnly, clearing his throat.

The man removed the pipe from his mouth and looked down at him with a friendly expression. Were you saying something to me?

Well, I'm curious to know, hmm, what a jacket such as that might cost.

This jacket? It didn't cost much, said the man. It has a top-quality lining and was bought abroad. It cost . . . let's see, wait a moment, yes, it cost about the equivalent of two hundred and thirty Icelandic kronur.

The farmer appeared to have difficulty swallowing: two hundred and thirty kronur!

A first-rate article of clothing. Dirt cheap, considering the quality.

Maybe I've been missed . . . I'll . . . knit . . . a white cap and a red jumper . . . In a strange manner the low quavering voice penetrated the hum of the engine and the rattling and creaking, just as if the words were whispered in the ear and their sound clung persistently to it.

Well, I'll be damned, exclaimed the man in the leather jacket. She's dreaming! She's talking in her sleep!

So it seems, said the farmer.

It's quite extraordinary how old folk can adapt themselves comfortably to travel, said the man in the leather jacket. They sit quietly where they are put, don't worry their heads about anything, and take a nap when the rest of us are sweating our guts out.

The sweet young thing with the fair hair began once again to croon to herself: En Dag er ikke levet uden Kaerlighed.

V

At long last the brow of the Kambar Pass was reached. Here a scheduled bus was waiting to receive the samples of humanity that were on their way eastward, and to deliver others that had to get to the town. (Why had they not stayed at home and counted up to 15,728, waiting for the going to improve?) The storm had finished its symphony, the sky was beginning to clear and the wind to die, stars were twinkling and the moon casting beams on glittering snowdrifts and rounded peaks, on the endless open plains and faint far-off ranges.

You're devilish late, said the driver of the bus from the east.

What do you expect in this weather? replied the other.

The passengers of the snowplow stretched their legs and remarked, Ah well, now we're over the heath. Then they took out their purses and paid the driver, each handing him the money, and shuffled about him relieved, emitting tobacco smoke and repeating, Yes, now we're over the heath. When all had paid their due, the driver recollected himself: Where's the old woman?

I believe she's asleep, said the farmer.

The brisk assistant acted upon this, caught hold of the door handle of the vehicle and called in, No more sleeping now! We're across the heath!

The old woman did not move.

We've reached the top of Kambar! You've got to get into another bus, the man called.

Since the old woman still failed to respond, he climbed inside the vehicle, lifted her up, and carried her outside. When he tried to stand her on her feet, the saddlebag and paper-wrapped parcel fell on the snow.

She won't wake up, he cried in alarm, and laid her gently on the frozen ground with the saddlebag for a pillow.

The moon cast a pale light on the thin, beaklike nose of the old woman, her half-closed eyes and open mouth. In an instant all had gathered around her, both those going east and those going to town. Oh Lord, said the sweet young thing with fair hair, and there was a sob in her throat. Oh Lord! The naïve-looking youth thrust a hand under the belted overcoat of the old woman and felt the left side of her chest.

I can't feel any heartbeat! She's ice-cold!

The man in the leather jacket drew closer as though meaning to make sure that this was right. Perhaps she has fainted, he said. She must be got to Hveragerdi without delay.

The farmer turned to the driver of the snowplow. Has she paid? he asked in a low voice.

No, replied the driver coldly, she didn't pay me.

FIRE

Petur Palmason, retail merchant, shook his head and sighed deeply as he turned the pages of the newspaper. Continued on page eight, he muttered. How on earth is it going to end?

A plump woman in her sixties with red cheeks and a good-natured expression turned restlessly beside him, making the bed creak.

It's past twelve, she said. When are you going to switch off the light?

I'm just finishing this article, he replied absently. It's an ugly situation overall, I must say! Farming, the fisheries, industry, trade . . .

It'll get no better for you keeping me awake, said the woman.

Petur Palmason perused the paper for a while, then began once more to shake his head and sigh.

What's the matter? asked the woman. Are you unwell?

No, he answered with a touch of irritation, I was only thinking about the disastrous overall situation. I'd like to know what they intend to do about it.

Who?

Why, the government, my dear. The government and the National Assembly.

What do you suppose they'll do? she said. I think they're used to this sort of thing. There'll be plenty of wind blown off in the new year!

Petur Palmason considered it unnecessary to acknowledge such unfitting remarks. In fact he had long realized that his wife had no understanding of either politics or political economy. He ran his eyes once more over the concluding words of the article on page eight, then gazed thoughtfully before him.

Well, he murmured, the outlook is anything but glowing. Farming, the fisheries, industry, trade . . . nothing but deficits and mounting debts.

Can we do anything about it? asked the woman.

No, he replied, and put down the paper. No, it's not our fault, he added, at the same time removing his dentures and dropping them into a glass of water on the bedside table. But someone ought to have a sense of responsibility, my dear.

Ai, that everlasting sense of responsibility! said the woman, and she turned over onto her other side. Let's go to sleep!

Yes, my dear, it's high time we did so, said Petur Palmason, and he switched off the light, adjusted the pillow under his head, pulled the quilt up to his chin, and yawned. In a few minutes they were both asleep, in spite of the ugly situation and dubious overall outlook.

He woke maybe a little over an hour later and looked about him in wonder. His wife was breathing heavily beside him, but the room was intermittently filled with a flickering light. Jumping immediately out of bed, he looked out the window and started back in dismay. The house of Nikulas Nikulass, the trawler operator, that beautiful new building on the other side of the street, was on fire. The top story was ablaze.

Petur Palmason popped in his dentures and hurriedly slipped on his trousers and shoes. Without pausing to wake his wife he then dashed downstairs, half-dressed and hatless, threw open the front door, bounded straight across the road, and rang the doorbell of the house of Nikulas Nikulass, the trawler operator. There was no response. The house was locked and bolted, and not a glimpse of light was to be seen in the windows. He rang again and again and then beat on the door with both fists. Fire! he shouted repeatedly. The house is on fire!

Who's that?

Petur Palmason.

Did you say Palmi Petursson?

No, Petur Palmason, the merchant, your neighbor, he shouted. There's a fire on your top floor!

A retail trader, said the voice inside. All nylon stockings finished.

What stockings?

He's not at home, said the voice. He's away.

Don't you understand plain language? yelled Petur Palmason. Your house is on fire!

I have told you, my good Palmi, Nikulas is not at home, said the voice inside. He's away.

What's that? Where has he gone? asked Petur Palmason, and he was so perturbed that he continued to beat on the locked door.

Stop making that racket, said the voice. Nikulas is away. He has gone to Siam-Diam.

What did you say?

He has gone to Siam-Diam. Good night. All nylon stockings finished.

The house is on fire, yelled Petur Palmason. Phone the fire department.

Stop creating a disturbance, said the voice inside. Go to Siam-Diam instead.

Where the devil is that?

Ask the man in the moon, replied the voice.

Petur Palmason looked upward, pale with fury and horror. The roof of the house was blazing fiercely. Yellow tongues of flame reached out from the burst windows and a wolf gray column of smoke coiled endlessly in the light of them, vanishing into the darkness of the night. He could hear the crackle and inrush of air. It was clear that the house would be burned to the ground if the fire company was not summoned at once. The flying sparks would also set fire to the houses of Jonatan Asgeirsson, the bank manager, and Magnus H. J. Arnason, the wholesaler. After that the flames would spread to the wooden houses below and grow to such a magnitude that they could hardly be extinguished. The whole district would be consumed, maybe the whole town. Shops would blaze, fuel tanks explode, the cathedral collapse, banknotes and savings books be turned to dust and ashes. Dear God! Only two days before, Jonatan Asgeirsson, who by the way was a member of the honors committee, had greeted him warmly, walked with him a short way along the street discussing the situation and outlook in the economic affairs of the nation, and said time and again, You're one of the few men who have a sense of responsibility. Those were his very words.

Petur Palmason pulled himself together and ran from the house, ran like a madman down the empty street, jumped a fence to take a shortcut, rushed along passages, across gardens, and down pathways, tore past frost-covered trees, and did not stop until he reached the fire station. To his astonishment, he found the doors securely locked, and no light was to be seen in the windows here any more than elsewhere. It was as though the city was dead.

Who's in charge here? he shouted and began to pound on the doors, even snatched up a piece of iron that lay on the pavement at his feet and rained blows on the massive oaken portal.

What's this all about? inquired a sleepy voice inside.

The house of Nikulas Nikulass, the trawler owner, is on fire, he shouted, shaking all over with his efforts.

Well, I'll be damned, said the voice.

Jonatan the banker's house is in danger, too!

What the blazes? said the voice.

And the house of Magnus the wholesaler!

You're a regular firebrand, aren't you? said the voice. What's your name?

He yelled his name through the keyhole and repeated hoarsely, It's on fire! Nikulas' house is on fire!

You're making me mad, said the voice. Are you a parson?

No, I'm a retail trader! The firemen, for God's sake, the firemen! The roof is ablaze!

A shopkeeper, corrected the voice. The firemen are not here, my dear Palmi, You'll have to fetch them yourself.

Where have they gone? asked Petur Palmason, ignoring the incorrect name. The fire will spread everywhere if it isn't put out at once! My house will catch fire as well!

What can I do about it? said the voice. The firemen aren't here. They've gone to Siam-Diam.

Where is Siam-Diam?

Ask the man in the moon, replied the voice. Ask Namurt to help you. Good night!

Namurt?

Petur Palmason stopped beating on the doors and stood for a moment utterly at a loss on the step of the fire station, half-dressed and perspiring in the cold night air. Involuntarily he glanced upward, and—do you know?— the gable of the building, above his head, was beginning to smoke. The fire station itself was burning. Beyond the chimney a golden red glow filled the sky as flames mounted from the house of Nikulas Nikulass, the trawler owner. Perhaps the residences of Jonatan Asgeirsson, the banker, and Magnus H. J. Arnason, the wholesaler, were already ablaze. Only two days before, the bank manager had said to him, You are one of the few men who have a sense of responsibility. Those were his very words.

God almighty help us all, whispered Petur Palmason, shaking and trembling from head to foot, and the piece of iron fell from his grasp and rang on the pavement. The police, he thought, and he started running. The police will have to take action.

He had become strangely weak in the knee joints and ran half-bent through the silent street, gasping for breath, with his knees giving way at every step as though weighed down by a heavy burden. The shops were as dark as the dwelling houses. Not a soul was to be seen outside, not a glimmer of car lights. When he had only a short way to go to the police station, three questionable characters carrying large bottles of spirits rushed out at him and drove him into an alley.

Let me go! he cried. Let me go!

You'll never get to Siam-Diam, they said. You're so old!

I'm going to get the police, he groaned. There's a fire!

We are young, they said. We're going to Siam-Diam.

He tried to slip past, but they intercepted him, waving their bottles.

Let me by! I order you to let me by, he said. I'm getting the police!

I say, one of them asked, what do you have in your bag?

Bag? he queried, surprised, but at the same instant noticed that he was holding a small gray bag and that it was unbelievably heavy.

Just wait a minute, old man, they said, and they opened the bag. They took out of it a set of *Sagas of Icelanders,* leather-bound, *The Hymns on the Passion,* Jon Vidalin's *House Readings,* the *Poems* of Matthias Jochumsson, a collection of folktales, a book of heroic lays, an ancient Bible which Petur Palmason had inherited, and finally, a pair of knit gloves in three colors, with an ornamental pattern, which his mother had given him when he was confirmed nearly forty-nine years ago.

They were seized with a fit of uncontrollable laughter:

Ha ha ha, he's a funny one!

FIRE

After that they fastened the bag again and strapped it on Petur Palma-son's back.

Reverend sir, they said grinning, we bid you good-bye.

He took to his heels and ran from the alley. Soon after, he was standing outside the police station. There was a light in the window, thank God. He rushed breathlessly up the stone steps and would have thrown open the door, but it was locked.

Devil take it, he exclaimed, and pounded on it with all his might until a ghostly voice from within inquired what all the noise was about.

The house of Nikulas Nikulass is on fire, he shouted.

I know, said the voice.

The bank manager's house is in danger!

I know, said the voice.

The fire station itself is on fire!

I know, said the voice.

You must help! My wife could be burned alive!

We are leaving, said the voice. There are only two of us left.

Leaving? For where? Petur Palmason asked, paralyzed with horror.

For Siam-Diam, replied the voice. Come with us!

What? Come with you? said Petur Palmason, catching his breath. To Siam-Diam? he repeated foolishly. Then it finally dawned on him that they had no intention of trying to put out the fire or prevent it from spreading to other houses. Traitors! Villains! he yelled, kicking the door. Have you no sense of responsibility, you dogs? Must I teach you how to live? Must I break every bone in your bodies?

At that moment the key was turned in the lock.

He was confronted by two giants in shining uniforms with gold braid, ribbons, and truncheons, revolvers in leather holsters, massive bags on their stomachs, and hideous masks that reminded him of deep-sea divers.

Namurt, they said nodding to one another. Mota, they said, and stripping him of his bag, they emptied the contents and hurled them into the night.

My wife, said Petur Palmason, close to tears, my Gudrid will be burned alive!

Namurt, said the giants, and they grew yet bigger. Mota, they said, and seizing him by the shoulders, they stuffed a gag in his mouth and snapped handcuffs on him.

After this they led him for a long time along twisting passages, narrow alleys, and dark streets, and finally threw him into some kind of vehicle, whispering to each other in a strange language. Then raising their hands to their masks like soldiers, they slammed the door and climbed into another compartment of the vehicle.

Namurt, they said. Mota.

Then the light went out. Petur Palmason heard the hum of an engine and rolled to and fro on a cold serrated metal floor. He missed his bag and began weeping. I can't bear it, he told himself. I'll die. After that he tried to remember some prayers his mother had taught him when he was little, repeated them silently, together with the Lord's Prayer and the words of blessing, closed his eyes, and waited for what was to come.

He could not tell whether he was a long time or a short time in the dreadful vehicle, but suddenly he felt it stop. He was dragged out, the uniformed giants put fingers in his mouth and removed the gag, took off the handcuffs, dusted him down, and smiled and bowed to him.

Namurt, said one. Mota.

Come along, my friend, said the other. Come along.

They were standing outside a splendid palace surrounded by fountains. Petur Palmason had never seen anything like it, even in dreams. They led him up white marble steps and into a magnificent hall where everything gleamed like gold and silver or glittered like crystal and pearls. A banquet was being held in the hall. Firemen and policemen stood at attention, munching, along every wall, while people in formal dress with potato flowers in their buttonholes sat at a long table heaped with delicacies and provided with every sort of drink. Nikulas Nikulass, the trawler owner, was there. Also Jonatan Asgeirsson, the banker, Magnus H. J. Arnason, the wholesaler, three editors, five cabinet ministers, many members of the National Assembly, two economists, and one pyramid diviner wearing a woman's hat with a yellow speckled ostrich feather on it. Wherever Petur Palmason looked he saw familiar faces, or faces that seemed familiar. Even the host who sat in the seat of honor, with glasses on his nose, smooth and mild-looking, as if he had never had an evil thought, reminded him strongly of pictures of a head of state on a distant continent. He stood for a time in the middle of the floor, paralyzed and confused, disheveled and ridiculous, then, contriving to collect his wits, stammered fearfully, The . . . the fire must be put out!

Keep calm, my dear sir, said Nikulas Nikulass, raising his glass. Mota!

Skal, said Magnus H. J. Arnason, the wholesaler. Namurt!

There's nothing to fear. We're here, as you see, said the bank manager, smiling.

My wife will be burned alive, he shouted. The firemen must come!

You are improperly dressed, said the pyramid diviner. Get yourself a woman's hat with an ostrich feather. And a potato flower in your buttonhole!

Hmm, said the host, and rising from his seat, he walked up to Petur with slow, dignified steps, adjusted his glasses, bowed, and said in a friendly voice, Welcome to Siam-Diam, Palmi Petursson. Now you have got rid of your bag. Would you be good enough to sweep the floor in the cellar?

I? Sweep the floor? he asked. Then beating his fists together, he leaped in the air and was on the point of telling these people that they hadn't a scrap of a sense of responsibility, when he was grabbed rather firmly, so that he started up gasping for breath.

What a dreadful commotion, said his wife. You woke me up!

F-fire, he stammered. The house is on fire!

What foolishness has got into you, man? she exclaimed, and shook him again. Stop this nonsense, and go to sleep!

Then she lay back in bed and turned over several times before dropping off to sleep again.

Thank God, he had been dreaming. The fire, the voices, the bag, the giants, the ride to Siam-Diam, Namurt and Mota—these had all been a meaningless farrago of dream. Nevertheless the terror and dread which had possessed him during this strange nocturnal journey was still with him. He moved closer to his wife and patted the quilt with a palm of his hand. She slept soundly, snoring without the slightest sense of responsibility. It was as if she breathed peace and serenity upon him, though he could neither sleep nor rid himself of the apprehension that all was not well. In the end he got out of bed and crept softly to the window. The night was bright and clear. He gazed for a while at the houses on the other side of the street: the house of Nikulas Nikulass, of Jonatan Asgeirsson, and of Magnus H. J. Arnason. The frost glittered on the roofs in the moonlight, and in fact he had never before noticed what secure and imposing buildings they were. Such houses were sure to stand for centuries, if they did not happen by mischance to catch fire.

TRANSLATOR'S AFTERWORD

The popular culture of Iceland that I imbibed in childhood . . . is of an ancient Nordic life-wisdom combined with a Christian faith whose fairest expression is found in the New Testament, and interwoven with a classical Icelandic literature and the experience of generations through the centuries in an intimate union with their harsh land, their sufferings and struggles, their joys and sorrows, their courage and endurance. This popular culture imparted a dignity to the very act of creation, awakened a love of stories and poems, and stimulated a poverty-stricken people with no hope of schooling to acquire knowledge and enlightenment. It taught them to place human values above wealth and power, kindness and justice above rank and renown.

These words are freely translated from a speech Ólafur Jóhann Sigurdsson gave in Danish when, in 1976, he received the Nordic Council Award for Literature in Copenhagen.

Ólafur Jóhann was born in the southwest of Iceland on September 26, 1918. He spent his childhood years on a farm in the district south of Thingvellir, the meeting place of the medieval Icelandic assembly, close to the Lake of Swans (Álftavatn), which was to give its name to his first book, published when he was only sixteen. That collection of childhood memories won for him an immediate reputation as a young writer of promise.

During the thirties, years of depression in Iceland as elsewhere, he moved to Reykjavik, the capital, and lived precariously on what he could earn from jobs that enabled him to continue the writing to which he from early days had determined to devote his life. He worked as a parliamentary messenger, for a newspaper, in publishing, and for many years, as a proofreader.

In the spring of 1943 he married Anna Jónsdóttir, daughter of a doctor from the northeast of Iceland. They had two sons, one who is an oceanographer, and the other, also a writer, who is a senior executive in the Sony Corporation and lives in the United States.

Ólafur Jóhann read widely in European and American literature, and during the winter of 1943–1944 attended literature courses at Columbia University in New York City. Back in Iceland, his growing reputation as a writer was sustained and enhanced by a steady flow of short stories, novels, and poems. Following the great masters of Icelandic language and literature, especially the Nobel Prize winner Halldór Laxness, he soon developed a style and lyrical quality of his own, in both prose and verse, which he harnessed to his vision of a changing world. An Icelandic critic has remarked of him, "His formative years in the period between the wars were in many respects unique in the history of Iceland: a bridge between the old and the new." The works of Ólafur Jóhann reflect the drastic changes that took place in Iceland during a period in which a backward rural community was turning into a modern technological society—changes that in the rest of Europe had extended over two centuries. Iceland's isolation ended abruptly in the aftermath of two world wars, in as many generations.

Ólafur Jóhann, like other young writers of his day, was first led to adopt a radical attitude in politics, especially with regard to the presence of an alien power, in the form of a NATO base, in the newly independent Iceland. The traditional beliefs that were so deeply ingrained in him, however, saved him from falling like many others into simplistic ideological traps, and an emphasis on personal values prevailed in him. Another critic, perhaps reflecting reactions among some of the Icelandic intelligentsia of the day, has remarked, "All the works of Ólafur Jóhann Sigurdsson, his poems and his stories, are presented with strong moral feeling and a sense of responsibility. Some readers are not too ready to be offered such by an author. But what matters most is that the author has the artistic power to present his convictions in such a way that the highest artistic demands are fulfilled. This Ólafur Jóhann has succeeded in doing. His stories are finished creative works in every respect. His taste and skill in handling language are exceptional."

In 1948, I was engaged in research at the University of Iceland under the supervision of the great Icelandic scholar Sigurdur Nordal, who directed me to Ólafur Jóhann as a potential literary successor to Halldór Laxness. That was the beginning of an association and friendship that was to last until the author's death forty years later.

Ólafur Jóhann had an excellent knowledge and understanding of English: he had translated John Steinbeck and Richard Llewellyn, among others, in his day. The collection of stories here is the first comprehensive sample of his works available to English-speaking readers, although his tales have appeared in many other languages. The volume is the fruit of a close collaboration between author and translator over the years, with every word, every phrase, and every nuance of style having been subjected to a thorough scrutiny and discussion and the final version adopted only when both parties were satisfied.

As a master of Icelandic language and style, Ólafur Jóhann offers the translator both a challenge and a rare satisfaction. It is hoped that *The Stars of Constantinople* will give something of the same satisfaction to its readers, and go some way toward doing justice to the author's remarkable talent and his highly personal, yet universal, vision. Some critics have found his writings marked by pessimism, gloom, and even despair about the future of mankind. But one of them has pointed out that "in the innermost nature of Ólafur Jóhann Sigurdsson is to be found . . . an unshakable belief in life and a respect for the glory that lies before our eyes"—not least, perhaps, the eyes of a remembered childhood:

> You feel no fear at the whine and hiss of the whetted
> steel of this time or bullets that hit their mark.
>
> Nor do you catch the cries that rise from cities
> when iron-gray force bears fire and blood through the world.
>
> Held by flowers of the dale in a tender embrace
> the spring's light brings to you a daylong promise.

Grass-blades give you shelter, and unshaped dreams.
Great and unconditional their defense.
(*A Child*)

This is the vision to which Ólafur Jóhann Sigurdsson clings in a world that seems to have lost its bearings. For the bitter winters of a harsh land hold the promise of a returning spring. And the child in him constantly recalls this vision in the dark days:

The warm fingers of the sun
stroke the golden dandelion
and the lamb with budding horn
where the lamb-grass campion blushes.

Oyster catchers, curlews call,
marsh snipes nest among the rushes.
Soon the marsh will quicken all,
white with waving cotton grass.

Mists of early morning calm
kiss the cliffs farewell and pass,
while the sea pink on the sill
lifts a head to spread its balm.

Blissful days, with nights as sweet:
the river winds by limpid pools
through the dells where little feet
clambered once with naked soles.
(*On A Spring Day*)

In these short poems, Ólafur Jóhann speaks for himself.